Turnbull, Agnes Sligh

The winds of love

THE WINDS OF LOVE

By Agnes Sligh Turnbull

Novels

The Rolling Years
Remember the End
The Day Must Dawn
The Bishop's Mantle
The Gown of Glory
The Golden Journey
The Nightingale
The King's Orchard
Little Christmas
The Wedding Bargain
Many a Green Isle
Whistle and I'll Come to You
The Flowering
The Richlands
The Winds of Love

Nonfiction

Out of My Heart
Dear Me: Leaves from a Diary

For Children

Jed, The Shepherd's Dog
Elijah the Fish-Bite
George
The White Lark

Volumes of Short Stories

Far Above Rubies
The Four Marys
This Spring of Love
Old Home Town

Agnes Sligh Turnbull

THE WINDS OF LOVE

HOUGHTON MIFFLIN COMPANY BOSTON

1977

Library of Congress Cataloging in Publication Data
Turnbull, Agnes Sligh, date
The winds of love. I. Title.
PZ3.T849Wj [PS3539.U76] 813′.5′2 77-1592
ISBN 0-395-25341-1

Printed in the United States of America

v 10 9 8 7 6 5 4 3 2 1

To
My Granddaughters

Suzanne O'Hearn
Kristine O'Hearn

Love is a great thing, yea
a great and thorough good.
For it carries a burden
which is no burden, thinks
nothing of trouble, attempts
what is above its strength,
pleads no excuse of impossibility.
And it completes many things
and brings them to a conclusion
where he who does not love
faints and lies down.
Love watcheth and sleeping,
slumbereth not.

THOMAS À KEMPIS

THE WINDS OF LOVE

Prelude

IT WAS after their first deep, satisfied sleep. Kathy stirred, turned, and moaned a little. At once David woke, his arms around her. "Darling, what is it? Was I — did I — oh, tell me what's the matter? Why, you're trembling! Tell me, darling. You must tell me!"

She nestled closer to him. "I'm ashamed to have wakened you. It's nothing, really. It's just that I always get a little bit frightened at — the wind."

He laughed. A deep rich laugh full of genuine humor. Kathy remembered it was because of such a laugh she had fallen in love with him. They had met at a cocktail party and the crowded room was filled with the noise of bits and pieces of chatter and small titters from the latest gossip and interesting news imparted from friend to friend, when suddenly above it all came a man's laugh, deep, rich, and genuine, born of amusement. She looked and saw David, his head lifted a little, his whole strong face pleasantly animated; she looked at him, listened, and fell in love. Even as his eyes met hers, he separated himself from the couple he had been standing near, and with a word or two, left the group, and came straight to her. That was how it had all begun.

David had stopped laughing now as he drew her still closer. "The wind," he repeated. "That seems so odd to me because I've always rather liked hearing the wind at night. It makes me feel so comfortable and secure, somehow. And now, with you beside me, I'll love it more than ever. How did you come to feel afraid of it?"

"Well," Kathy said, "I guess it goes back to my childhood. My grandparents had a house at the beach one summer and I spent it with them. My nurse and I had a little cupola room on the third floor and the wind simply howled and cried through it, right from the sea. By morning all was quiet and I believe I never told of my night fears then, but they did bother me afterward . . . And now, as I woke up and heard how boisterous the wind was now on our *wedding night,* I felt scared somehow."

"Poor little lamb!" David said, as he held her cheek to his. "I'll never let you be afraid again . . . of anything, least of all the wind. Let me tell you how it was with me. I was happy at boarding school. You know, some kids aren't. And one song we sang so often was a favorite of mine. I never could remember it all, but it began this way.

"Over the chimneys the night wind came
And chanted a melody no one knew" —

I forget the other words, but it was to the effect that it meant something different to many people, and it ended with:

"It is God's own harmony."

You see how my thoughts tend to run? Why don't you think of it that way when you hear the wind? It was God's own harmony we heard on our wedding night. Aren't you content now, darling? If I dared, if you wished, I'm sure I could bring all your happiness back. The wind has died now and the daylight is beginning to come in. What do you say?"

She put her lips on his face, then whispered her answer against his cheek.

Chapter One

IT WAS the incredible, the miraculous time of the year. It was the days longed for, expected, and yet, with human wonder, feared lest the miracle could never come again. It was the time of unnamed essences which the weary nostrils drank greedily: the pushing up of shoots through the cold, the gentle bursting of bud and leaf, the pungent fragrance of the first daffodils, the miracle of crocus blooms under the trees. It was all this and more than the heart could take in or the mind conceive: it was spring!

Katherine Davenport stretched her arms above her head and drank, breathed, and smelled the newborn air of the season. The greatest wonder, she was thinking as she always did, was the dual nature of spring. On the one hand, an elixir filled the veins with fresh hope, fresh ardor, as if all humans were citizens of a world just discovered. But, on the other hand, there was the calmness and peace of spring. "The storms of winter are over, my children, so relax now and enjoy the sweet mildness of my weather." She stopped, laughing. "A peroration to spring. Well, it was deserved."

She started up the broken flagstone of the lower garden path, snapping off a few early daffodils as she went, thinking they would be bright on the dinner table — Oh, she hoped David would not be late tonight. As she passed through the little white gate in the low fence she and David had built long ago to separate the more sophisticated front lawn from the lower, pleasantly casual garden, she heard children's voices shouting a "Counting Out" song.

"Oka, boka, stona croka
Oka, boka, two
Engine — Number Nine,
O-U-T, spells out go you!"

Katherine laughed. She had sung those very same words as a child. How strange that the primitive rhyme and folklore persisted from generation to generation, when more important gems of thought were lost along the way.

She waved to the singers, two her own and two neighbors, and stepped up on the side porch.

"Oka, boka, stona croka," she repeated, smiling. "How literary can one get?"

She opened the door leading into the dining room and then stopped dead on the threshold. David, her husband, stood there, his hands gripping the back of a chair, his face stone white.

With a cry she ran to him. "David, what is it? Oh, you're sick. Sit down, dear. I'll call the doctor at once. Oh, David, what happened to you?"

He fended her off gently but firmly, as she came up to him.

"But what is it, then? You look so ghastly . . . I know!" She said suddenly, holding her head high. "The promotion didn't go through! You lost the vice-presidency! You couldn't ever think I'd care enough to make you look like that. Why, David, it is only a relative thing. Don't you see? We can just forget the possibility and be as happy as before all this came up. If it's the promotion —"

"It's not the promotion; it's not that, Katherine. The promotion came through. I'm now the first vice president."

"David, I knew it would come. And —" She hardly breathed as she asked the next question. "And the year in France?"

"That is practically mandatory."

Her face was pale. "Then something is more serious than I

thought. You must already have seen a doctor. David, you must tell me, my dear, just what is wrong. Don't wait any longer."

I'm going to tell you. I've been trying for weeks to tell you and each time I come up to it, I can't do it. Today I left the office at two o'clock for I couldn't live with it on my mind any longer. The worst is I can find no way to begin except to blurt out the awful, unbelievable truth to you, Katherine . . . I'm in love with another woman!"

"I don't believe you." Her reaction was instinctive.

"It's true. I wish to God it were not. You deserve to know how it all came about. I'll tell you as well as I can."

"David, you look so awful standing there. Tell me this incredible thing if you must."

He sat down, looking away from her. "The woman is Celia Mills. When Brownie retired — good old Brownie — I had to have a new secretary. Miss Mills applied and Harbison hired her, subject to my approval. I was startled when I saw her. She is so very — beautiful. The other fellows all teased me and I took it as a joke. I felt so secure.

"Then after some weeks I knew I was not secure. I couldn't go on working in the same office with her." He stopped, swallowing painfully. "I went, then, to Harbison and made a clean breast of it. He was understanding and respectful. He said he would take Miss Mills into his own office. I felt that the problem was solved." He paused. Katherine sat stunned and did not speak. "I soon found that even the change did not cure me. I had to go into Harbison's office now and then for a paper and when my hands happened to touch her, it was like fire. I knew then I had to fight with all that was in me. And, Kathy [the old nickname slipped out], you must believe I have fought until now I am weak from the struggle. I'm at the end of my string, as it were. I know I have to give up."

"How did you fight?" she asked.

"Well, first I began coming home earlier to spend more time with you and the children, but I realized I was just a sort of wooden man. You must have seen I was different."

"I thought it was the business strain."

"I tried and tried and finally gave up. I asked Harbison to send me on any trip that came up. As you know, I was often away. But it was no good. Then I began taking walks at night till I was exhausted, while you thought I was working late. But, strangely, this brought about the climax of my struggling." He looked away across the room as though it was hard to explain his next words. "One evening I stayed in the office to finish some work. Suddenly Celia — Miss Mills — came rushing in; she had forgotten her sketch. She goes to art class two evenings a week. And there we were for the first time alone together. We knew then that we couldn't go on as we had been doing.

"So, Katherine, although you must hate me as much as I hate myself, I have to have my freedom. This thing is like a fire in me. I can't fight it any longer. I've come to the end. The next move, I'm afraid, is yours."

"What do you want me to do?"

He recoiled as though she had struck him. "I didn't want to name the horrid word," he said. "I didn't want to. But surely, after all I've told you, you realize I must ask you to give me a divorce."

There was silence and then Katherine said, slowly but distinctly, "And, David, that is what I will never do."

"You can't mean that. You couldn't be so cruel to me."

"It is for you to judge which of us is the cruel one. Have you seen Tim?"

"Yes. I stopped at his office as I came down."

"What did he say?"

For the first time a faint relaxation touched David's ashamed face. "I couldn't very well repeat it all. He did call me a dirty dog and told me to get down the stairs before he threw me down. Then, being Tim, he was at the foot of them before me, and he will see you soon. That is good. He's not only your brother, but the best lawyer in the area. You may feel different after you talk to him. I'm going now. I have work to finish, but I simply had to come. I'll sleep in the city at the company suite. I have clothes there."

"And the children?"

"I'll be back. I can't see them now." As he went to the door he said, "Katherine, try to forgive me."

When she was alone her head dropped on her arm on the table and a great oblivion enfolded her. It was sweet and comforting, this complete absence of thought, and she yielded completely to it. When she half woke, someone was bending over her, shaking her gently.

"Hold your head up, Kathy. You did give me a scare. When you faint, you do it on a big scale. Here, drink some of this soup. I don't know what it is. I found it in the refrigerator. Come on, Kathy, get awake now."

She drank the hot broth obediently, but her head was still heavy.

"Are you sure all this is real, Tim?"

"I'm afraid so, dear. Come over to the couch and lie down. I'll feed the kids and get them to bed and after that you will have gotten hold of yourself and we can talk a little. Come on."

She lay very still, hearing Tim's explanations to the children. Mummy had a headache and he was putting them to bed later. He had a brand-new story to tell them about a rabbit. She roused to eat some of the supper Tim had prepared and sat up, her head all too clear for remembrances of things past. She wanted now, desperately, to talk.

The children said good night and she heard Tim busy above. They adored him — the fount of all songs and stories, the inventor of games and frolics.

"You should have six kids of your own," David used to tease him.

"Oh, I'll practice on yours," he would retort airily.

Now he came into the room, sat down beside Katherine, and took her hand. "I still don't believe it," she said.

"Nor would I, if I hadn't heard it from his own mouth. I don't think I could repeat all I said when I heard his errand." His own stricken face eased slightly. "I think I called him a dirty dog and threatened to throw him down the stairs. And then I thought to myself, 'My God, this isn't a client, I'm speaking to; it's *David,*' and I hurried after him and said I'd come to you as fast as I could."

"You feel, then, he's really in earnest, sure of himself?"

"I'm afraid he is."

"Have you ever seen the girl?"

"Once. I was taking a client to lunch and Harbison knew him. As we passed his table, he stopped us and then introduced the girl with him. It was this Miss Mills."

"Is she beautiful?"

"Yes, she is, I have to admit," Tim hesitated. "But a little scrap of description from somewhere floated through my mind. It was 'icily regular, splendidly null.' I don't think she's null, though. I would guess she has brains; but her face does look carved, it's so close to perfect."

"Didn't she smile?"

"Yes, and then she came alight, as it were. I can see how she would attract a man. But, as for David, it still seems utterly incredible."

"I don't know how I can go on living now. My heart is broken. There can be no mending for this."

"Yes, dear, you will wake up tomorrow to a new day, a terribly, terribly hard one, but one in which, at least, you can breathe and work. The worst shock is over now. You are strong and you are brave. You will slowly emerge to live your own life and feel a new freedom. I've seen this happen to other women."

"But I'm not giving him a divorce, Tim. Not now, not ever."

"You're — what?"

"Just what I said. I told him when he asked that I would not give it. Why should I? I've been a good wife and I still love him, and one day . . ."

"Oh, my dear, I hope you're not building on the hope he will forget all this and come back to you!"

"It could be, but I won't count on it."

"You *mustn't*, Kathy; I won't have you living in a fool's paradise. I've seen too many women who have done that and it's wrecked them. Always waiting, expecting, hoping for what never comes. It's hard for me to say this to you but when a man wants another woman as madly as David seems to want this . . . this one, I don't think he gets over it. What makes you even think of such a possibility?"

"Well, it's hard to explain; there were the deep feelings, of course, but also we had such fun together — silly little rhymes and quotes. They say that sort of thing helps to hold a marriage safe, but it didn't do it for ours." She drew a long, shuddering sigh.

"What sort of things are you talking about? Give me an example."

"I can't think of one special thing. They were just interwoven with our daily conversation . . . Oh, I do remember one that *we* thought was funny. One morning at breakfast, away back before anything had changed, while I was pouring the coffee, David looked at his watch, then took it out of its bracelet and held it to his ear. Then he shook it and looked mystified. 'But "it was the *best* butter,"' he said. And then we laughed and laughed, all through breakfast."

"Yes," Tim smiled, "and of course I do it too. I love the Mad Tea Party. I quote a bit of it once in a while to throw a stuffy prosecutor off his beat, but, my precious little sister, you must remember that there are thousands upon thousands of lovely, desirable young women with a good sense of humor too, who were never brought up on the children's classics as we and David were, never read *Alice,* for instance."

"And suppose another woman like this Miss Mills would

hear David say such a thing and think he was a bit crazy and answer, 'Well, of course it was the best butter. I always buy it at Shave and Harts.' What then?"

Tim stood up. "Listen," he said, "it's time you stopped supposing and went to bed. You're white and shaky. I'll carry you up. Come on. You get into bed. I'll check the kids and the house down here, then make you a good stiff toddy and take it up to you, and I swear you'll sleep like a baby."

"You musn't carry me. That's ridiculous."

"That's highly sensible. Here you are, light as a feather; here am I, strong as an ox, ergo, I carry you, my lady, and no more words from you. I'm not only your brother, but your lawyer. I have authority. Come On! Up you come!"

"Oh, Tim, could you stay here tonight? It would help."

"Of course, I had thought of doing that myself. I'll check everything after you're in bed, bring you your toddy, and then find everything I need in the guest room. It's nice that I'm a frequent lodger."

"Dear, dear Tim."

He carried her easily up the stairs, making light remarks and laughing as he did so; he saw it helped her keep back the tears. He deposited her gently on her bed, then stood looking down at her.

"After the potent beverage I'll bring you, you'll sleep like a tot and wake to a miracle. You will see the sun in the sky, the flowers blooming, the children at play, and hear the usual sounds. Don't think of problems for a while. You needn't hurry. By the way, you were pretty shaky. Do you need help to get ready for the night? Once, as a very young attorney, I had to help a matron undress a jail lady. I haven't practiced since, but I'm pretty clever. How about it?

Katherine managed a weak laugh. "No thanks, Tim. I can get myself ready. It's an unexpected comfort to have you here."

"For me too. Okay. I'll check on everything and be up soon with your potion. Take it easy, now."

When she lay still, as last the hard tension of the last few hours broke. All she had said, had felt, all she had restrained herself from feeling and saying, somehow drifted away. She felt limp, inert, weak to the point of hesitating to move an arm or a leg. She could hear Tim's movements vaguely below and at last his entrance into the bedroom with the heavy tall coffee cup.

"Here you are!" he said. "And sip it slowly; it's mighty hot. I'll watch that you don't burn yourself."

It was potent indeed, but it tasted good. He had put honey in it as David used to do.

When she had slowly, sip by sip, drained the cup, Tim put out her light and said good night very quietly.

"I'll leave your door open and if you should want anything, just call. I'm a light sleeper. My guess is you won't think of anything, but if you do, keep your mind on Mother's old poem. She used to keep it beside her bed.

'Forget thyself and all the world
Put out each feverish light
The stars are shining overhead
Sleep sweetly then, goodnight.'

Well, there are my sentiments, but I don't think you need them." And he was gone.

Katherine felt a delicious numbness steal over her — a complete relaxation of body and mind, more general than she had just been experiencing. Her mind refused to remember anything with clarity, only faintly, the words. "It was a dream" seemed to rise from the depths. Then it too was gone and great waves of oblivion like those of the sea, swept Katherine into a sleep.

When she woke next morning, she was lost for a few minutes — back in former days. Oh, she was late and, she thought, David would miss his train. And the children? Then the silence of the house brought the truth like a mental avalanche. She remembered. Evidently Tim had made himself some coffee, given the children their cereal, and started them off to school with Helen Hunt's children next door. But how could she have slept through the usual sounds, even though they were muffled? Shock? Tim's potent toddy perhaps? But it had been the silence that had wakened her at last.

She dressed as quickly as she could because of her unsteady legs and went down to the kitchen, where from the coffeepot spout a streamer in Tim's handwriting waved:

"I gave you a good one, didn't I? I have to leave, but do, my dear, take things quietly. I can't come again until tomorrow, but will see you then. Love, Brother, lawyer, bartender."

Katherine smiled, felt her head growing more normally alert after coffee and toast, then tidied the kitchen and walked slowly into the living room. There in the bright sunshine she sat down to take stock of her day — this new day, with its dreadful overhanging cloud. The main point was that it had to be lived. It could not be erased or slipped behind a calendar. She had to deal with its hours as they passed.

She glanced down at her engagement book. There, staring at her, was this: "Conference with Miss Darby about Davey at four o'clock."

Well, Katherine thought with a sigh, here is something to take up my mind for a while at least. There was, indeed, the problem of Davey. He was nine now. Nature had delayed in giving David and Katherine the desire of their hearts. They had waited long years in secret despair, when suddenly little David, the beautiful, perfect baby son, arrived. As though nature was bent upon making amends for her delay, in less than two years, a little girl, all sweetness, dimples, and curls, at once called Kit, was added to the family. It was early apparent that while she was, as David put it, as smart as any female ever needed to be, it was also clear that Davey, as he was known, had an almost abnormally keen intelligence. So bright indeed was he that in school he felt rather too sure of himself. He always knew the answers without apparently listening to Miss Darby's questions. This habit, this quality of mind, had brought about the disaster of a year ago. Katherine still shuddered as she thought of it.

Davey had come home one day breathless with excitement and joy. "Guess what?" he had yelled as soon as he was within his mother's range of hearing. "Guess what?"

"What, Davey?" Katherine had said. "You look like a Roman candle ready to burst."

"It's — well, you'll never believe it. Miss Darby just told us today. On Friday our whole grade is going over to the city in a bus, and then —" He stopped for breath. "And then we'll all get off at the Museum of Natural History and we'll take our lunches in paper bags. Miss Darby knows a place we can eat and then go to the zoo. What do you think of that, Mother?"

"Wonderful, past believing," Katherine had said.

"Isn't it? I don't think I've ever been so happy. Wait till I tell Daddy and Kit! She's so young! She can't go *anywhere*." His tone was definitely superior.

When David came home, the whole beautiful project was described again, with flourishes and ruffles: "The only awful thing is having to wait all through Wednesday and Thursday. I think it will kill me. Say, I forgot to tell you — we boys have to dress up. Miss Darby says she's not taking a bunch of hoodlums over there, and we've got to wear jackets and ties. I wish you'd help me pick one, Daddy. I'd like to look real sharp."

The intervening time finally passed. Came the eve of the great day, Davey was too excited to eat his dinner. He arranged his clothes for quick dressing in the morning: his new slacks were laid carefully over the chair in his room, his white shirt and blazer hung on the back, fresh underwear and socks neatly placed. It was hard to get him to bed, but at last he had said his good nights and gone to his room. In a flash, though, he was back with his small brogans in his hand.

"They're not shiny enough," he explained. "I forgot them. Can I use your brushes and things, Daddy?"

He set to work almost feverishly, and finally, with the leather polished like glass, he made a final trip up the stairs, calling gaily as he went. "Be sure to wake me on the dot, Mother. Some of the kids are sure to be early. Besides, I'd like to see the old bus come in. Gee, it's going to be neat, all right!"

"I guess we won't need to set the alarm clock tonight," Katherine remembered that David had said with a grin.

"I'll probably not sleep a wink. I believe I'm more excited than Davey. I want him to get the very last minute of sleep he can, though; he's as nervous as a witch tonight, and I don't want him to tire out before the big day is done. Set the clock for eight. Of course, we'll be up long before, but we'll take no chances and if we waken him, then he'll have a whole hour to get to the school house."

"You checked the time?"

"Oh, right away. He just said, 'We all meet at the front steps same time school starts.'"

"Sounds reasonable," David said. And, at last, with the clock set, they went to sleep. In the morning David and Katherine had been up for more than an hour before the clock chimed eight.

"I'll go wake him while you finish the breakfast," David said, and hurried to Davey's room. But the clock had barely stopped striking when the telephone rang. Katherine answered at once, to hear Miss Darby's voice, sharp and anxious. "Mrs. Davenport? What's wrong with Davey?"

"Why, nothing." (Katherine recalled now how brightly she had answered.) "He's getting dressed. He's —"

"Mrs. Davenport, it's five past eight now. The driver says he can't wait any longer or he'll miss his connections. I told the whole grade to be here by eight sharp or a little before and they're all here but Davey. Apparently he didn't listen. Now we've already waited five minutes; every child was here by eight. I made the driver hold a little because I was so sure Davey would come."

"Miss Darby!" Katherine's cry had been hysterical. "We'll have him there in ten minutes, or even less. But wait —"

"We can't. The bus is starting now, as soon as I get on. I'm sorry —" The words floated back as the faint echo of the great grinding bus machinery started.

David and Katherine had stood, staring at each other, speechless. Then David laid his hand on her shoulder.

"I've fought through a war, Kath, and I suppose I was as brave as any, but I can't tell that child what's happened. I'm afraid you'll have to."

She went slowly up the stairs to Davey's room. He was dressed, sitting on the bed, one shiny brogan on, the other in his hand.

"Gee, Mother, they shine all right, don't they? I'm glad I polished them. Say, I'll be ready —"

"Davey!"

At her tone he looked up. "Anything wrong? Has old Darby fouled anything up? Just like her —"

"Davey, something dreadful, something terrible has happened. You children were all to be at school not a minute after eight and before that, if possible. Every other child understood. They were all there, waiting for Miss Darby. She made the driver of the bus wait till five past eight, she was so sure you would come."

Davey was standing up now. He had struggled into his other shoe and was tearing into his jacket. "Well, hurry, Mother! Daddy said he'd drive me over. I'm ready. Let's go!"

"But Davey, dear, you'll have to understand. The driver couldn't wait. The bus is — is gone!"

"You mean it's gone and left me?"

"I'm afraid so, darling. Oh, I'm so sorry."

There was one great, despairing cry which seemed to fill

the house, and then, even harder to bear, nothing at all. Davey sat on his bed, stone white, and would not speak. She and David had done and said all they could think of, Katherine remembered, while their own hearts ached for his utter misery. But he did not respond. He only sat there unconsciously, stroking one polished brogan.

In midafternoon, the Principal, kind man, called to say he had heard of the tragedy and would Davey care to come over and help him design the fifth-grade blackboard? Davey slowly changed to his school clothes and went. At supper he was almost airy. He had seen some of the kids as they got back and the trip wasn't so hot, and Bill Waters even said the whale in the museum *stunk*!

"That's the way," Davey had remarked with a great show of cheerful wisdom. "Sometimes the very things we look forward to and want so much are not — "

Davey suddenly excused himself and went upstairs, where they could hear him being very sick.

For weeks, while the wound slowly healed, it seemed, indeed, as though, even so sore and bitter, it had really, in the classic phrase, yielded the "peaceable fruits of righteousness." Davey was less cocky and arrogant, listened intently to instructions, and his reports were good. For months all seemed well. But now, as Katherine looked down at her desk, there were the old, familiar, damning words: "Conference with Miss Darby about Davey at four o'clock."

As she drove into the school parking lot, she watched the departing hordes of various ages, listened to the cries and shouts die away on the spring air, and knew she could put off the evil moment no longer. She went through the great front door, encountered the familiar and peculiar elementary school smells, and went up the stairs to the proper room. Miss Darby had left the door open and rose now to greet her guest.

"Sit down, Mrs. Davenport. I'm very glad to see you; I've about come to the end of my rope with Davey."

"Oh, dear! I thought things were better now."

"I know. I think we all felt, for a long time, that the terrible disappointment last year had taught him a lesson. But now he's been worse. Just yesterday he made a fool of me. And I can't stand that." Miss Darby's strong, bony face twitched with emotion.

"Oh, I feel so wretched about this. What did he *do*, Miss Darby?"

"Well, it was like this. I had given the grade a very hard arithmetic problem. They would need guidance; so I told them to listen carefully and make notes if they needed to, and that I would tell them step by step how they could work it out. Every child listened intently but Davey. He looked out the window, at the ceiling, yawned, leafed through his book, never looked at me as I explained the steps. I made up my mind for once to humble him. So the minute I finished, I said, 'Davey Davenport, please rise.

"The children had all noticed his attitude and were eager to be in at the kill, as it were. 'Now,' I said, 'repeat all I have just been saying step by step for solving this problem.' And what do you suppose happened? There, with the other children all watching him and then me, waiting for him at last to be humbled, he did just that!"

"Oh, Miss Darby!"

"He began at the beginning and practically word for word, repeated all I'd said. It was incredible. And when he finished, the whole room clapped, for Davey, while I stood there, in front of them all, as red as a beet. Children understand everything. They knew what I'd tried to do and that Davey won. I felt today I could hardly face them and I really must have help. 'I was hoist with my own petard!'"

"Oh, Miss Darby, I can't tell you how distressed I am that this has happened. I will do anything to cooperate with you. There must be some way to change Davey. I'm so ashamed of him. Have you any idea what I could do?"

"Well," Miss Darby said, "last night after this had happened, I lay awake a long time thinking and I came up with one possibility. I know your little girl, Mrs. Davenport, your little Kathy. Now, she is the prettiest child I ever saw — dimples, curls, big blue eyes. No father could resist fondling and playing with a little girl child like that. Now, I reasoned, it could be that, without realizing it, Mr. Davenport gives more attention to her than to Davey, and that a kind of jealousy is what's eating Davey," she finished, dropping from Shakespeare into common vernacular. "He may feel he just has to show off to compensate. What do you think?"

Katherine was indeed thinking. She suddenly knew that the spinster had divined what the parents had not. She hesitated and then, trying to keep her lips steady, she spoke.

"Miss Darby, we have been a little blind, I think, but there will now be a cure. I will tell you something because I know you will say nothing until it has to be made public. My husband is leaving me for another woman. So, except for visits, the children will be alone with me, and I will make it up to Davey."

Miss Darby's face had frozen in vicarious anguish. "When did you first know this?" she whispered.

"Yesterday afternoon was the first."

"And yet you came here *today* to see me for a conference?"

"Of course," Katherine said. "I knew it was about Davey. I have to think of the children now more than ever."

Miss Darby reached her bony hands across and grasped Katherine's. There were tears on her cheeks. "Mrs. Davenport, you are a strong, brave woman. If ever you want to confide anything at all in me, my heart is safe for a secret. God bless you, my dear. I'll be especially kind to Davey and I know you will. Little Kathy will always have love and attention poured on her. Maybe Davey needs something more."

As Katherine drove home, the strong clasp of Miss Darby's hand and her perceptive understanding comforted her. David had, and perhaps she herself had, quite unconsciously, been wooed by little Kathy's beauty and charm. Davey, worshiping his father, longed for more of his attention, and while David was a devoted father, listening to all conscientiously, to all of Davey's reports of his day, little Kathy always seemed, as it looked in this new light of understanding, to come between, to insert her own little problems and prattle of tales until she had taken her favorite place on her father's knee and from there surveyed her brother complacently. Davey would toss his head, make a few cutting remarks in regard to his sister's youth and general ignorance, be mildly reproved for the same, and settle down with a book.

Yes, she and David had been blind to Davey's problem. The woman who had never born a child but who understood children had discovered it. A pain, almost physical, knifed through Katherine's heart. From now on, there would be only visits to the children from David and she would point out to their father Davey's need. But he adored them. He would come often to see them! At supper she told Davey she had seen Miss Darby and she had told her something quite wonderful about him.

"That's hard to believe," he responded in his most grown-up voice. "She's mad at me. She thought she'd catch me yesterday with her old arithmetic problem and I fooled her. I said it right back to her and all the kids clapped and she got as red as a turkey gobbler. She's mad at me, all right."

"No, Davey, you're wrong. She's not a bit mad. She told me you did a wonderful performance."

"She did?"

"Absolutely."

He laid down his knife and fork. "Well," he said slowly, "I'm a dead tomcat if she said that. Old Bony!" he added slowly. "You see, she's always yak-yakin' at me and, gee, I thought she'd blown her top this time."

"Don't call her Old Bony, Davey. She's really nice when you are nice to her . . . Now, Kathy, tell us about your day."

The evening was easier than Katherine had expected. The children did their homework, listened to some records, and went to bed. Mary Hastings, one of her dearest friends, who lived diagonally just across the way, came on her duty trip to collect for the Heart Fund and, after a brief call, went on to stop at various other houses.

"I've a long stretch to do, so I thought I'd start this evening. The children are busy with some school project, and Bill," with a little laugh, "isn't half through with the sports section."

Katherine forced a laugh too. "Good luck! You're a noble citizen!"

When Mary had gone, she put out the lights. The spring darkness was warm and sweet. She felt relaxed to be alone. Tim was distressed that he had to be out of town in connection with a case, but Katherine sat down on the front porch, relieved to think her own thoughts. Strangely, there was much to think about apart from David's heartbreaking news. There was Miss Darby. She knew, suddenly, that when she had to unburden her soul to someone — her inmost soul — it would not be to a close friend, or Tim, or her rector; she would tell Miss Darby. Something told her there was strength to be found there and that between them they would work out Davey's salvation.

She sat quiet in the all-enfolding darkness, only the dim light from a distant porch making the opposite street faintly discernible, until Bill Hastings, Mary's husband, raised the dining room window and shade a little, leaving a glimpse of the scene within. The children, all four of them, were working at the table; Bill had his paper spread before him. Once there was a burst of laughter and then all was quiet.

Katherine sat thinking of Mary and Bill. Their romance had begun in High School when he, tall, handsome, and powerful, had been captain of the football team. Mary, quietly and worshipfully, had marveled that this god should have chosen her for himself. Mary had once told her this. Bill had gone through college on a football scholarship and, upon graduation, he and Mary had been married. The years, with four fine children, came to make their union more complete.

But sometimes Katherine had wondered. Bill adored his wife and would no more have left her for another woman than he would have thrown her to the lions. He was a devoted father and a good automobile salesman, whose favorite diversion was a poker game with some of his buddies and plenty of beer on the side. Mary had majored in English at college, belonged to a very select reading group here, and had quietly built up her own library, including much poetry. She was a fond wife and mother, but still Katherine, in the light of her own tragic revelations, kept wondering and probing. Mary had grown in depth and beauty of mind. Bill had remained the big football captain. The two families had been neighbors and close friends for years, but the Hastings did not go as a couple with the group to which David and Katherine had belonged. When she had once questioned her husband, he had laughed. "Why, Bill's all right. I like him. But he's just too *hearty*. And he can't talk about anything but the latest games. Oh, you know!"

Katherine knew. She loved Mary. She sat on now thinking, until she knew the hour must be growing late. She was about to get up when she saw two figures slowly, very slowly, walking along the pavement across from her. Her eyes, now accustomed to the dusk, recognized them. It was Mary and Harold Brown, who lived at the end of the street. She was late and he was walking her home. But as she watched, she discerned something different. They were not speaking. Once in a while, they paused and looked into each other's face, then slowly, silently, walked on.

Katherine sat, clutching her heart. Even then she knew the mystery. The two opposite her stopped at last where the Hastings lawn began, out of sight of the opened shade. They looked once more at each other; then Harold took Mary's hand, raised it to his lips, placed a kiss within it, and closed the other over it as though to guard something precious. He turned then and walked back toward his own home. Mary stood for a long minute, her head bowed on her breast. Then, as though given an order, she looked up, straightened, moved steadily toward her own front walk, and opened the door. At once, faintly, shouts of welcome came from within.

Katherine shivered in the growing dark. Mary and Harold Brown loved each other, though she had never realized it before. Harold was an English professor in the small college just beyond the town. His wife, Hilda, had once told her of their romance. Harold had been excessively shy at college and she, Hilda, evidently dynamic to a degree. "I had to make all the advances or I never would have got him," she had said complacently. "I was president of the student council and so sort of drew him out of his shell." She was still president of various clubs, headed numerous committees, thrived on organizations. In between she was a good cook, for she liked food only too well. She had produced three nice children, now in High School, and was a kind wife and mother. This was Hilda, overweight, overtalkative, overzealous in all kinds of good causes, overpossessive, and overfond of husband and children.

And there was between Mary and Harold that hidden kiss. There would be nothing more than that, Katherine knew. And because of this, the four Hastings children and the three Browns would, that night, go happily to bed, knowing that their familiar world would not come crashing over their heads; there would be no desolation for their young hearts. As surely as the sun would rise on the morrow, their parents would be there, watching over them, blessing them as they started their day. They would be safe.

Katherine sank suddenly into her own particular and irremediable sorrow. Strangely enough, she found herself longing for those hours a year ago before the alien fire had burned David's heart . . . when together they had smilingly watched Davey's polishing of his little brogans and making his preparation for the great day, and then together had shared the cruel blow of his disappointment. She could even share all the child's anguish if only David were beside her, sharing it too, close and secure as for so many years they had been.

He had told her he had fought against this new love. "Don't ever think I haven't fought," he had kept repeating.

Well, she thought to herself, as the tears for the first time streamed down her cheeks, I have seen two people tonight who have fought — and won.

Chapter Two

For two weeks day followed day with the numb, resistless beat of Katherine's heart. There was no word from David, though she had a feeling Tim had been in communication with him. Occasionally he brought in the word divorce as though to accustom her to the sound. A small doubt sometimes assailed her. Could her instinctive and definite reaction be wrong after all? Then an incident happened to establish her decision.

The children came hurrying home together from school one afternoon. Davey's eyes were red and teary and Kit was trembling.

"Mother, Mother!" they cried as soon as they reached the garden where they could see her. And then they clung to her as those about to drown cling to a raft.

"Children! What's the matter. Davey, tell me what frightened you?"

Davey raised his head from the sanctuary of her skirt. "The kids . . . " he said. "It's what the kids told us. Billy Hart was the worst. I told him he was a liar and I socked him on the nose. But, oh, Mother, tell us it isn't true."

"Listen, Davey, you must control yourself. Tell me, please, what you heard. At once," she added.

"Well, Billy Hart was the worst. He said he'd heard his folks talking last night and they said Daddy wasn't ever coming back and was going to marry someone else," he choked, "and that you were going to get a divorce thing that would make us like the Weston kids and have to live —" he choked again, "— six months with you and six with the other woman. And, Mother, I couldn't stand that. Tell us —"

It was little Kit, her small hands unsteady, who found her voice. "You aren't getting this divorce thing, Mummy?"

Katherine's voice rose strong and clear. "I certainly am not." She could feel the children relax. "And Daddy? He isn't going for good? Oh, Mother, he *couldn't* do that!" Davey hung upon her reply.

Katherine thought fast. "Of course not, silly. Now this is how it will be. Daddy is a very big man in his company now. He's vice president and may one day be the real president of the company. He will have to spend much time not only in Paris, but in other cities, like London, for example. We all couldn't go along and be moving around all the time. So Daddy will be away a good deal, but will come back once in a while for weekends, when he can play with you and tell stories and talk to you more than ever. See?"

"And you?"

"Why, I'll be right here. Where else would I be?" She gave a little laugh. Always afterward, as she remembered, she was proud she had managed that laugh.

"And no divorce thing? Not ever?"

"Not ever."

"Well, it sounds all right to me then," Davey said judicially. Okay with you Kit?"

Kit could only nod, with the tears still on her cheeks.

"Well, please go right up to the bathroom and wash your faces; then come down for milk and cookies to calm yourselves," their mother said.

"Kit does look dreadful," Davey pronounced. "We were both pretty shook up, I'm telling you, and poor Kit," he added with an unexpected burst of tenderness, "she was shaking all over and she *leaned* on me — can you believe that? So I sup-supported her all the way back." Katherine drew the little girl close and pressed her own cheek to the tear-stained one.

"And you wouldn't ever send us away to live with someone else like the Weston children?"

"Never, never, my darling. Don't believe stories you hear. Come and ask me first. Oh, my dear children, please, please, don't worry. We are safe and happy together."

They started up the stairs to repair the ravages of fear and the fight. Halfway up, Davey leaned over the balustrade. "Mother," he called jubilantly, "I gave Bill Hart a real sockaroo on the nose! You should have seen the blood. It was *beautiful!*" And he disappeared above.

Katherine felt weak enough to faint without the addition of the *beautiful blood*. That would have to be dealt with somehow later on. But when the children, washed and brushed, came down to fall ravenously upon the cookies, she felt an inner strength gathering. She would need it all, for Tim was coming that evening — as he said — to talk business.

It was always a gala meal to the children when Tim came to join them. That night he was especially full of new riddles, crazy antics, and puzzles done with the cutlery. But at last, after the treat of one story apiece when they had gone to bed, there was quiet in the children's wing and Tim came down slowly to sit with Katherine in the living room.

"Well, my sweet," he began, "I suppose you know that the evil day cometh when business machinery rears its ugly head. I've put this off as long as possible to let you catch your breath, but David has kept calling me. He wants to come out next Saturday, if you agree. His idea would be to take the children for a nice drive into the country to a farm if we can locate one. I can, as a matter of fact. They would see the animals and feel it was all a big deal. I don't know why on earth we've never thought of this farm before. We're too suburbanized. We take children to the city to a ballet or a museum and they never know which end of the cow the milk comes from."

Katherine laughed feebly and he went on. "He would take the children to lunch, come back here right after, send them out to play, and then sit down with you — and me — to make arrangements."

"What arrangements?"

"Oh, you know the main thing. He wants a divorce. I just made bold to ask him if his feeling for this other girl was still the same. He said yes, more than ever and if I didn't get on with things, he'd get another lawyer. I think the man's gone crazy, myself, but crazy or not, we have to deal with him. What is your answer to his plan?"

"About coming to take the children out? I think the idea is really inspired."

"Yes, and the divorce? Shall I now get things started?"

"Tim, I will not give him a divorce. Before, I had moments of doubt. Now, after what happened this afternoon, I have none. I am adamant."

"Kathy, you can't do that, dear. It's really not quite *gentlemanly*. Do you realize that if you refuse his request you will be dooming him to what the old Puritan ethic called 'living in sin'?"

"I'm not dooming him. He is choosing it for himself. I have been a good wife and since I have lost all pride where love is concerned, I will say I still love David. If he chose to come back to me, even now, I would receive him. It's like that with me. And after this afternoon —"

"Good God, you are a wonderful wife. But what happened today? You haven't made that clear."

So she told him, word for word, as clearly as she could remember. Tim's face grew more and more grave as she talked.

"You say little Kit's hands were trembling?"

"Yes, she was so frightened. My hands used to do that when I was a child and even yet do sometimes." She paused a moment. "They did the day David told me."

"But how did the children get all these ideas about what they feared would happen?"

"Oh, that groundwork has long been laid. Two children they both know come from a broken home. In the terms of that divorce, the father has the children during summer vacations; the mother has them during the school year. But the children hate the time they have to spend with their father and his new wife. They don't like her and she resents having children dropped upon her every summer. The father tries to compensate, so the neighbors say; but the wife then feels he is neglecting her for them and *they* are wretched because they have to miss their accustomed summer in their grandmother's cottage in Maine. A whole sad business! I think the mother in the case should have fought for her rights. The neighbors say she was so paralyzed from shock when he told her, she just let him get away with everything." She went on.

"Those children, of course, told all their friends at school just how everything was, giving plenty of details. Do you get the picture now?"

"All but one thing. How did David and you get into the story?"

"That's so. I was struck by that after the children's outburst. Then all at once it seemed clear that the leak had come from Andy MacNeill. He's the accountant for the company, you know, and his office is right there. He would get all the business rumors and then someone out here must have seen David go into your office twice without coming to the house. That's true, isn't it?"

"Afraid so."

"Well, there is enough put together to start a family conversation which the MacNeill youngster overheard and threw at Davey today."

Tim's face was still very grave and he sat silent so long, Katherine kept watching him anxiously.

"Would you accept money from David?" he said at last.

"For the children's needs, yes. I know he can afford it and perhaps, for the taxes and upkeep of the house. For myself, of course, I would not want to take anything from him. As you know, I have some funds of my own, thanks to our parents, bless them."

"The money part is a bit sticky. Where do your personal needs begin and end? You have to eat. You have to run the car. I think you'd better leave the financial end to David and me. But as to the divorce . . . I'm in a bad spot. David and I have always been close friends until all this wretched business came up. I felt you were wrong in holding out against the divorce, but now, in the light of the children's fears, no matter how unfounded, I can't go on with it." He put his head in his hands.

"Timmy dear, you mustn't take this so much to heart. Let David get another lawyer if he must."

"No. That I will not do if I can avoid it. If you refuse and sign nothing at all, I don't see how you can ever be coerced, but I don't want you to be harassed in any way by one of these sharpies. A fellow in law school always said they could go through the eye of a needle and come out on an elephant's back. So they can, damn them. I'll stick, if David will let me. And I'll stand with you about the divorce. That's going to be a big blow to him, Kathy."

"I've had a big blow myself, let me remind you!"

All was settled for Saturday. The children were hilarious with delight. It was to be Daddy's day, Katherine explained to them, but when they got home from their trip, they must go out and play, leaving Uncle Tim and Daddy to visit with her quietly.

On the day itself the morning drizzle settled into sunshine by the time David drove up to the house. The children were waiting outside with Katherine just behind them, so when the call came, "Hurry, Davey and Kit! Get in fast; we have a big morning ahead of us," it seemed natural enough for all hands to wave and for David and Katherine to call out to each other.

As the car sped away, the one left behind went in to sit

quietly in the living room. It was not a time for tears. The hurt was too deep and she felt it in the very tissues of her body; it was a longing, inescapable and essential. No surface tears could assuage it. It was for David, her man, who had been lover and husband in one; to whom she had given herself body and spirit. Or so it had always seemed to her.

She had watched him as he sat in the car, handsome and dominant, with something of a vital happiness in his face. His new love (if it really was that) and then the great business success! He had worked hard toward this and now it had been achieved. What man would not show confidence in himself and all the world at such a time?

All at once, almost automatically, she raised her head. *She* had helped with his success. Never until this moment had she realized how much. An old line flashed into her mind: *"Thy gentleness hath made me great."* She had contributed this. She had made their home a gentle place where a nervous man could relax. She gave her breast where a tired head could rest. Through all those years of ambition, she had shared his dreams, his moods, his certainties, and his doubts; and she had gloried in the sharing, for they for so long had been one. Would he indeed ever have reached his high place on the company ladder without her constant understanding and support?

In any case, she felt strangely comforted as these thoughts filled her mind and she began to set the table with her prettiest china and the epergne in the center dripping with the first white lilacs. When Tim stopped by to speak again of dinner plans, he repeated his views.

"I think, after our conversation, *especially* after that, he will want to get straight into the city. If he wants to wait over to discuss anything more with me, I'll take him to dinner."

"But the children won't possibly understand and they'll be so disappointed. If he would care to stay here, you could come and it would give the day a perfect finish for Davey and Kit."

"Could you stand it, feeling as you do?"

"I have to learn to stand things."

"Where do you get your strength, Kitten?" He hadn't called her that for years. It took her back to their childhood.

"I don't know. You just do what you have to. And I do still say my prayers. By the way, Tim, so should you. We were brought up the same way."

"I know. Only you stayed in the fold and I was a wandering sheep. Say, I've had a thought. No kidding. I'm in dead earnest. How would you like to have me go to church with you and the kids next time you go? Okay? That is, if it wouldn't throw the rector into a fit when he saw me in the pew!"

"Tim! You know I don't like you to talk that way."

"But I tell you I'm serious. You don't suppose I was thinking of my soul's salvation, do you? I have two good, practical reasons for my suggestion. One is that I think it would raise your spirits to have a big, strong — oh, don't let's be modest — handsome man in the seat beside you rather than to be alone. Wouldn't it?"

"Of course, Tim. You *are* thoughtful. I can't ever thank you —"

"The other reason is that rumors will soon, I fear, have to be dealt with in some way. Meanwhile, I feel it will be good for you and me to be seen together in public places — church, for one — so that all may know you not only have a male escort, but male protection. Well, I'll sound David out later about the dinner. Everything looks very pretty here. Including you," he added.

Katherine followed him to the door. "You asked me where I got strength. You won't believe it, but a lot of it comes from you, Timmy."

"Tut, tut, and likewise, nonsense!" he said. "See you later."

When the sightseers returned, it was not hard to send the children away. They tore off to tell their friends of the wonders they had seen. The three older people sat down in the living room and Tim said, "Go ahead, David, you begin."

David looked strained and embarrassed. "I feel like the proverbial cur, Katherine, to bring this hurt to your heart, but I can't help it. It's beyond my control. I have already explained. We will not go over that again. I do ask you very humbly to give me a divorce. The finances will be easy to take care of and, as to the children, I would only ask visiting rights and perhaps two or three weeks spent with me in Paris or London, whichever would be —"

"David!" Katherine's voice was a cry. "Oh, David, stop, please. You are all wrong. You are assuming I have changed my mind about the divorce, but I have not. I will not agree to one."

David was white. "What do you mean? What possible reason would you have for denying me? And you, Tim, agreed with me, you doublefaced —"

"Hold it!" Tim said. "I did agree with you and I tried honestly to show Kathy what I thought, until yesterday afternoon."

"Well, what happened then?"

"You tell him, Kathy. Don't leave out a thing."

So she told him the background of the children's knowledge; she described their fears, their tear-stained faces and Kit's trembling little hands. David turned and stood looking out the window. Then anger seemed to sweep over him. "But this is not really honest. You know if we had a divorce, nothing would be like the stories they heard. That scene with the children was terribly touching and dramatic, but it was more hysterical than true. Surely you know that everything could be explained happily to them."

"Except for one thing."

"What's that?"

"Why Daddy is living with a new wife."

Tim stood up quickly. They could hear the children at the

gate. "Come on, David. Let's go cook the steaks and then after an early dinner you can come up to the office for a bit and still get back to the city early."

"Sorry, Tim. I've got to leave now."

There were cries from the doorway. "But, Daddy, this was to be our day with you — the whole day — and Mother's made strawberry shortcake because you like it so well, and we're having *artichokes*!"

"Whew!" Tim whistled. "If you can pass up this dinner, you are a strong man, stronger than I am, David. Why don't you end the day gloriously for the kids, then come up to my office and cuss and discuss things a bit. You can still get back to the city in good time, since it's so early now."

A cry rang out from Davey before his father could answer. "Why, he hasn't seen the rabbit! He *couldn't* go without seeing it, Mother. Come on Daddy. It won't take but a minute."

David's hands were grasped by the smaller ones and he was led to the end of the lower garden. In a small house a snow-white rabbit was delicately munching lettuce.

"Isn't he *beautiful*?" the children asked together, and then, "Now you have to guess his name. We make everybody do that. Don't tell him, Kit," Davey adjured.

"Well, now, that oughtn't to be too hard," David said. "I guess it's Timmy, for Uncle Tim."

"Wrong," the children shouted. "Guess again! Don't tell him, Kit," Davey added.

David stared contemplatively at the rabbit, while Katherine, from the back door, felt a new sharp ache of loss as she watched the reality of father and children together.

At last he spoke. "It wouldn't be . . . I suppose it couldn't be *Peter*!"

They fell upon him rapturously. How had he guessed it so quickly? It had taken Uncle Tim all evening. When dinner was called, there seemed no time for change of plans. Before anyone realized any irregularity, they were all in their usual places at the table with the children's talk full of the visit to the lower garden and its inhabitant.

"But what I don't understand," Tim began, keeping conversation on a safe level, "is why you named that lovely white innocent rabbit for that famous iniquitous rascal who disobeyed his mother, sneaked into Mr. McGregor's garden, nibbled all his bean tops, lost his new jacket —"

"Hid in a wat'ring can," Kit put in, carried away by the story.

"And finally got back home dirty and disheveled."

"Dish what, Uncle Tim?"

"All mussed up," their father explained.

"And was put to bed without any supper. Just camomile tea. A rascal if ever I knew one. And why name your pure, white bunny, as I say, for that iniquitous —"

"What does that mean?" Davey demanded.

"Very, very naughty, indeed," David explained.

"But we didn't name our rabbit for the one in the story. Kit picked it out of a rhyme. Say it, Kit. It's sort of childish, but I went along with it."

Kit spoke clearly and sweetly:

"Peter, Peter Pumpkin-eater,
Had a wife and couldn't keep her;
He put her in a pumpkin shell,
And there he kept her very well."

"Now what about that!" Tim said. "My mind is certainly relieved. And the moral is that what the world needs are more pumpkin shells. Very, very good, Kit!"

"I think it's nice," Kit said complacently. "We like pumpkins and Cinderella's coach was made out of one, so —"

"There we are!" agreed Tim. "Now let's settle down to serious eating. What a dinner, Kathy!"

It was, indeed, excellent and even though David was quiet, it was evident he was hungry and able to enjoy the food, even under the circumstances. The children, for once, were allowed to talk uninhibited, so the chatter was bright and full of laughter, with Tim guarding against any awkward silences. When they all rose, replete, from the table, the children said good-by to their father and thanked him for the day.

"When you saw Peter and stayed to dinner, it just made it perfect," Davey said.

"And come back soon," little Kit whispered, holding his hand tightly in hers.

Tim left at once, saying he would be in his office for any sort of consultation. "I think there are a few things we might want to say, David. And, oh, thanks for that luscious meal, Kathy."

In a few minutes the house was quiet. Katherine closed the dining-room door and with one accord she and David went to the porch and stood, screened by the vines, each awaiting the voice of the other.

David spoke first. His voice was deep and angered. "I would never have believed you could be so hard, Katherine, so vindictive. I asked you humbly for a divorce, the only way to dissolve a marriage, and you refused me. How *could* you be so cruel, knowing what sort of life you would be making me live? I'm a decent man."

Katherine's eyes were flooded. "No, no, David, you are all wrong. The truth is I still love you. You see, I have no womanly pride left . . . only the feeling that I can't bear to have us torn apart, and our home broken by a decree. Can't you understand my feelings? It's like — " A small smile, albeit a sad one, touched her lips as she thought of some lines they had often read together years ago. She paraphrased one now: "Let no man dream but that I love thee still."

David looked at her strangely. "After all I've told you of my feeling?"

"Yes, and I'm not *making* you do anything, as you say. You are the one who is making the choice. And I'm not hard and vindictive. My only fault is that I —"

"I wish you hated me. It would make it easier."

"I know. I've sometimes thought of that too."

There was a long silence and then David came nearer. "Katherine, if you still love me as you say, then would you not give me the honorable happiness I ask you for? Won't you change your decision?"

"I can't, David. Won't you change yours and come back to us?"

"You know I couldn't." Then he turned quickly toward the steps. "I'm too shaken to talk to Tim tonight. I'll go on into the city as fast as I can." And he left.

Katherine went back to the ruins of the beautiful dinner and slowly began to bring about order. Perhaps it was prearranged by nature that women should always have dishes to wash and floors to sweep even when their hearts were breaking. They could make a snowy bed, they could hang bits of white linen on a line in the sunshine, and something of their inner pain would be eased. Men did not have such solace. Their hands were not trained to minister to their hearts. Most men, unless they were true craftsmen, would, in emergencies of the spirit, curse their particular fate, drink too many drinks, or sit in blind impotence, waiting for the first dark mood to pass.

At all events, Katherine, while thinking these thoughts, cleared the table, put away the silver, left the dishes in the washer, called the children in, and, after the bedtime rituals, went back to relax on the porch, where a full moon was making its silver lighten up the street and the yard. She sat beyond the vines so she would miss none of this beauty.

All at once she noticed a man walking slowly along their sidewalk. He was of medium height and strongly built. He wore a gray suit and the kind of soft straw hat most men had discarded. Under the edges there would seem to be grayish hair. He had stopped at the fence she and David had had fun building across the front of their property years ago. He stood now, drawing long breaths of the lilac-scented air and looking beyond the front lawn to the lower garden where there was much early bloom. Katherine could see his face quite clearly in the moonlight from her vantage point. She liked it. It looked strong and kindly.

At last he spoke, very low, but the tones were resonant. "Beautiful!" he said softly. "Beautiful!" And then, with a last look toward the garden, went on down the street.

Katherine felt a small warmth in her heart. What a charming compliment to her garden! She had worked hard on it to help heal her hurts. Now here came recompense. She wondered who the man was. While she was pondering, the telephone rang and she went indoors with a rapidly beating heart. It couldn't, though, be David, she knew, or even Tim. The voice that answered was that of Miss Darby.

"Now don't be scared," the lady began crisply. "This isn't about Davey. He's so good, I'm afraid he'll sprout wings. This is me, Mrs. Davenport . . . Gracious, I'll have to learn to say, 'It is I.' . . . Well, what I want to know is is it too late now to come over for some advice?"

"Oh, you couldn't be more welcome."

"I'll be right there."

When she arrived, it was evident that she was nervous and excited, so Katherine gave her a cup of coffee and insisted on the whole story at once.

"Well," said Miss Darby, "Joseph Harris —"

"You mean the Principal?"

"I do. I've known him a long time. He called me into his office and asked if I thought I could teach High School English. And he's got my records and knew all the time I taught that for ten years after college. The sneak!" she added affectionately. "Then he wanted to know why I changed, and I told him I began to feel I'd always be an old maid and not have any children of my own and I wanted to be among youngsters, so I had gone into primary work."

"And now?"

"I told him I'd take a try at the English and especially since they were caught in such a bind. Oh, I didn't explain that. Miss West of the English department is engaged and her fiancé has the sudden offer of a good job overseas. He wants to be married within two weeks and take her with him. And as I was leaving the office, what do you suppose Joe Harris said to me? He said, 'Now don't you ever fly off to get married on a week's notice and leave us in the lurch like this lovesick young thing.' Imagine saying that to *me*!"

Katherine saw on Miss Darby's cheeks a faint rise of color, which, in a young girl, could almost be taken for a blush. "Mr. Harris is so nice," she said. "And so very kind to everyone," Katherine said.

"A little *fresh*, I called it!" Miss Darby answered. "But, Mrs. Davenport, I haven't come to my reason for being here now. I had to give you the background first, as it were. But the point is, I've never paid much attention to how I looked and now suddenly, going before the older students, I care terribly. I want to look a little up-to-date and as — as good-looking on what we have to go on as possible. I wondered if you would sort of supervise me a little on a new hairdo and a couple of dresses. Would you?"

"Yes, yes, a thousand times, yes." Katherine told her. "I will love to help you. I simply *need* such a pleasant project just now. Are you pleased at getting into High School work?"

"Well, I do hate to leave my little folks, but I will enjoy the feel of Shakespeare under my tongue again . . . But how are things going with you? I've been selfish, telling all my own news. Dear Mrs. Davenport, is your situation better?"

Katherine shook her head. "This has been a hard day, so I'd rather talk about you. Some other time I'll pour out my troubles. Let's plan now what to do first."

At the end of an hour it was settled that Katherine would arrange an appointment with her own hairdresser. "We'll begin there," she said. "You have lovely hair, only you've kept it so tightly brushed and braided around your head, no one has noticed how pretty it is. We'll show them!" she added spiritedly.

By the time Miss Darby left, much of feminine arts and wiles had been divulged and a definite campaign agreed upon. At one point Miss Darby said "I think I'll tell you why I'm so dead anxious to be made over. I was in the hall yesterday and I heard two High School girls talking. One said, 'Who do you think we'll get for English now?" And the other said, 'Hadn't you heard? They've switched Old Bony to us.' I'm called that!"

"You won't be when I'm through with you," Katherine said, smiling, but with a grim determination in her tone.

When Miss Darby left, her eyes were moist with a strange delight. "I wouldn't have asked any other woman but you to do this for me," she said. "I'm so grateful."

When she was gone, Katherine put out the lights and went to her room, knowing sleep would be long in coming. She lay thinking of all the events of the day, feeling her last conversation with David was even harder to bear than his first confession. She thought of Kit's rhyme explaining Peter's name. Of all things for her to come up with right then — "Had a wife and couldn't keep her"! There should be another more fitting about the wife who couldn't keep her husband. She tried to make such a jingle and finally gave it up. Her head was weary with repetitive thoughts.

She decided to concentrate upon Miss Darby. Here there would be a bit of real pleasure and also something other than her own troubles to which she could cling. She wondered if there might indeed be a thin little thread of affection between the spinster teacher and the bachelor Principal. Well, no harm in giving him a shock as well as the students. She went over all the possibilities of her campaign until at last her tired head grew drowsy. But it was not of David, nor Miss Darby, either one, who crossed her last consciousness. It was of the person she called to herself The Gray Man who had looked so long at her garden and said softly, "Beautiful! Beautiful!" I wonder, she thought dreamily, who he was.

Chapter Three

THE TRANSFORMATION of Miss Darby was more startling than even Katherine herself had dreamed. When in the beauty salon her thick braids were unbound and the abundant hair with a faint russet tinge hung loose over her shoulders, Henri, the master, gave himself up to true Gallic delight. "But what hair! What length! What thickness! Mon Dieu, what a joy to work with that! You shall see, madame, what we shall do for you!"

"Well, I'm in your hands. I think I need some improvement, so go ahead and do whatever is necessary," Miss Darby returned, her expression a mixture of fright and anticipation.

So Henri, the skillful one, went to work, calling upon his most clever minions to assist him.

Once, with hesitation, he managed to tell his client that he felt she probably had tried to wash the hair herself sometimes and that a little of the *savon* had remained in it.

"I know the word for soap," Miss Darby said at once. "You may be right. Well, we can see what your shampoo will do."

"One thing, it will make it one tiny, tiny more light in color," he replied complacently.

"None of these rinses, mind you!"

"Please relax, madame, and let us get to our delightful work!"

When all had been accomplished, the abundant hair cut, shaped, washed, trained in rollers and under the dryer, Miss

Darby was lead to the front salon and seated before the large mirror, while Henry, with brush and comb, prepared for the final triumph. When it came, he danced about his work, viewing it from every angle, speaking much volatile French, while Katherine looked and marveled and Miss Darby stared at the mirror and said nothing at all. For her head was now covered with soft waves, a shade lighter than the very dark auburn, artistically arranged by a master hand so that the whole beautiful coiffure was indeed a crown of glory.

When Miss Darby spoke at last, she was angry. "I know just what you did, you Henri. You cut off all my own hair and put a wig on me. Now you've got to make that right somehow, though I can't see how. I feel sick —"

"A wig? But listen to her, Madam Davenport! I shall show her tout de suite."

He reached over and clutched a curl between his fingers and pulled it sharply.

"Ouch!" cried Miss Darby.

"You want more proof, yes?" asked Henri wickedly.

Miss Darby laughed and rose from the chair. "You must forgive me, Henri. You see, I couldn't believe that could possibly be my own hair. I can't even believe it's myself I see in the mirror. Oh, I can't thank you enough for what you've done to me. You say you want to see me again in two weeks?"

"No longer. I must check on my beautiful work. Two more little things perhaps Mrs. Davenport will see to. If you'll just go out through our cosmetic alcove you can get them. One eye pencil, soft, and the other, a lipstick. Let the girl there select it. With your hair. Madame Darby, you must be careful. But a *soupçon* will make such a nice difference. Women must watch these small aids to beauty. What a pleasure to have served you, madame!"

The bill was arranged, the cosmetics purchased, and as though the Angel of Beauty was brooding over Miss Darby, a hasty and tentative look in a dress shop ended in the purchase of two becoming dresses.

"Why, this is all too good to be true for one morning," Katherine said. "By the way, when will you be seeing Dr. Harris again?"

"This afternoon at four. We're to have a conference. You see, this week is a sort of interim for me when I can glance in on my successor occasionally and also find where I start in English. We have only a month left and Dr. Harris would like to rearrange the curriculum for next fall. I'll enjoy doing that."

"Will you do me a favor?"

"As if I could ever repay you!"

"Come over this evening and tell me how Dr. Harris liked your hair."

Miss Darby looked flustered. "Dear knows," she said, "how he'll take it. He's pretty conservative. He will probably think I'm an old fool trying to look young. But I'll tell you!"

When she came that evening, she was definitely ill at ease, but with all her nervousness Katherine was more struck by the physical change in her than she had been earlier in the day. The trace of lipstick applied by the cosmetic girl and the sketchiest arch of the eyebrows were still present, along with the white cowl of the new dress collar and, above all, the beauty of the hair.

"Come on, Miss Darby. I've been a party to all this. I'm dying to know what Dr. Harris said."

"But — but, dear Mrs. Davenport, I can't — I couldn't tell you. I was so shocked for he never — I never heard him — I really wouldn't want to repeat — "

Katherine laughed. She realized it was the first real laugh she had had since all her own trouble began.

"Oh, Miss Darby, let me guess. I think he took one good look at you as you are now and then said, 'Well, I'll be damned!'"

Miss Darby almost flew out of her chair. "Oh, did you hear it? Some student must have passed the office, listened, and told you. Oh, I'm so terribly embarrassed — "

"Listen, Miss Darby, I didn't hear anything. Nobody did but you. I was only guessing. You see, I've known several men very well. My husband, my brother, and my father too, and I'm sure I've heard each of them at one time or another use those words when he had a big, pleasant shock. It just struck me that maybe Dr. Harris might have said the same thing. That's all there is to it!"

"You really think that was it?"

"Why, certainly. Then I imagine when he got over his amazement, he said some very pleasant things."

"Oh, he did. I couldn't — I really never expected him to — to — I was very much surprised — *moved*," she ended, sitting down again. "But that first expression — I'm so glad you explained about it. I'll tell you now, though, the nicest thing that happened to me — next to Dr. Harris' c-comments," she added the word primly. "When I was leaving the office, two students passed and *they didn't know me*!"

With normal feminine excitement they went over all the events of the day and when Miss Darby left at last, a changed woman, Katherine felt a sense of loss. For all the last hours her mind had been away from David and her own personal problems. Now, tomorrow, there would be nothing to fend them off, to keep them out. Strangely enough, there was.

She was doing a bit of weeding when she heard the sound of the gate hinge. She looked up and saw, standing hesitant there, The Gray Man, as she had mentally dubbed him that night in the moonlight. She rose at once and went toward him. He had doffed his Panama hat and now she realized he was much more handsome than she had guessed in that first evening view of him.

"Good morning," she said brightly. "I'm glad to have the chance to thank you for your lovely words about my garden as you stood there by the fence a few nights ago. Would you care to come in and see it at close range? It's really nothing wonderful, though, I warn you."

He watched her hesitantly — indeed, she thought, a little humbly.

"I couldn't be more eager to accept your invitation, but I think first I should explain why I was standing here at your gate. You see, I've been a man, as Mr. Keats would say, 'long in city pent,' My business kept me there, but as soon as I could get away I never went on one of the usual *vacations*." He paused and smiled and as he did so, she liked him completely. There was a charming warmth in it.

"It must be an old inheritance in my bones. What I did was *gardening,* at home, of course, but wherever I could find a place to work, I offered my service free for the pleasure of dealing with flowers instead of figures. Do you understand my story at all?"

"Yes, I do. The only thing is, it's seems too wonderful to believe. Were you really thinking of working in my garden?"

"Well, you see, I took a fancy to it, as we all take fancies to various people, I suppose. I came by chance to this delightful old town and felt it might have garden possibilities. That first evening I knew I had found what I wanted when I saw yours."

"Please come in," Katherine said at once. "You should see it before you get too involved."

As they moved back, she explained that the arrangement had been all her own and his practiced eyes might find much that needed changing. "If you really decide to work in it," she added.

"If you decide to allow me to be an assistant gardener," he rejoined, and they both laughed.

It was more than pleasant to Katherine to point out her favorites and see his skill in discovering others. He drew breaths of satisfaction as he walked beside the tiny stream at the end of the lower garden.

"I believe watercress would grow here if we treated it tenderly," he said. "I think you would like that, and the violets — the Johnny Jump-Ups — I think should all be put along the little bank. Too bad we can't get any wild thyme!"

Katherine laughed delightedly. "Oh, you're a Shakespearean gardener then, aren't you?"

"Don't tell me you are! Why, this enhances everything. Oh, by the way, do excuse me for not introducing myself at once. I was so eager about the garden I forgot my manners. My name is Philip Andrews and I'm stopping at the hotel here."

"I'm Katherine Davenport and before long, there will be two small people who will be terribly interested in everything you do."

"Good! I like children," he went on. "I should think this lower garden should be left practically as it is — it's what I call a *natural* garden. The tiny stream sets the motif, as it were. But in the upper one — ah, I have ideas! When I have looked it over again carefully, may I make a little sketch of what is in my mind?"

"But, of course."

"Then you could make your own suggestions or possibly accept mine. But the point is you must be completely pleased."

He began his study then as a doctor might study a patient, bringing forth a little pad and pencil upon which he made notes. He made remarks to various flowers also as he touched them. "Good!" he would say softly to one. "Nice and straight." To another a mild rebuke: "That's not the way — to bend over like that. Here, I'll give you a little stick to lean on. Now, look up at the sun." He glanced back at Katherine once. "Have you ever heard that flowers grow better when you talk to them?"

"Yes, I have. But I'm afraid my conversations are more stilted than yours."

"Oh, I'm an old friend. I guess they know me. I really think there is truth in the adage, though."

When he had made his careful rounds, he suggested to Katherine that they might sit down while he made a sketch from his notes, for her approval. "And as I explain my ideas," he added.

"Please do. I'm excited already."

"Well, I think this upper garden should have a touch of formality. Not too much. That wouldn't suit the charming old house, but just enough to give it a bit of — well — elegance."

He sketched quickly and Katherine, with her lively imagination, watched beauty grow under his hand.

"I would first suggest a low brick wall along the lower side to separate this from that. Flowers like to stand in front of a wall. Gives them confidence, I fancy. I would suggest letting it grow a bit taller as it reaches across the back. There your garden seat could be and you could go up to it by a little brick walk, bordered on both sides by all your most fragrant and dignified flowers — white phlox, stock, nicotiana, along with Canterbury bells and snapdragons." He stopped for breath. "There are two schools about rose plants. Some say they must all be in a bed to themselves. I don't agree. If each rose has plenty of room to breathe, it will flourish near other flowers. I am very fond of mingling roses judiciously with their neighbors. You can always have a whole bed somewhere but oh, the satisfaction of using their color and fragrance here and there to enjoy all through the garden. So I would have a choice rose here and there frequently. Does any of this make sense to you?"

"It sounds perfect, but how will I get the walls built?"

"I didn't tell you, but I'm sure there was a mason somewhere among my great-greats. I never feel more satisfied than when I fit brick on brick. Don't worry. It will go fast."

"But there is an element of expense involved," Katherine said hesitantly.

He smiled his gentle, disarming smile. "Please understand. I am at an age when I don't need to continue working for my living. I can use my assets, such as they are, as I please. Most men in like positions do various things: they tear all over the world in travel, they collect paintings, they endow colleges. Well, I make gardens and, in a sense, endow them. Are you content now?"

"More than that. I'm amazed and happy."

"Then we're ready to start. I will go about this afternoon and pick up some faded bricks and find a good nursery, and tomorrow I shall appear in my work clothes and begin as Philip, the gardener, to all and sundry."

Before he left, however, the children came, hanging to Tim's hand. Introductions were made and after a chat in which it was plain Davey and Kit had accepted "Mr. Philip" with quick acclaim, they walked with him and Tim came inside to talk to Kathy.

"For heaven's sake," he said, "fill me in on the details. Who is this man and what's he doing here?"

"Didn't you like him?"

"Well, yes, as a matter of fact, I did. But I'm still a little mystified. He seemed to me to be holding something back. He wasn't open about where he lived, why he was in the town at all, and what I'm most concerned about is why he happens to be working for *you*!"

She began at the evening he had stood at the fence, softly praising her garden and told him all his story as he had given it to her.

Tim whistled. "It seems a queer setup, but it may be all right. I studied him, of course, while we talked. First of all, he is patently a *gentleman*. Then he's a very cultured one. You can tell at once. But he's holding something back. I threw out half a dozen little leads about his home, his work, and the city generally. He gracefully parried everything which seemed like a question."

"But you like him?"

"Unqualifiedly. That is, three fourths of me does or seven

eighths, or whatever. The other fraction of me has a question. And I don't like mysteries except in novels. Tell you what I'll do."

Tim patted her shoulder. "I know the hotel people pretty well, especially the manager. I'll see what he has to say. They all have a sixth sense about people. And, Kitten dear, keep your distance and your dignity. Even if he has charm — and he certainly has — he *is* a stranger. I think I'll make it my business to drive up rather late sometimes and sleep in my room here. It won't hurt to let him see I've had my coffee with you."

"Oh, Tim, you lawyers do have the wickedest thoughts. I won't let you mar Mr. Andrews' kindness with your ridiculous suspicions."

"All right! All right! Just play it cool, Kathy. And as to my wicked thoughts, they're my stock in trade, you know."

The next morning the stranger arrived at nine, clad in a neat work suit, evidently made for gardeners, for there were pockets where various tools could probably fit. Almost at the same time, a small truck drew up on the drive which ran along the upper side of the house and deposited a load of beautifully faded rose-pink bricks. The driver began bringing them by bushel basketsful over to the garden where the wall was to be built. The stranger was delighted. He called Katherine to witness the color.

"It's almost impossible to find bricks like these, but the hotel manager, who knows everything, took me right where they were. I can hardly wait now to begin to build."

The driver brought a tub of what Katherine assumed was cement and Mr. Andrews announced his procedures.

"We must move the plants where I have to kneel or stand to work, but if they could be set with their feet in the little stream, they will not be harmed."

"I'll do that," she said. "I'd like to be doing something."

"Good. Then we dig a very small trench into which we put

just a bit of gravel. So! And then at last I will really *begin*. I'll help you finish moving the plants first."

When Katherine watched the wall rising layer upon layer, she could hardly contain herself. "Play it cool," Tim had told her. How could she, when her excitement rose by the minute? This was a miracle. Steadily, speedily, brick upon brick, the stranger's skillful hands worked as though he were one with his materials.

"It's going to be *beautiful*!" Katherine kept exclaiming. "You are right. It will add real elegance to the garden. Oh, I love it. But how fast you do it!"

"It doesn't take long when you know how, and it's a very low wall. We should have this side done by one o'clock. The one at the end may take a bit longer. I've been thinking of the upper side. Brick there would be too much. What would you think of a row of little pointed evergreens?"

"Lovely."

"Then we'll do that. I'll talk to the hotel manager, a delightful chap and a perfect repository of useful knowledge. He'll know the right place to go for them when we're ready. Do sit down and be comfortable while I concentrate hard on my work."

When the children came, they were entranced. "Oh, Mother, you should have told us. We've missed a whole morning watching him. Will you be making the wall this afternoon too, Mr. Philip?" Davey asked.

"Oh, yes. I shall say until at least four o'clock. At which time," he added with a twinkle as he eyed Katherine, "would it be possible to have a cup of tea to celebrate our first bit of wall?"

"Oh, of *course!* And what about lunch? I have some sandwiches all ready. We'd love to have you join us."

"No, thank you very much. I'm ashamed to say I eat a workman's lunch and they make quite a fuss over it at the hotel. So I mustn't disappoint them. But as to tea, to which I invited myself, I accept with the greatest pleasure."

The sun was kind that afternoon, bright enough, but tempering its rays to those who had to work beneath it. Mr. Philip, as he was now freely called, took only a short time for lunch and then began to add to the wall. Two feet high he had planned and two narrow brick widths thick: it seemed almost a living thing creeping steadily along under his hands. He had helpers now. Davey and Kit on the other side, carefully handed him brick by brick.

"Wonderful! Now we go faster!"

"Oh, I could have been doing that," Katherine said, chagrined.

"No, dear lady. Your heaviest work should be cutting the flowers when all is done."

She laughed, noting to herself how many occasions there seemed to be for laughter; then went into the house and on to the kitchen. She had a feeling the stranger might be old-fashioned enough to like gingerbread. On the assumption she baked a panful, set it to cool, split English muffins and spread them ready for the broiler, put the tea things where the children could carry them easily to the side porch overlooking the garden where they would eat, and sat down to quiet an inner tremor in her heart.

She sat on, knowing she was tired, listening to the voices outside and wondering if Tim had found out anything at the hotel about the stranger, The Gray Man, Mr. Philip. Every hour she was with him, she not only admired him more, but felt a mystery. She must have drowsed a little, because she was wakened by wild childish whoops and a masculine "Hurrah." She hurried out at once and saw the little wall completed! Even during the building she had not realized what real beauty and elegance it would add. She was, for a moment, speechless with delight.

"What a lovely gift you have given us! How can I ever thank you?"

"You have," he said, looking very directly into her eyes. "I like it too. I'm always ashamed to be so proud of my work, but I have to admit it. Now, if you'll excuse me for just a few minutes, I'll go back and remove some of the cement from my garment."

"We have a flower sink," Davey volunteered, "where you could wash your hands."

"Thank you, but I'll feel better to change. I won't be long."

When he returned, he was handsome in the gray suit and proper shirt and tie. The children led him to the big wicker chair as the place of honor beside the tea table.

Katherine explained that they had built this side porch so they could look right into the garden and watch the changing afternoon lights upon it.

"You watch them too? To me, the most golden of all brightness is the western light just before the actual sunset. Oh, what a charming setting here! If every workman was served a cup of tea at the end of his day, it might put off all union wrangling, stop strikes and who knows what? Should we propose the idea?"

Katherine smiled as she filled the cups. "The trouble is, they might not all like tea. I've heard many workmen prefer beer."

"That's true. Perhaps we'd better just let the world wag along without our advice. How are my helpers?" he asked, turning to the children. "Do you know your work has a real name? It's called "tending the mason," and you did it very well."

The gingerbread was an inspiration and the muffins crisp and hot. There was much laughter and the mood one of happy gaiety. When the children at last left to find their playmates, Katherine remarked, "How blest we've been so far in the weather! It's been perfect."

At once Mr. Philip leaned forward.

"'Shall I compare thee to a summer's day?'" he quoted.
"'Thou art more lovely and more temperate:
Rough winds do shake the darling buds of May . . .
But thy eternal summer shall not fade.'

"I'm afraid my quote is not quite exact, but that sonnet is one of my favorites. *'The darling buds of May!'* Imagine the Earl of Oxford or anyone except Shakespeare writing that!"

They discussed the old controversy with some vehemence and then Mr. Philip drew out his little notebook and pencil and began to sketch.

"You see, I've done some thinking as I worked and last night before I went to bed and I've concluded that I made a mistake about that rather higher brick wall at the back. Too much brick. So! For your approval, I suggest we let the end of the wall already built, curve into a little patio with plants all behind it. You could have your garden seat there and a couple of chairs perhaps. Then a little brick walk would lead up to it, this patio, bower, or whatever you wish to call it. How does the idea strike you?"

"Oh, very, very well. In fact, I had wondered about the other wall — whether it would give a sort of heaviness to the garden. This sounds perfect — if it all isn't too much to do."

Mr. Philip turned his disarming smile on her. "You may not believe me, but this is going to be pure fun for me. But now I must be going. I've stayed too long, but it's been the most delightful tea I've ever known. When I spoke of a workman's tea hour I really wasn't hinting, you know."

"And Shakespeare did write so many sonnets," she returned. And they both laughed as he left.

That evening Tim came, studied the wall, went up to say good night to the children, and then sat down to talk to Katherine.

"Your new little wall is a lovely thing. It adds what Mother always referred to as 'indescribable charm' to your garden. And I'd swear it was built by a professional hand — at least, by someone who has built a lot of walls."

"Why do you look so sober, Tim? Did you go to the hotel? Did you find out anything wrong? Please don't keep me uneasy."

"Yes, I went to the hotel and had a long talk with John

Boles, the manager. What I found out was that from him down to the women who clean the rooms, everybody there is his absolute slave. Boles couldn't praise him enough. Such a fine gentleman who knew just how things should be done, so kind to everyone and so generous. And he *dressed for dinner!* It gave a tone to the hotel and now occasionally a few other men do it too."

"Did he explain why he was there?"

"Oh, yes. Substantially what he told you. I asked to see the register, said I was interested in handwriting or some such thing and he spread it open. There was the name Philip Andrews written in a rather odd hand, beginning strongly and then tapering off a bit. But what really disturbed me was what followed. It said simply, 'The Willows, Landers, New York,' and he explained to Boles that he didn't want to be bothered with any calls or messages, so set down a madeup address."

"Well, couldn't his idea be a reasonable one? Haven't men put down fictitious addresses before and even names?"

"Usually when they have a strawberry blonde or a redhead with them. Which is not the case here. Boles stressed what a quiet man he was. A little brandy after dinner and then a walk maybe and after that to his room to read until bedtime . . . So," Tim ended, "now I've told you all."

"And you're satisfied now?"

"Let's say reasonably. I'm entirely satisfied with your little wall, though I think it's one of the prettiest bits of masonry I ever saw!"

The town of Lemming was, in the first place, only a broad strip of green bordered by two softly rounded hills: A few hunters camped there occasionally but it was not until revolutionary times that enough settlers had made their homes there to give it importance. After the war was over, many men who had learned of adventure through arms left to go westward, but there remained a strong nucleus of those men content to ply their trades or work their small farms on the rounded hills.

As years passed, population grew, churches and schools were built, a railroad finally included it in its journey and the little settlement of Lemming became first a thriving village and then a large and busy town, keeping with it something of the earlier peace along the tree-lined residential streets. It was this that attracted city people as they passed through on pleasure drives, sometimes to try out a new automobile. It had been so with David and Katherine Davenport years ago.

"A nice place to live out here, if one could," David had remarked.

"But it would be possible," Katherine had said eagerly. "Oh, I would love it if the commuting would not be too hard for you."

"We'll look into it," he had said. And in two years they were established in the comfortable old house with its porches and gardens.

Katherine especially had thrilled to the kind of life she found here. She was essentially a friendly person and she rejoiced in the neighborliness of her community and her street in particular. She knew all the families on it; three of the women besides Mary Hastings were her closest friends. They had been kind about her trouble. They had not spoken David's name in a way to hurt her, though they soon knew the facts. But now, on this sunny morning as she prepared breakfast, she was wondering how they would receive Philip Andrews' story. Tonight was Bridge Club too, and she must prepare them somewhat. So she called Celia Bradley on the phone and suggested she come by and see what was going on in the garden."

"Katherine! You don't mean it. I've been simply dying to come in and yet I was hesitant about it. Everyone wonders how you found this marvelous gardener when most of us have trouble even getting a man to cut the grass. What's he like?"

"Come and see," Katherine said, "but don't stay long. He doesn't like to be interrupted in his work."

She wondered how the meeting would go. She had discovered that he had the social gift of meeting people with absolute courtesy and then escaping quickly and with easy grace from those who didn't interest him. It was even so with Tim which puzzled her. Anyone, she felt, would be interested to talk with Tim. Such intelligence! Such wit! Did Philip Andrews feel instinctively that Tim's mind held a question concerning him? But she didn't need to worry about Celia Bradley. That lady came breezing in at midmorning, calling, "Hi, Katherine! Show me the garden and the marvelous man who's working miracles in it!"

They went to where Philip Andrews was beginning on the curving patio and he rose at once for the introductions.

"Oh, Mr. Andrews, I'm so excited about all this and the wall is simply adorable. Won't you tell me all about how you ever happened to get here, to this town and this garden? I'm *so* interested!"

Katherine trembled inwardly, but Mr. Philip smiled at Celia as he would have to Kit.

"Well now, it's like this. When I'm on vacation, as I am now, I drive around through town after town until I find one that captivates me, as Lemming did; then I walk about in it until I see a garden I long to get into; then I ask the lady who owns it if I could pull a few weeds for her or plant a few flowers, and see —" He made a little expansive gesture with his hands. "See what we arrive at!"

"That's fascinating! And the bricklaying?"

"Oh, I'm not a professional. I just like to do it. It makes me remember all the mathematics I never learned in school, when I build a wall. And I have an idea if Ovid had been taught to lay bricks he would have made a wonderful mason. But, good heavens, I mustn't detain you with nonsense like this, and I'm working on a sort of schedule, so I must get on with it. It's been delightful to talk with you, Mrs. Bradley." And with a graceful gesture he returned to his bricks.

Celia was completely charmed and as completely baffled as she discussed the conversation with Katherine in the house. "I really didn't learn a thing," she said, "but he's simply divine. Can I tell the girls about him at club tonight?"

"Of course. All there is to tell."

The Bridge Club met across town that night and Tim, as he sometimes did, drove her over to the home of her hostess and picked her up afterward, eager to hear what was said between bridge "hands."

"Of course they drank in Celia's report and asked me all kinds of questions and each, it seemed, had a different theory about his coming. But one always rose to the top."

"What was that?"

"They've all been so sweet to me and now they feel Providence has provided me with a new interest, so that I won't think of anything except my garden."

"Not a bad idea. As to theories about him, I've had a few new ones myself. Might he be a clergyman unfrocked? If so, he'd never mention his profession, certainly. In a way, it fits him. Or a lawyer, disbarred from practicing? Not such a good fit, but possible."

"And I've thought of a professor, sick of the classroom and wanting to get far away from it. Oh, apropos of teaching, there's one person I do want to invite over to meet him. I'll have to fend the girls off, for he wouldn't like them swarming around. But Miss Darby would be different. I haven't seen her for some time."

Tim laughed. "Trust old Tim here to find out the gossip. I can tell you what she's been up to. Several times I've had occasion to pass her house in the early dusk and there she was on her little patio with a man looking like Dr. Harris and they were both imbibing something from tall glasses by means of sippers. I'm terribly afraid it was *lemonade.* It surely didn't look like Bloody Marys. It distresses me to witness these Bacchanalian revels, but I thought I ought to let you know!"

"Oh, Tim, you are incorrigible. I'm so happy if it was Dr. Harris. But you mustn't make fun of them, especially of Miss Darby."

"I wouldn't think of it. Since you've made her so good-looking, I could even make a pass at her myself."

"Now, stop it, Tim. I want to speak to you about something else in a serious way since we've started out on this line."

"I have a vague feeling I may have heard it before."

"Oh, you have. I still yearn to see you happily married. Don't you ever consider it?"

"Oh, I have. I've made up my mind at last."

"Tim! That's wonderful. Tell me, dear . . . everything!"

"After duly weighing the matter, I've decided that when I find a girl as nice as you, I'll marry her the next day. If she'll have me," he added.

"Oh, *you*!" Katherine said. "Such a thing to say just when I was really getting excited. Well, I'll just have to put all my matchmaking skill upon Miss Darby then."

"Did I ever tell you," she added, "how I really came to fall in love with David?"

"No."

"It was because so many little things about him reminded me of you."

Tim did not answer at once and then said quietly, "Thank you. That's the nicest compliment I've ever received."

"No word from him lately?"

"Just the check from his bank." And they began to talk of other things.

With surprising swiftness day followed day until in the aggregate, they became one and then two weeks. The brick patio curved in grace before a planting of young lilac bushes. The walk, Katherine's favorite of all the new masonry, moved with an almost human beauty through the garden, the sunlight bringing out the fair pink and rose of its composition.

"And, Katherine," they had advanced easily to first names,

"there must be a Sun Dial. I'll attend to that. And remember to set it at sun time. It pays no attention to Daylight Savings. What wisdom there often is in material things!"

The teas continued, though usually without the children, who grew tired of grown-up talk. So Katherine and Philip wandered easily through bits of philosophy and poetry and, most of all, the seasonal needs of the garden. Sometimes she invited a guest experimentally. Miss Darby was a success.

"Now, I'm no gardener. I can't tell boneset from honeysuckle, but I can appreciate what other people do. And to me that little wall, there, is the prettiest thing in this garden. It's so firm and sound and you can rest your heart on it."

"What a perfect compliment!" Philip said. "Thank you. I hope by next summer there will be a glory of Madonna lilies there. I'm quite sentimental about that; for when I was a boy of seventeen or so I sang a bit and one song went:

'The lilies clustered fair and tall
They grew beside the garden wall.'

A shadow crossed his face. "I remembered that only a few weeks ago. Now it's completely gone."

"Don't worry," Miss Darby said crisply. "I forgot the Lord's Prayer yesterday."

He laughed and the shadow passed. "I do know the last two lines, though:

'I stood alone outside the gate
And knew that life was desolate.'

How's that for a mournful seventeen? And why do the very young seem to turn to sad songs and verse at a time when they should be most buoyant?"

"Oh, I know," Katherine put in. "I came across some verses I had written in that period and they are all about death and unrequited love, and yet I was a completely happy young girl. It is strange, isn't it?"

"Well, I have a theory," Miss Darby said. "You see, it's in the teens that the great tragedies first hit young people and usually they don't feel them as actualities. They think of them as dramas, like something on the stage. So they dramatize them in their mournful songs and sad verses and in this way, in a sense, have dealt with them and so can go on their normal, happy way.

"Later on, poor young things, they learn life's tragedies are all too real and may impinge on their own lives and then they crave bright songs and verses to comfort their hearts which before needed no comforting. Oh, dear me! Excuse me for talking so long. It's the school teacher in me, Mr. Andrews. I must go now, Mrs. Davenport. It's been a lovely tea."

"And you've given me a great deal to think about, Miss Darby. May I walk with you as far as my hotel?"

If it was evident that Mr. Andrews was relaxing in friendliness toward the townsfolk in general, it was even more apparent that their interest in him and his work had grown. Every day now, it seemed, a woman and often, indeed, a man stopped at the white gate and, if Katherine was in sight, begged to come in for just "five minutes or so" to see this unusual garden. And Philip, instead of withdrawing courteously into the background, acted as though he had grown to like all the callers and showed real pleasure at their praise. Katherine wondered if he had never received such friendly praise before.

The debris was all cleared away and loads of blooming plants arrived now often in the little truck which had brought the bricks.

"Where do you ever find them?" she asked.

"Oh, it's Boles, the hotel manager. He pulls them out of his hat, I think," Philip said lightly.

One afternoon he varied his usual routine. "Would you be

home this evening if I should drop in for a little while? I have a very special sonnet I've been committing to recite to you without a book. Would it be convenient?"

"Of — of course," she answered a bit nervously. "That would be delightful."

"Would eight-thirty be a suitable time?"

"Yes, quite. I'll be trying to guess the sonnet."

"The first line is one of the most beautiful in the language, I think. Maybe that will give you a clue. I'll see you this evening, then, and thank you."

Katherine's hands were a trifle unsteady as she drew several dresses from her closet, deciding what to wear that evening. And yet, she upbraided herself, there was no cause for emotion. Or — was there? She stopped to ponder. There were several disturbing things. She had once caught a glance in Philip's eyes which had made her start a new conversation quickly. There was Tim's unrelenting question which amounted to a warning. There were her hands now fumbling a bit over the dress at the thought of his unusual request to come for the evening.

"Oh, nonsense!" Katherine summed it up. "I'm only imagining things because being admired goes to any woman's head a bit. And, as to Tim, he's so immersed in cases and intrigue, he can't see a simple situation."

She made coffee and set the small cups and a liqueur on the end of the living-room table. Philip came on the dot of the hour, so to speak, and stood for several minutes looking at Katherine in her long, soft dress of blue.

"Do sit down. I have some coffee, in case we might need to be braced for Shakespeare. You know, I'm so curious and eager about the sonnet."

Philip was at once his charming self. "Perfect! Coffee is the one thing the hotel seems to be unable to bring to perfection. Ah, this is delicious. And liqueur too. You do know how to cheer the spirit, don't you? And by the way, I'm admiring your room. It's lovely. The first time I've been in it, you know."

"Oh, that does sound inhospitable of me, but the weather seemed to demand the porch."

"We couldn't give up a single tea. But I'm glad to see the inside of your house. It has a rare combination of delicacy and a sort of strength. I congratulate you."

The talk drifted soon to the garden, the new flowers they had both forgotten on their lists, the new planting against the wall. "I know," he said suddenly, "Canterbury bells! We almost left them out. We must remedy that."

After a time Katherine said she was waiting for the sonnet, and could it not begin now?

"Oh, yes. I'm eager for us to share it together. The first line, I think, is, as I told you, one of the finest in the English language and the alliteration defies all criticism. It is so effortless, so inescapable. Well, I'll begin." In his low, resonant voice he spoke the first words:

"'When to the sessions of sweet silent thought
I summon up remembrance of things past . . .'"

There was a sudden triple knock on the door. It was Tim's signal that he was coming in. Before Katherine could cross the room, Philip had reached the door and stood facing Tim. Philip's back was to her, but she could see Tim's face grow pale and his arms reach out and grasp Philip's with a deadly grip. They stood for only a couple of minutes, then the color seemed to come back to Tim's face and he dropped his arms. "I'm so sorry," he said, trying to speak naturally. "I'm afraid I interrupted a lovely visit. Do forgive me."

But Philip spoke before Katherine could finish her request for them to sit down.

"I really must be going. It has been delightful, Mrs. Davenport, and thank you very much —"

"But we've only begun on the sonnet," she said, her voice trembling.

"We'll finish it another time. I must be getting to the hotel now." And he left.

Half shuddering, she watched Tim carefully locking every door before he sat down. "And now I'll try to tell you. But it's a sad story, Kathy."

"But first, why did you hold his arms when you came in?"

"I was trying to save my life, I guess. I've never seen such blind rage or anger on a human face before. I thought he meant to choke me.

"Well, to begin before that, you surely must know the poor man is dead in love with you. And, as I've told you before, he has enormous charm. I don't know your feelings."

"Oh, Tim dear, I'll tell you about them later. But I want to hear his story now. I'm so mystified and frightened."

"Well," Tim spoke slowly, "it's a sad-enough story. As you know, I felt a strange uneasiness about him, so I hired the finest detective I know. At first all clues seemed to be nonexistent and then slowly he came out of the tunnel. He found Philip's son Phil. The last name is Armour. The son gave the facts briefly.

"His father had been one of the greatest actuaries in the country, with an enormous salary and a genius for investment on the side. His hobbies had always been gardening and reading to rest him from figures, he said. About ten years ago he and his wife had been taking a driving trip through Europe when, in a tiny town in Italy, there was a terrible auto accident. The wife died, but Philip survived physically with only touches of amnesia as a result. They found later however, that he, the gentlest of all men, as his son said, was occasionally seized by fits of rage which endangered his own life and that of the one causing it. He had to be under constant guard for safety.

"The son said they had built a combination hospital and country home with plenty of space around for gardening, but here he must stay! Even though under the strictest surveillance, at times he escaped and then Phil, the son, said he was frantic as the search went on, for there had been several near-fatal accidents. He sent word now, having heard of his whereabouts here, that there must always be at least two people with him until he could — could come for him in the morning."

"You mean they're coming to take him away — to take him back? Oh, Tim, he has made all the plans for certain planting tomorrow. This is too cruel. I can't go through with it in the morning."

"Yes, you'll have the strength. You must wave him off gaily and tell him you'll write him about the flowers. You'll do it. But why not go up now and rest, even if you can't sleep. I'll stay tonight and be around in the morning. Oh, Kathy, I had to do what I did. And I'm glad the strange thing happened this very evening. You'll understand better."

"I do understand, Tim, and I love you for all you did. I'm only stunned. I'll go to my room and sort out my feelings, and I'm glad you'll be here tonight."

Promptly the next morning, which was mild and sunny, at nine Philip appeared in a fresh work suit and spoke gaily to Katherine on the porch. "A perfect day for gardeners. I can't wait to get at this new planting."

His looks and tone were normal as he had evidently forgotten all about the episode of the night before. He was kneeling before a clump of heliotrope when a large car stopped before the house. He evidently felt it unimportant and went on with his work until a voice behind him said, "Why, hello, Dad!"

Then he got quickly to his feet and faced his son. "Phil!" he said. "How did you get here?" There was both amazement and fear in his voice.

"Well," the young man laughed, "it was a little like the

story of the Purloined Letter, you remember? So close no one thought of looking. Of course, we were naturally anxious to know where you were when you just sort of took French leave of us, as it were; but we were thinking of faraway places, never of Lemming, so relatively close to the city. Nice town, this."

"Oh, it's delightful! I've made friends here and the hotel is surprisingly good. Couldn't you stay on a few days, Phil? Oh, how could I forget my manners? Mrs. Davenport, my garden hostess, my son, another Philip, her brother, Mr. Dalzell."

And then for the first time he looked past his son at the strong-looking men waiting near the car and his face hardened. Phil acknowledged the introductions gracefully. "I'm sure, Mrs. Davenport, you've given my father great happiness here. I thank you too. But, Dad, I'm afraid we must start back at once. There is so much waiting to be done. We can stop at the hotel while you change and collect your things. The manager there is quite an admirer of yours. He wants you to promise to come back next summer."

"You mean," Philip repeated, "you want us to leave *now!* But I've just begun to set out the heliotrope. It's very hard to find. My beautiful day was all planned! I can't leave now."

"I'm afraid we must, Dad. And wait till you see the gardens when you get back. They're needing you badly."

Even this did not move him. He kept looking piteously first at the unfinished garden and then at Katherine.

"Let's say our good-bys now and be on our way, Dad." With these words he shook Katherine's hand. "I can't thank you enough. And you too, Mr. Dalzell," shaking his hand warmly, "have done us a great service. I'll be writing you."

Then Philip, looking hard into Katherine's eyes, said, "I've been happier here these weeks than I've been in many long years. Also, even with listeners — it can't matter now — I want to tell you that I have loved you more, I think, than I've ever loved a woman." He raised her hand, kissed it, then released it, turned, and walked quickly with his son toward the waiting limousine. There he got into the back seat with the strong men.

Katherine tried to keep waving gaily as the car moved slowly away, but tears blinded her. Tim, however, watching clearly, saw that Philip never looked back.

Chapter Four

WHEN THE LIMOUSINE had rolled out of sight, Katherine signed for Tim to come into the house. His face looked drawn and anxious. "I grieve that this had to come upon you on top of everything else," he said.

She kept wiping away the tears which would not stop. "It's so cruel, so unutterably sad. My heart simply aches for him. Holding onto the heliotrope till the very last, when he saw he was beaten. And then leaving so quickly. And with *such* a confession!"

"Yes," Tim said quietly. "That's what has been worrying me. I — I didn't know just how *you* felt."

"How *I* felt? Oh, you couldn't possibly think I was in the slightest in love with him. You surely know me better than that. But I checked my other feelings carefully and I realized I had a great tenderness for him and that our companionship had been real friendship of a sort of healing kind for me. The fact that, although I had been discarded (to put it bluntly) by the man I love, another man of charm could find me attractive and even, I guess you could say, desirable was a little balm to my hurt. So now you know it all."

"I'm glad it is just as you've told me. I was afraid you might have been shot with two barrels as the saying goes and that would be too much. Don't brood over this more than you can help. I love and admire you, as always, and I'll run in this evening."

During the coming days, while Katherine tried to avoid looking at the not quite finished garden because of the tender sorrow the sight brought, she was amazed at the reaction of her friends and town acquaintances. Generally, due to Mr. Boles at the hotel and the type of news osmosis that pertains to a suburban community, the story of Philip Andrews' (or Armour's) sudden leaving was soon known and discussed everywhere, not with mere interest, but, on the part of most, with a sort of affection. The strange, mysterious gardener, for a time coolly aloof, had melted under the warmth of spontaneous friendliness and made, in the few weeks of his stay, a place in their hearts.

So they came now to tell Katherine how much they missed him and to comment upon the story as they had been told it, that, due to some brain damage after the accident, he occasionally had a seizure which needed special care and his son felt better to have him at home. If Mr. Boles, at the hotel, suspected anything more, he kept his own silence, only telling all and sundry what a terrible "miss" it was to all of them to lose the lovely gentleman.

At Bridge Club the women all sympathized openly with Katherine in a way they never dared to do after David left.

"You will feel lost now about the garden when you've had such good times working with him on it."

"And he was so handsome and charming!"

"Oh," Celia said, "let's come out with it. What we all wonder is whether or not you fell in love with him. Then we'll know better how to treat you."

Katherine smiled at their eager, affectionate faces. They were her friends.

"I can set your minds at rest at once about that. I did *not* fall in love with him. I was perfectly aware of his charm and of the happy congenial quality of our days together. I was — how shall I say it? — I was *fond* of him, but it was not love. My heart aches with pity for him, but it was not love. Of course I shall miss him and I can hardly look at the garden, but that's all there is to tell, girls."

"Good!" said Celia. "Somehow I'm glad, no matter how much I liked him. If he had been completely well and you had been entirely free, Katherine, would it then have made a difference at the end?"

"None. I don't think real love can be put on and taken off like a dress." She did not let her eyes glance around the group as she said it.

"Okay. Now that the air's cleared, we can talk to you all we want and not be afraid of hurting you. Come on, let's get to the game; I've got a good hand, partner!"

One person who had been a devoted admirer of Mr. Philip, as she called him, was Rose Hastings, daughter of Katherine's close friend across the street. After he was gone, the girl still made many excuses to come over: the garden, the recipe for gingerbread, the number of a certain sonnet. At last one day she spoke hesitantly.

"Mrs. Davenport, I have a problem. I think I've decided how I want to solve it, but I'd like to talk about it. Could I tell you about it privately sometime?"

"Why, Rose dear, of course. I would love hearing about it. When would you like to come?"

"Soon, if I could."

"Well, there's no time like the present. What about tonight about nine? The children are sure to be quiet then."

"Wonderful — and thanks."

She came in a white dress, her hair hanging loose, looking even less than her seventeen years. Katherine made her comfortable and then said, "Now, do begin. I always feel important when anyone asks my opinion."

Rose was nervous. "You've met Tom Renton, haven't you?"

"Yes, once or twice at your house. I liked him."

"Oh, he's so — so wonderful," Rose went on. "You see, we began to date in our sophomore year and now next year we'll be juniors and we've been talking things over. We do feel we want to go to college, but if so, that makes five years to wait — I mean, to wait until we'd be married. And, Mrs. Davenport, do you understand the expression *living together*?"

Katherine kept a serious face. "Oh, yes. I've heard that many times."

"Well, you see, it used to be done more in college, I think, but now a lot of high school kids are trying it and think it's wonderful. There's a fine reason for it, you know."

"What is that?"

"Why, if a boy and girl live together they will find out whether they are really compatible for marriage and may save themselves from making an awful mistake later on."

"They should be compatible," Katherine said. "For instance, if the girl likes to sit and read all evening and the boy likes to listen to a new Rock and Roll album —"

Rose waved this aside.

"Oh, they would know this anyway."

"But now, there's breakfast," Katherine went on. "Many a good marriage has had to adjust to that. Here's a man, let us say, who likes bacon and eggs and muffins and the works, while his wife almost gags at the sight of all that food so early in the morning, and wants only coffee and orange juice. Now there's a —"

Rose waved this aside also. "Oh, Mrs. Davenport, I didn't mean things like that. I meant finding out whether we were *sexually* compatible. For sex is the most important thing in marriage, isn't it?"

"Well," Katherine said thoughtfully, "it is certainly very important, but I wouldn't say the *most* important. There are so many factors that go into making a good marriage. I wonder, Rose, if you and Tom were thinking not so much of the future as of a desire to experiment with sex relations in the present?"

Rose's sweet young face was cast down. "We thought we were working on a problem in a mature way. We felt a little proud of ourselves, I guess. But now I'm — a little uncertain —"

"I'll give you the best advice of all, dear. Talk this whole plan over with your mother."

"*Mother*!" She cried. "Why, it would shock her out of her skin!"

"I don't think so. I suppose you realize she's a very beautiful woman."

"My *mother*? Why, I think she's nice-looking and I love her terribly, but I never thought of her as beautiful!"

"Well, she is, and because of that I imagine a number of men over the years have admired her."

"You mean she's had — had *affairs*."

"Mercy no! She set out to make a home and have a family and that's what she's done. But I somehow feel she would be very understanding."

"But if she is dead set against our plan — then what?"

"Well, you and Tom can think it all over again and decide what you want to do. There would be practical matters to consider if you were 'living together,' as you say."

Rose's face all at once became lighted again. "Oh, we've planned everything. I've got an allowance and Tom has a really good one; so we could easily afford a room with a hot plate and stuff. One of my friends is living with her man and she washes his things in the sink and got a little electric iron to press them. And she says when she's doing that she just feels wonderful — so *close* to him, you know."

Katherine studied the table. "Well, dear child, tell your mother everything and see how she feels about it. She has wonderful judgment."

"But the trouble will be that she's sure to tell my father and he'll blow his top for sure. He's so funny about *sex,* Mrs. Davenport. He acts shy about it. Last week at dinner my brother used a word everybody knows about the — the sexual act and my father got up and left the table. I don't think he even knows the *words*."

Katherine tried not to smile. "I imagine he knows them all, but just doesn't care to have them used at the dinner table."

"Well, maybe so. And I do thank you for letting me talk to you. In one way, it has helped just to talk about it. In another way, I'm afraid your advice may upset everything if I follow it. But I didn't like deception anyway, so we'll see."

Katherine kissed her tenderly. "Come back whenever you want a listening ear," she said. "I couldn't be more interested."

When Rose had left, Katherine sat stunned. She had heard that the breakdown of so-called moral standards had begun among the High School students, but she had refused to believe details, partly because she had her own problems to engage her mind. But now, here was Rose, sweet young Rose, with her virginal white dress and her hair hanging in a soft shower over her shoulder. Had she really given the child any advice? Only to talk to her mother. Mary, poor Mary, would have to cope with this new problem. But the thing that shook Katherine was that it apparently was not an isolated one. The teen-agers, the young of heart, were somehow being pushed by books and articles, the media itself at times, out of their normal innocence into sex knowledge and situations with which they were not yet ready to cope or should not be.

To change her train of thought, she picked up David's last two letters to the children. Charming letters they were, dealing much with Peter, the white rabbit; with a small lake on which he had seen children sailing little boats; of a cat that came to sit on the windowsill each morning to be fed. He hoped they were well and Mummy too, and they must be sure to do everything she said. The letter was dated from Paris.

Katherine felt the stab in her own heart diverting her from the other distressing thoughts. She folded the little letters as though the paper had a human quality and, even as she did so, she heard Tim's special rap at the door. She hadn't seen him for some days now, and even if it was late, she was glad he was going to be here.

He looked tired, almost grim, and threw himself down wearily on a chair.

"I've just lost my faith in human nature, and it's taken all the starch out of me," he said.

"Tim dear, you look dreadful. What's happened to make you say that. You're always on the side of the angels!"

"Do you know Madeleine Fulton?"

"Of course. I've never been really intimate with her, but she's in our Bridge Club. She's our gifted member. She has a lovely voice and you know she always brings the house down at the Lemming Club plays. What about her?"

"Well, that's it. Too many gifts, but I fear too small."

"Now, just what does that mean?"

"She wants a divorce."

"I don't believe it!"

"True, nevertheless. She wants me to take her case and I have refused."

"But, Tim, she must be crazy. With a fine husband like Bob and plenty of money and her three fine boys — what's the matter with her?"

"Well," Bob said, "she feels her talents are being wasted in a stupid suburb like Lemming. Her words. She wants to cut loose, get an apartment in the city and, as she puts it, find herself. She's been submerged in small things. She's sick of Bridge Club, church bazaars, and PTA meetings."

"But she knows there is more to life out here than that. What's she going to do in the city?"

"She's seen an agent and he is much pleased with her. He has a new musical comedy in which she just might be good for a part. I think he can be playing her for a sucker myself, but there's no telling. She's so excited."

"But what about Bob?"

"Well, she says it's all going to be civilized. When she's in her city apartment it will be wonderful to have him come over and take her out to dinner. So *civilized!* And at that, I'm ashamed to say, I lost my temper completely. I said you'll dress your prettiest for your husband and then send him home to an empty house and a cold bed. I don't call you civilized. I call you a damned selfish, cruel woman. That was dreadful for me to say."

"But exactly true. Oh, Tim, what of the boys?"

"The two older ones are in college and each in a good fraternity. They are taking it lightly, she says. Promising they'll all come over for her first night and all that. But she says the youngest is taking it a little harder. But she's sure he'll snap out of it soon. She will have him over at her apartment and they'll go to shows and, of course, she'll be back and forth here."

Tim paused. "She said she did not expect to leave Bob without sexual comfort. Her words again. They should each be free to find new relationships if they wished. I asked if she had ever mentioned this idea in front of Lucien — that's the young boy — and she said certainly, she had tried to be quite honest about everything. Oh, I'm worried about that boy. I know him. He used to do little things for me in the office when he was just a kid. He's sensitive and as good as they come. What a home that woman pictured for the boy!"

"It still doesn't seem real to me. Oh, I wish there was something I could do!"

"That's really what I came for now at this late hour. I can't get the situation out of my mind, chiefly because of Lucien. I came to ask if you would go to see Madeleine. You know her. You could explain that I regret my hard words — that's true enough, and then, woman to woman, speak of her boy and also what would happen to her if after a couple of years she did not get a place in musical comedy or whatever, and is left alone and without a career and would like only to come back to Bob and the family and by then he could have made other plans. Oh, you know what to say. It surely would be worth trying, Kathy."

"She hasn't left yet?"

"She's got another lawyer — a shyster if ever I knew one — but it will take a little time for the divorce unless she takes off for Mexico. She's rented an apartment, though, I hear, and is busy packing. Will you go to her, Kathy? Soon?"

"It's a real intrusion of privacy."

"It's a duty when you think of the boy."

"Why don't you speak to Miss Darby? He's sure to be in her English class and trust her to have found out all about him!"

"That's a wonderful lead. I may even stop to see her tonight. And you'll go to Madeleine?"

"I'm ashamed to, but I'll do my best. It seems odd in my position."

"It's your position that should make it easier. Good night, my dear, and many thanks. We'll keep each other posted."

The next morning, feeling unsteady and uneasy, Katherine found herself at the front door of the large colonial Fulton house. Hannah, the long-time housekeeper, answered her knock. There were traces of tears on her black cheeks.

"I'm surely glad to see you, Mrs. Davenport. Nobody's been here since the word got around. Everybody acts like we got the plague or something. I feel that way myself. I feel we've been struck with lightning, mebbe . . . I do hope Mrs. Fulton will see you. She's packing. I don't know what. Come in and I'll tell her."

The word came back that Katherine was to go on up if she didn't mind the confusion. Once there, she stood, startled, facing the woman in front of her. She hadn't realized how alluring Madeleine's body was. She was wearing only an old negligee, for comfort in packing evidently. Her usually immaculate hair hung carelessly around her face, her feet and legs were bare except for worn bedroom slippers, and with it all there was a grace, an instinctive beauty which in this woman was born for dramatic expression. Katherine felt it with something like a stop in her heart.

"Well," Madeleine was saying, "I see the carrier pigeons have been busy. I thought I'd kept my affairs very quiet. Or is it the Bridge Club which has spread the news?"

"Neither," Katherine said, a strange softness in her voice. "It was my brother Tim who really wanted me to come —"

"I hate him!"

"He wanted me to bring you his apology for losing his temper as he did and saying what he did. Please forgive him."

"Well, that's at least a step in the right direction. But was that all the reason you came?"

"No," Katherine said honestly, "it wasn't. I was stunned and distressed at your plans. I really wanted to ask you if you couldn't reconsider and reach some sort of compromise."

"*You* ask *me*!" Madeleine laughed. "Of all people, *you*!" Your own husband did just what I'm planning to do. He was weary of the same old round. He wanted something new and glamorous and exciting; so he left you, got himself a beautiful mistress, and went to Paris! Do forgive my bluntness, Katherine, but in coming here you didn't consider *my* feelings."

Katherine gasped but said nothing.

"What is so different about me? I have some gifts which nature gave me. I want to use them before it's too late. I've given all my best years to Bob and my boys. Even Lucien is now seventeen. Am I to have nothing? Nothing of all that I crave? Of all I'm sure I could have if only I'm brave enough to take it. I ask you!"

"But . . . but . . . Lucien?"

"Well, what about Lucien? He'll be eighteen his next birthday. He's practically a man. He's got all kinds of interests and I'll have him over to the apartment often. He'll love that and he won't be waking me up there at two o'clock in the morning to tell me he's got the combo going at last and they did some hot stuff that night, and —"

"But, Madeleine, can't you see? Can't you understand?"

"What is this — an inquisition?"

Katherine blushed to the roots of her hair. "Oh, I'm ashamed and embarrassed. I only want you all to be happy. I've only one suggestion and then I'll leave. Couldn't you have your city apartment and try for your career, but not be divorced? Still keep in close touch with your life out here? Couldn't you?"

"No!" the other said sharply. "That would defeat the whole purpose."

All at once, in a completely unconscious gesture, she raised her arms. The soft chiffon of her negligee fell from them like wings. Indeed, Katherine thought, as she watched her, she looked very much like a bird poised for flight. "I want to be free," she said.

Katherine moved quickly to the door. "Please forgive me for coming," and she slipped down the stairs and out of the house as quietly as she could.

All the way home she had an uncomfortable lump in her throat. Worse still was a sort of physical ache in her heart. She ached for Bob — good, kind, steady Bob, who perhaps never realized he had a caged bird in his home. She ached for the older boys trying to imagine exciting "first nights" while they kept from thinking of how holidays would be at home. She ached for Lucien. Oh, Lucien, with his big news of the combo! But Madeleine! Could it be that she had been the true actress during these years? Had she played her greatest role as loving wife and mother, while in her soul she longed to be *free* as she had said? She pictured the night she had been wakened by Lucien. Even then and times like it she might have managed through her annoyance to say, "Wonderful! That's thrilling! Now, go get some sleep!" And the boy would go happily to bed. Katherine knew that her heart most strangely ached, though, for Madeleine, who had played her part only too well.

Tim came that evening, eager to know how her interview had gone. When she tried to describe the situation as she felt it quite likely was, Tim's face grew more and more grave.

"You're a perceptive gal, Kathy, and you may have hit the whole thing right on the nose. If so, you see how terrible it will be for Lucien. If she has seemed to him a loving mother and he's felt close to her, you can imagine how the foundations will all fall under him now. The marvel to me is how quiet it's all been kept. You'd think the town would be buzzing with it. For one thing, Madeleine has got herself a good lawyer, to my surprise. He's older than I am and very slow and steady. I know he'll take his time, hoping that at the end of interlocutory she'll have decided to stay."

"Meanwhile, she is definitely moving to a furnished apartment. I rather think, as she seems to be taking only her pet linens, drapes, bibelots, and things that will go in boxes. But now what can we do about Lucien?"

"I've done one thing on my own," Tim said. "I stopped in to see Miss Darby and dropped a hint. She's got a mouth like a clam. She's been worried too, but never thought of family trouble. Says he's been a straight A student and now doesn't look at a book and that he's worked for weeks over this combo and just when it was making real music, lost all interest apparently. Then she added the information that stabs me most of all. She said he thought his mother was the most wonderful person in the world."

"Oh, Tim! Where do we go from here?"

"At least I'm going to keep an eye on Lucien. In the evening especially. Miss Darby thinks he's got a girl and I let it go at that, since, strangely enough, the real news hasn't spread. We'll just have to watch and wait, I guess, and keep our mouths shut."

For several weeks everything seemed outwardly normal

about the Fulton house. Promptly at seven Hannah came out and swept the front porch and sidewalk; at eight Bob left for his train; at eight thirty Lucien started to school, and after that those living near could hear Madeleine "vocalize," as she usually did. "Ah-ah-ah-ah-*ahhh*." Then one night at the Bridge Club, to which Celia had once said a baptismal certificate was necessary for initiation, Madeleine told her news quickly and brightly, as though she were speaking of a trip to Bermuda.

Everyone sat stunned until Celia spoke first as usual. "I don't believe a word of it. If it's true, you're crazy and if it's not true, you ought to be ashamed to get us all stirred up this way."

In a few moments they were all talking seriously and, most importantly of all, Madeleine herself told them the gist of what she had told Katherine. The others, after their first expletives, had sober faces with now and then a look of half wistful understanding. Did any of them ever feel they too wanted to forsake household cares and be *free*?

"All except me," Katherine told Tim that night. "I have no right to judge Madeleine, because I was never tempted. When I had David and the children, my house and garden and friends and you — Tim, I was so perfectly content, so utterly happy!"

"There! I told you when I can find a girl like you —"

"Now, don't start on that. But, Tim, you would be so good to a wife."

"Sure! Sure! And beat her with a stick no thicker than my thumb!"

Katherine laughed. "Where did you ever hear that crazy thing?"

"Oh, I think it's in some very old English book of law. Crazy people, these English, but they do come up with a good idea now and then. Well, I'm going to keep my eyes open, especially in the evenings. Lucien is always the last one in and he leaves his car in the driveway; so I can keep tabs. Of course, now the beans are spilled, everyone will be talking the thing over tonight."

"I'm afraid so. Madeleine said she had found a perfectly darling little furnished apartment, so she's just been sending boxes by express — clothes, special linens, and oddments she likes to have around her."

"Will she be back soon?"

"She thought not for a while, as her agent wants her to be in close touch if anything comes up that has a real part for her. The first one, I take it, didn't work out as he hoped. Meanwhile, she has the promise of a role in a children's play and is learning the lines. Also, the agent told her not to despise commercials, which need good talent and pay good money."

"Well! She may have found herself a sensible agent at that! What's the matter, Kathy? You have tears in your eyes. Oh, my dear, the same hurt?"

"It's what I said about being so happy before. That was true, but all the time with it I was dreaming of our year in Paris. Tim, you'll never know —"

He put his arms around her. "Dear Kitten," he said with the childhood pet name. "Ah, poor Kitten! You've been so brave, I haven't talked enough to you about that. What a bitter, cruel disappointment coming as it did! Sometimes I think I could wring David's neck for the hurt he has brought to your tender heart. Cry it all out now, dear. You've been too brave all along."

She nestled against him. "I think I needed to be comforted just now. I don't often cry except when David's letters come for the children and then, as soon as I'm alone, I break down completely. This has helped me, Tim. You'll never know what a support you have been. What would I ever have done without you? Now, I'm better . . . really. I hope I haven't wet your nice clean shirt."

"Are you sure you are all right? Shall I stay now and fix you a hot drink or something?"

"No, no. I'm quite myself and it will do me good to get on with my regular nightly routine. Bless you for everything! Keep me posted about Lucien after Madeleine goes."

Her leave-taking was so quiet that after it there was no outward change at the Fultons'. Bob took his same commuter train, read his paper, and did his puzzle as usual, and, always a quiet man, said little to his fellow passengers. Lucien, according to Miss Darby, appeared to be working a little harder, but did not have much to say, though she tried to draw him out. After a few weeks the gossip died down with nothing new to feed upon, except occasional bits and pieces from Hannah, who reported she cooked good meals but no one seemed to eat much. Then at last she confided to a neighbor, with tears, that Mrs. Fulton had come downstairs after the others had gone one day, carrying a suitcase, and had got into a cab and said, "The station, please." She had really *gone* and had given Hannah a beautiful big gold locket the night before and told her to look after the family and said she'd be back soon. But it didn't look right, somehow, to Hannah. Nor did it to all those who knew the circumstances. Discussion again waxed heavy, but failed at last because of the quiet and dignified departure of Madeleine and the apparently normal routine of the household she had left behind her.

Only a few kept watching Lucien. Dr. Harris, of the kind heart and discerning eye, lent him a book on architecture, knowing it was one of his many interests; Miss Darby tried to get him to take the lead in a dramatization of *The Merchant of Venice,* which he declined; and Tim, faithful Tim, cruised about each night trying to spot Lucien's little red sports car. He gradually learned the boy's habits and schedule. He was not a member of the real gang which got many of the parties going and sometimes ran afoul of the police. But evidently he had many friends, was entirely sociable, was well liked, and drank only beer. "A nice young seventeen-year-old," he reported to Katherine. "I wish I had one like him."

"Well, if you'd —"

"No sign of a girl that I can see. I really wish it were that more curable disease than the other situation. I'm going to keep my eyes open. Miss Darby says she doesn't quite like the look on the boy's face. He seems to keep about the hours the kids all do nowadays, but still he may not be getting enough sleep."

At four o'clock one morning the telephone wakened Katherine sharply. It was Tim.

"Kathy," he said. "I'll give you the good news first. Lucien is going to be all right, but it was a very close call. Garage shut and the car running. At two I saw his car was not out and the big doors closed, and I had a hunch. I yelled for Bob, who had been asleep. Together we got him out, but we all but fainted ourselves. The neighbor next door heard the noise and called the ambulance right away. At the hospital they gave it all they had. How those doctors worked! They thought at first it was too late, but they kept on. Now he's breathing naturally. The reason I called you now is to ask you to make a big pot of coffee and a good breakfast. Bob is here with me and he's pretty well shot. I'll bring him along and you can feed us both and say your private prayer of thanksgiving while you work."

"Tim! Oh, Tim!" But he had hung up.

When the men came she was ready for them. The odor of coffee and rich breakfast smells filled the house. Tim had recovered much of his usual jaunty appearance, but Bob's heavy shoulders still drooped and he found it hard to speak.

"No liquor, Kathy," Tim said at once. "Just coffee and lots of it!"

As they drank it, cup after cup, the dark lines on Bob's face seemed to lift a little and while he insisted he couldn't eat, it was evident when he tasted the good food that he fell upon it as though he had pangs of real hunger. Katherine kept quietly supplying his plate and Tim talked just enough to stave off any silences.

"My darling sister, would it be too much to ask for a little marmalade for the muffins?"

"Good heavens! Did I forget that? Oh, I am sorry! I'll get it right away," Katherine said. When the men were both supplied, she thought it was time to speak. "Bob, have you called Madeleine yet?"

He looked up, frightened. "No. I want to, but I'm not sure when I should tell her or how. It's all pretty complicated."

"I think not," Katherine said. "You see, in any crisis, a woman wants to be right there in the middle of everything. If I were you, I'd call her now without wasting another moment. Tell her what happened, that the danger's past, but that you want her to come out at once, that Lucien will need her."

Bob looked helplessly at Tim.

"Don't ask me, Bob. I don't know anything about women. Listen to Kathy, now. Her advice is always good."

"But, you see, I'm not sure I'm in a position just now to order her to do anything."

"Yes, you are. In a case like this. Go ahead, Bob. There's a telephone in the little study. Don't wait. I'll keep the rest of your breakfast hot."

Bob walked slowly over to the study and closed the door behind him. The two outside heard the low steady murmur of his voice for several minutes, then a cry from Madeleine. After that, Bob's voice seemed to grow stronger until some words came through clearly.

"What the devil does it matter *what* it costs? Just come as fast as you can. Good! Have the driver drop you off at the hospital. I'll be waiting there!"

When he came out, much of the strain had left his face. "You were right, Katherine. She said if I'd waited till night she would never have forgiven me. She's coming at once. Getting a driver to bring her, since all the trains now are the ones going *to* the city and not from. And if it's not indecent of me, I really would love another muffin."

Before the men left again to check at the hospital, Bob found thanks impossible, but he said he did have a question.

What should they say? He had thought it might be good to say Lucien had been sound asleep and just not enough awake to switch off the car. How about it?

Tim was very serious. "In my experience in and out of the law, I've found it's best to tell the truth. It will stand up and do more to quell rumors than any made-up story. Hardly anyone will really *ask* you about this, Bob. But if anyone does, if I were you I'd tell it straight. In no time things will settle, and people will forget all about it."

"Thanks, Tim. I think you're right. I'll go now and give Hannah all the news and then wait around for Madeleine."

When Tim called Katherine up in the morning after a good night's sleep, he was in great spirits. "A rough time it was, but all is going well now. Madeleine is at the hospital, but when I went over I didn't see her. One of my doctor friends was a witness to her arrival, though, and asked me if this Mrs. Fulton wasn't interested in the stage or something. I said I believed she was, somewhat, and then — listen to this! — he told me she didn't have to go into dramatics to get a kiss like the one her husband had given her when she got there. 'Holy Jehu!' he said. So, my dearest sister, maybe God is moving in more mysteriouser ways than even the old poet thought who wrote the line. Well, with this little idea, the defense rests."

The community was rocked by the news of the near tragedy. As Tim had advised, Bob and Madeleine told the facts simply and straightforwardly if they had to speak of them. But the town was shaken. Its citizens had become, in a measure, inured to scandal, which seemed on the increase; but this was different. This struck at the heart. And many fathers of teen-age sons who had put most emphasis on discipline now surprised their young people by an attitude almost of tenderness and suggestions of little fishing trips or city jaunts together. But practically everyone of every age was affected. There was first the relief, and then the black shadow of what had been so close to reality. The latter was always connected with the question of what Madeleine would do now.

It was nearly three weeks before Katherine heard her familiar lilting voice on the telephone, asking if she might come over. When she came, she was, as always, pretty, smartly dressed, and poised, but with a serious expression new to her. "I came," she began promptly, as was her wont, "because I owe you a debt and I want to pay it as well as I can. It goes back," she added slowly, "to the day you came to talk to me about my leaving home. I was mad at you for coming. I resented all your advice then —"

"It was utterly presumptuous of me. You had good right to hate me."

"Oh, it was courageous, and there came a day when it helped me. But that's my story. There was a woman quite a bit older than I am who had the apartment next to me. I've always spoken to her in the hall and I had a feeling she was an actress, but was 'At leisure' just then. Sometimes at night we saw a show together and got to be friends.

"Then, one evening, the one before I got the — the call from Bob, she asked me to come in. She was sobbing in actual despair. Her experience didn't exactly parallel mine, but it was mighty close to what you said might one day happen to me. She said she'd been on the stage for years in small parts and road companies and so on, but she began to think she could do bigger things if she were not tied down. So she got a divorce and came to New York. Some months later she did get a really good role, but after a short run the play folded. The same with the next, and then there seemed nothing for her but bits and pieces. All at once, after a long time of this, she was sick, she said, of the whole thing — learning lines that never got her anywhere, rehearsing for plays that never got put on, going about from agency to agency. Suddenly she knew what she wanted — it was to shake the dust of the stage off her feet and go back to the peace and safety of her husband's arms.

"Her desire was so violent, she couldn't wait. That very day she had called him up at his office, saying she had made a terrible mistake and would he take her back? She said she hardly breathed while she waited for his answer. Then his kindly voice had said, 'I'm very sorry that I can't help you, my dear, but I remarried a year ago and we are very happy.'"

The two women sat in silence for a few minutes. Then Madeleine said, "How could I comfort her when I felt her sorrow down to my very vitals because you had already pictured it as it could happen to me? I did what I could; then I went back to my own apartment and looked hard at myself, my life, and what I wanted to do with it. After that, I wrote to Bob and told him everything; I sealed and stamped the letter, ready to mail the next day. Before the day really came, I got Bob's call about Lucien, but I brought the letter with me so Bob knows I wrote it before I got that word."

"Madeleine, what did Lucien say when he saw you?"

For the first time she really smiled. "He just said, 'Hi, Mom, what brought you here?' And I said, 'Oh, I heard you'd been up to some crazy monkeyshines and I thought I'd come out and keep an eye on you.' I'll never forget our conversation. 'Can you stay a while?' he said. I said, 'For always. I found the city got on my nerves after the excitement wore off.' 'That's wonderful, but what about the apartment?' 'Well, your father thinks maybe we can keep it. He has meetings and hates to come out late on that miserable old train. And if I had been shopping and was awfully tired, it would be nice to stay in. You boys might enjoy it too.' 'Sounds great. You know something?' 'What?' 'Well, there's one thing that has kept bothering me. When you were talking to Dad about the divorce, you said you would both likely have new re-relations — I don't know how to say it.' 'You mean we might have new sexual partners?' 'Yes. That didn't sound right for you two, somehow.'

"And then, Katherine, what do you suppose I did?"

"I couldn't guess!"

"Well, I laughed. And it was the best laugh I've ever done. You see, to laugh in a play, for instance, and have it sound like a real one is about the hardest thing an actress has to do. Oh, I've practiced a hundred times. But this once, I swear, was perfect. And then I said, 'Lucien, have you ever heard of a *Sockaroo*?'

"'Oh, sure,' he said. 'That's what the kids say when they are going to give another one a bloody nose!'

"'Well,' I told him, 'it didn't have to mean a bloody nose — just any kind of a good hard shock. You see, it's quite a while since your father has taken me out for dinner and dancing. And I *love* to dance.'

"And then Lucien laughed. It was more of a giggle, for the doctors say he hasn't eaten or slept for a good while and is still weak. But he giggled."

"'Oh, Mom! You're terrific!' he said. 'I'll bet that shook him up all right. He'll take you dancing now, sure enough. If you'll just sit there, I think I'll have another little nap. You know, I've never been so happy in my life!'

"'Neither have I,' I told him. And that's my story, Katherine."

Chapter Five

THE MAIL one morning brought two surprise missives. One was an elegant, square, masculine-looking envelope which she opened with interest. As she somehow surmised, it was connected with Philip Armour, the gardener. It was a charming note from his son, the junior Philip.

"Dear Mrs. Davenport," it read, "in spite of my father's loss of memory, he still speaks of you and of the planting of your garden, and longs to go back, which latter, I fear, is not possible. But the thing he wants most is to get a Sun Dial for you, to put upon the brick walk he himself laid. So, after much search, we have come upon one which satisfies him. He wants the inscription to be poetic and different from the usual run. For instance, we found many which said, 'I record only the sunny hours.' But he would have none of that kind. Finally, in the basement of an old Frenchman's store, we found what my father and I both feel is the perfect one. The base is a solid but perfect copy of a Grecian urn and the dial itself has its inscription in French; which, translated, is: 'Time passes, friendship endures.' The whole business of the search, the delight of finding, the helping with the packing and crating, has all seemed in Father's mind to take the place of a visit to you. We hope you will like the Dial and accept with it our eternal thanks for your kindness.

Faithfully yours,
Philip Armour, Jr.

"P.S. If you want to communicate with Father after the gift

reaches you, perhaps you had better telephone me at the number given below. I will translate every word to him, explaining the message is for him but the operator got the 'Senior' and 'Junior' confused."

Katherine sat with the open letter in her hand and a tear fell upon it. There was a great happiness, though, behind the tear. She would love having the Sun Dial, but, more than that, it would furnish a permanent link between herself and Philip and also between him and the townspeople who had come to like and admire him and, in the end, pity him. He would not, like the flowers of the garden, fade away and be quite forgotten, but would be remembered each time they passed to look at the Dial and read its sweet legend. In a sense, because of it, the strange gardener would become a real part of the community. Katherine wiped away another tear — this too a happy one — and then turned to the letter unopened in her hand. When she read it, she smiled. It said, neatly and briefly, that it would give Dr. Harris much pleasure if she would be present at a conference in his office on Friday afternoon, the ninth, at half after two o'clock.

"A command performance," she said aloud. For no one ever pleaded a previous engagement to an invitation from Dr. Harris. They went! I wonder what this is about? she mused. The note gave no hint.

All day her mind was busy with the import of the two so different letters. She longed for the arrival of the Dial, but she had a twinge of uneasiness over the letter of Dr. Harris. Why was he calling a conference? And why invite her?

At early dusk she saw young Rose Hastings once again, as some weeks ago, crossing toward the Davenport house. Katherine hurried to greet her. "Oh, I've some news and I was eager to tell you. I'm so glad you came."

She drew the girl inside and told her of the letter from Philip Junior and of the coming gift of the Sun Dial. Rose seemed pleased and impressed, but there was an enthusiasm lacking.

At last Katherine said, "Did you come over to talk to me about something special?"

At once Rose's face lighted. "Yes, I did. I think it's really big news. You see, Mrs. Davenport, we at school were all just sick about Lucien's near miss. We can't get over it. And the thing that hit Tom and me so hard was that he did it because he thought he was losing his mother, that he wouldn't have a real family anymore if she left, and he couldn't bear it."

Rose swallowed hard. "And all at once we both realized what lovely mothers we have and what dear families and that what we were going to do would hurt them so and maybe sort of wreck the younger kids and we simply didn't want to do it. We decided to enjoy our dating the way we did before and leave anything more serious until later on. I think you'll agree."

"Oh, Rose, I couldn't be more happy over your decision. I think you'll always be glad you made it, and I respect Tom for feeling as you do. I only hope a lot of the High School students will have the same idea."

Rose shook back her lovely hair. "I doubt that," she said. "Most of them are pretty determined to keep on the way they are going. But anyway Tom and I don't feel badly to belong to a small minority."

It was a delightful talk. Small things came out about the Hastings home life, showing the deep, quiet waters that flowed beneath the experiences of the days. Though rough winds might occasionally roil these waters, the stream still flowed on; though a storm might beat upon the rock, it was never shaken. It stood fast. This beautiful picture of love at its best had somehow come to light in the heart of young Rose. So when Katherine kissed her good-by at last, the "God bless you" was very tender.

When Rose had gone, however, Katherine sat, sad and

stricken by the contrast of her own life and that of the Hastings. The stream of her wedded love had not run to the sea; the rock of her life's devotion had been shaken. Before she went to bed, she re-read the two letters which had come that day. Upon each there was the grip of reality, which just then she needed sorely.

The day of the conference with Dr. Harris seemed to come quickly. As she walked into the High School building, Katherine wondered again why *she,* having no students in that grade, should have been invited. Once in the office, she was surprised at the number of the guests. The furniture had been arranged to accommodate extra chairs, making perhaps twenty in all. True to his custom, Dr. Harris entered his office on the stroke of two-thirty, bowed, and took his place behind the desk at the back. Even in the small interlude between her arrival and Dr. Harris' entrance, Katherine was able to see how the plan had been evolved. For Lemming was a community of clubs. Dr. Harris had carefully picked a representative or two from each. There was the Athenia, made up of the extremely literate and generally cultured group; there was the Thespian, whose members were either actively engaged in the Players or in a wide circle interested in the arts in general; and there was the Mothers, whose only requisite for membership was a child in school. These women bore the burden of the PTA teas and other functions where chocolate cakes were more needed than papers on the poetry of Sappho. The Mothers were the fine, sturdy backbone upholding all lesser clubs.

Katherine looked squarely at Dr. Harris as he prepared to speak. He looked larger standing there than she always felt him to be and with a fleeting thought, she remembered how new High School boys looked at the blue eyes and said, "Here's a softie. Let's have some fun." But soon they learned the blue eyes could shoot steel sparks and the face turn grim. They ended by doing just what they were told and liking it.

Dr. Harris glanced again over his group and began to speak.

"My friends, I have asked you to come here today to confer with me because I am greatly troubled and feel I must have your help. You will recall how distraught all of us were a couple of years ago with the drug problem in our High School. At that time I consulted the best authority on possible means of overcoming it. He said he had found the best results came when alternatives were offered to the young people. As you know, we set to work on that. We instituted the square dances, which were and are enormously popular. Since our fears were largely for the boys, we started a new woodworking shop with a gifted teacher. You remember all the things we did. And slowly, surely, we got results. While we still have difficulties with marijuana and will surely continue to do so, the use of hard drugs has steadily diminished. I was so thankful for this, so filled with joy at the measure of our success — faculty, parents, working together — that I fear now there was also an element of pride in my thinking.

"And then suddenly I became aware of a new danger. With the drugs I had felt a terrible concern especially for the boys. Now there come from all sides to me reports about the girls which sicken me. For three nights I never slept, weighing and taking stock of this new problem. It is, in short, that great numbers of our high school girls, from fifteen years old up, are 'living with' the boys of their transient choice and, of course, having sexual relations with them. I felt something must be done or attempted.

"Now, in presenting this to you I realize I lay myself wide open to two major criticisms. One is that this phenomenon, in fact, is just part of the new age, belonging to the times and as such must be casually accepted. I do not agree with this. If a thing is wrong, it is wrong in any age or time. The second possible criticism is that we are here to teach intellectual courses and have no right whatever to move into the world of morals. I definitely do not agree with this. These young people are under our care for many hours each day. I feel we are under a heavy obligation to influence them for good in every way we can.

"My heart goes out to these girls who are bombarded from every side by books, articles, and T.V., on *Sex,* until their thinking is drowned in it before they are old enough to discriminate, to adjust to its various manifestations. They have snatched at the nearest, shall we say, concrete way to indulge in it. I may have explained this poorly, but I think you all know what the problem is among the girls and my distress because of it. I'm sure you feel this too. Has anyone a question at this point?"

"I have one," a voice spoke.

"Yes, Mrs. Gardner."

"You have referred entirely to the *girls* in this matter. Are the boys not equally involved?"

Dr. Harris stood quietly for a moment and then answered. "You have a right to ask that. I shall try to state my position. And, as we are all mature people, I shall speak plainly. You all know, I'm sure, what is meant by the Double Moral Standard. I hope no one will ever say I *believe* in it. But it is the truth that I accept it for two reasons: in the first place, when God made men and women, he made them with a difference. First, then, I would say that the sex urge is stronger in a young boy or man than it is in a young girl or woman. In the second place, in the sexual act, on the young man's part, it is, to a large degree, external; on the girl's part, it is entirely different. In her case, the inmost, holy, sacrosanct part of her body is invaded. There is deposited there something which, under certain circumstances, can become life itself. For these reasons I feel the attitude of the girls toward love and sex should be different. And so my great concern is for them. Have I made myself at all clear?"

There was only silence and intent faces regarding him.

"Then I would repeat that in this great problem our work is

to find some alternative interest which will keep sex from filling the girls' minds so completely. I would like now to throw the conference open for all the ideas you can present."

For a few seconds no one spoke and then Mary Hastings, mother of the young Rose, began. "Dr. Harris, this may be utterly crazy, but I have an idea."

"By all means, let us hear it."

"Well, before I came, I was folding up two beautiful quilts which my grandmother made for me. I suddenly wondered if we couldn't start a new 'fad' as it were, for quilting. We could have a display and even have a couple of frames set up with women who know how to quilt. Most of it is just sewing, but —"

"Oh," voices came breaking in from all sides, "that's a wonderful thought!"

"Why, we could collect all the most beautiful quilts we all possess and those we could borrow and this would make a marvelous display —"

"And there is a new method of making them. You just cut out a lovely pattern of cloth and appliqué it to the white background. It is stunning and easier than the old patchwork —"

"And there are so many old designs — the wedding ring and the lover's knot —"

The voices rose in a chorus of enthusiasm until, when a slight break came, Dr. Harris, smiling delightedly, spoke.

"Dear ladies, dear friends, in the common vernacular, I think you've got something. I am thrilled into real hope. This will need organization. Miss Darby, in a word, could you suggest how to go about this?"

"I am thrilled myself. I would suggest, first, a general chairman, along with our sewing teacher, whom I happen to know is much liked by the girls, to get what assistance they need in collecting the quilts. These are precious and must be handled and used with the greatest possible care. There will need to be many subchairmen, but I can imagine, eventually, a sort of quilting tea for the girls, as a great climax, with the lovely quilts displayed and a complete quilting frame setup being used. I can quilt myself. My grandmother taught me. The girls could have all details explained and make decisions about what they would like to try. It would all be something new and different and glamorous, if we make it go, for the girls to enjoy and think about. We might call this just a rough draft, but I'm sure it can all be worked out."

Dr. Harris looked positively aglow. "And we've even got a theme song! At the end of the afternoon or evening — I would rather favor the evening, for glamor — everyone would sing, 'It was from Aunt Dinah's quilting party, I was seeing Nellie home.' When anyone old or young starts singing that, they can't stop."

He dismissed his guests graciously. "More than I ever dreamed has come out of this conference. Thank you from my heart for coming. Won't you go home now and think of all the phases of the quilting plan and the possible party? There is sound substance as well as beauty in this idea. Bless you all! . . . Could I ask you to remain for a few minutes, Mrs. Davenport?"

Katherine's mind was full of ideas about the use which could be made of the quilts, so she raised an innocent and unperturbed face to Dr. Harris as he moved down and stood before her.

"Mrs. Davenport, before we begin on our plans for the quilting, about which I have great hope, I would like someone to speak briefly and with real sincerity to the girl students about this matter of 'living together' as it is called. I do not want a mother to do this, and certainly not one of the faculty. I have thought this over very carefully, and for this little talk I have chosen you."

Katherine's face was scarlet. "Dr. Harris, please! I couldn't. I am not a speaker and upon this subject, to a large group of girls, I simply couldn't. I'm so sorry, but — I couldn't."

Dr. Harris went on quietly as though he had never heard her. "I know you," he said. "I know your ideals of love and your attitude toward life in general. Young people like you. You speak gently but firmly about what you believe. There are a few precise points which should be brought out to the girls which they may never have thought of. I feel you are the one to bring them before them, wisely and tenderly.

"Please don't give me any answer now. I realize I have startled you. Won't you go home and think of what I have asked? Think of those girls as though they were your daughters. What would you tell them?"

He paused and then went on, "Talk to yourself in your own room. Practice out loud in sentences and paragraphs. You will find thoughts taking spoken form. Keep talking, but please say nothing more to me now. God bless you, Mrs. Davenport! Good afternoon."

Katherine found herself out on the sidewalk, stunned, speechless, and, most frightening of all, obedient. That's the way he does it with the students, she kept thinking. That's the way he did it with me.

She got in her car and drove home, still telling herself she could not, would not, do as he had ordained she must do and yet, all the while, knowing that she must. It was uncanny. For her to give a talk to the assembled High School girls on this, of all subjects, was simply impossible, and, Dr. Harris or no Dr. Harris, she would put it out of her mind. This was her latest decision as she entered her familiar house. Over dinner, however, the children questioned her anxiously. "Are you sick, Mother? You look very strange."

"No, dears. Just worried."

"Could Uncle Tim help?"

"I guess he will be coming in later on. He told us so. And please don't worry."

When Tim came, he pounced at once. "You can't dissemble worth a cent, Kathy. Something's on your mind. Now, out with it!"

She told him the story of the conference and the idea for the quilts. Tim was responsive. "By Jove! I believe you've hit upon something that will catch the girls' interest. Color, romance, all sorts of variations of designs, a nice chance for rivalry, an interesting dip into the past! It's got everything. Why don't you look happier over the idea?"

She told him then of Dr. Harris' quiet, implacable request of her. "And I can't do it, Tim. I won't do it."

He walked over to the window and stood watching the children who, sensing seriousness, had left the house and were raking the leaves. He stood for a long time thinking and then came back. His voice was tender but firm.

"You have to do this, Kathy dear. It's an obligation. It's the kind of thing you can't refuse. The hardest thing for me to tell you is that I'm very much afraid what you say or anybody else says will not make the girls change their ways."

"You feel it will all be worthless?"

Tim sat down and rested his head on his hand, thinking deeply.

"That was my first snap judgment, but let's look into this a little. In a group of girls that size there are sure to be some who either don't follow this new pattern or more, perhaps, who follow the pattern only because it is the 'in' thing now to do. They may not like what they are doing, may even be unhappy about it, but feel caught up with the wave habit of the crowd. Now, to these your talk might be like a raft to a drowning sailor. I know what you will say will be kind and sympathetic, but will also be straightforward and wise. I think, Katherine, you should ponder over this and then do as Dr. Harris asks."

"Oh, Tim! I thought maybe you would help me get out of it."

"I'm afraid all I can honestly say is that if a man were speaking to a group of boys, I might have some concrete advice. But you will know best about girls." He paused. "One thing I do know, but it may not fit in with your talk. Every man would *rather* marry a virgin."

He kissed her fondly, told her not to be afraid, that she

would soon find herself in possession of the best of her resources, and went out without more discussion.

Even the women at the conference who had come up with the thought of the quilts; even Dr. Harris, with his sublime optimism, had never imagined how this idea, carried over from a past day, would spread like wildfire among the girls. When it was all explained by the various committees in charge, with the sewing department head as chairman, there was at once a sort of instinctive response, as though the blood of generations of young women who had made quilts of all kinds as part of their heritage had now risen in the veins of their girls who had never before known much of the beauty and artistry hidden in these works of the past.

There began then, an opening of old chests and attic drawers, the carrying of carefully wrapped treasures from house to house to show unusual handiwork, to boast of certain designs. There was a flood of conversation between classes or wherever groups of girls could gather.

"And my mother says, our Sunflower quilt must be a hundred years old and as bright as if it was made yesterday!"

"And oh, Great-aunt Phoebe's Wedding Ring pattern is so lovely it makes you want to cry. If ever I could do anything like that!"

"They say some people now are hanging up quilts on the wall instead of tapestry! I can't wait until we have our exhibit and really get started."

In the midst of this most welcome general interest, Dr. Harris called Katherine on the phone.

"Mrs. Davenport, would you be ready to give that little talk I spoke of next Tuesday at 2:30? The girls will have a little free time then."

Katherine swallowed twice before she could answer. The insolence! she thought first, and then, The utter confidence! She realized this latter quality buoyed her up.

"I am frightened, Dr. Harris, of course, but as well as I can, I will give the talk on Tuesday at 2:30."

"Good! Don't be afraid. The minute you face the girls, the words will come. Miss Darby will meet you at the front door, since you are friends. She will escort you. Would you prefer to stand on the platform?"

"Oh, no. Please."

"She will arrange the microphone, then, for you so you can stand down on the floor level. I always prefer that too. Thank you, Mrs. Davenport. Thank you *very* much."

Katherine still felt shaky and uncertain as she set forth that Tuesday. She had thought, practiced silently and aloud, rewritten, revised, and thought again. Now she hoped that what she must say would be both straightforward and understanding.

Miss Darby seemed a tower of strength as she met her in the front hall and escorted her to the smaller of the two lecture rooms where there sat already what seemed to Katherine a very large gathering of girls. Miss Darby gave her hand a little encouraging squeeze and indicated a pretty young girl in the front row.

"Miss Kate Wills, chairman of the senior class, will now introduce you." She then slipped out quietly.

The girl, Kate, rose and spoke with ease. "We are glad to welcome Mrs. David Davenport as our guest today and will listen with interest to her talk. Mrs. Davenport."

It was time! Katherine looked into the sea of eyes and faces and they suddenly swam together. When she spoke, the words were unexpected.

"My dear girls, I had a little introduction prepared but I forgot it, for I'm really scared to death."

She could not have done better. There was a titter and then a wave of friendly laughter. The girl Kate rose after a few moments.

"We know just how you feel, Mrs. Davenport, for it's just the way we all have felt when we had to give our first speech in chapel. So now go right ahead, and don't be afraid."

There was, indeed, a general relaxation and Katherine felt a certain tension leaving her.

She started again. "My dear friends," she said, "I have come here because Dr. Harris asked me to do so and perhaps some of you may know it is hard to refuse him."

A lighter wave of laughter floated over the girls. They knew their Principal.

"The most difficult thing was the subject upon which he wanted me to talk to you. It was so intimate that at first I felt I could not do it. But as I pondered the matter, I realized that we here are all women together. You younger, and I older, but still women who will, sooner or later, know the great experience of love. So, with that as a bond, I'll start right in.

"For a time I didn't know that the practice of living together, as it is generally called, was so widespread. I knew it had been practiced to some extent on the college level and of course, in the case of many and various couples of different, usually older, ages. But that it was for many very young people, even high school students, a way of life, I somehow found hard to believe. I talked to some of my younger friends as to what they thought the advantages of this kind of living were. They all said that if a girl and young man lived together, it would prepare them better for marriage or perhaps save them from an unfortunate relationship later on by their getting to know each other better beforehand. I took issue at once with this idea. I felt it was a sort of cover up for the main reason, which, more likely, was experimentation with sex. A young boy and girl can, in normal dating and natural good times, get to know each other very well without any resort to sex relationships, I should think.

"Another reason given me was that if a High School girl refused to live together with boys, she would be completely unpopular. I am sure this is not so. I have known cases quite the contrary. If, for example, a boy should ask you for a date and you thanked him and told him you would love to go and then added, 'Perhaps I should tell you I don't go in for any sex behaviour.'

"If the boy says, 'Okay by me. I'll pick you up at eight,' and the evening proves to be a good happy one with another date coming up, then you've found a nice boy. If, when you reply to a boy with 'no,' he looks downcast and does not seem to enjoy the time particularly, even makes an excuse to shorten the evening, then you will be sure he was interested only in sex and you're well rid of him!

"More than that, girls who quietly stand upon their own moral principles, their own sense of values, will be respected by the boys and when they are being discussed — for of course boys talk — the pronouncement will likely be, 'There's a nice girl. You can trust her. You won't have any complications if you date her.'

"Now, as I have already mentioned, we know that many older young people and many still older than that have decided to live together for a certain time without marriage. I am not speaking of them. I am concerned with you High School girls in the first flush of your youth. This for you is the time of first kisses, the first gentle caresses, the first tender pairing off of boy and girl who suddenly find a new interest and a happy excitement when they are together. This is all beautiful and all natural and right and a part of growing up. But none of these includes the later part of sexual relations, or living together.

"I would like to speak seriously for a moment about love itself. Every girl and woman dreams of this: the great love which will someday come to her, filling her heart, making her eyes shine with joy as she thinks of the man who has caused this to come to her, the man she wants to marry and be with always, making his home, establishing a *family*! This is the Great Dream which comes to every girl, the Golden Dream! It also comes to a boy, but perhaps in a slightly different way. Just lovemaking itself is not quite the same between the sexes.

A few weeks ago Dr. Harris was speaking to a small group of women of this general truth. He said something which had never occurred to me before. We all know that a man and a woman are made differently. But what he pointed out was that when a man makes love, there is an external element about it. But when a girl or woman yields herself to a sexual act she is giving entrance to the most hidden, most sacred part of her sweet body, a part that nature quite evidently intended should be holy, ready at some time and under certain circumstances, ideal for the great miracle of life itself.

"The thought keeps coming back to me, which I would like to pass on to you, that, while there may be some unions which begin very young and continue on, even to marriage, there are perhaps many, many more which are only transient relationships. A boy and girl of High School age begin living together and after a time they become dissatisfied and separate. Then later another attractive boy wants to live with this girl and she agrees. This may not last too long either. So it is quite possible that during the years of High School and college or career later, she may have lived with a number of different young men . . . What then of the great Golden Dream of love? And what of the inner sanctity of the lovely body which has harbored so many transient guests?

"A great British poet once wrote a poem about all this. He began one line, 'Ah, wasteful woman . . .' His idea was that when a woman or girl gave love casually and too freely, she was wasting it, cheapening it. I have had the school secretary make copies of this verse and they are on the back desk if any of you would care to take a copy and see if you can understand his meaning.

"And now, girls, I'm not sure I have said anything that would be of help to you as you face all the problems that come into young lives, but I do want to give you my deep sympathy in all the questions you have to decide.

"And now, if I may, I would like to close with a thought

from the past. We all know of the glory that was once Rome, proud Rome on her seven hills, which seemed to dominate the world. It was a sort of golden city with its laws, its order, its rules of conduct and codes of honor. And then something began to happen. Slowly, almost imperceptibly, things began to change. The old rules began to be broken, behavior became different, almost indecent, the moral codes were rejected, and at last in all classes the family, which is the foundation of society, began to dissolve. And then Rome fell."

Katherine looked at the serious faces before her and smiled.

"I am not drawing an exact parallel between Rome and the United States. But I do believe, most earnestly, that our country is in danger. You all know how prevalent divorce has become even among young married people and in how very many ways families are broken up. As I said before, the family is the bedrock of society; if it is no longer a firm institution upon which we can depend, then our society is not stable.

"You all know too how the fine old qualities of morality, honesty, and integrity have been lost, not only in many private lives but in high places, reaching to our government itself.

"My hope, then, is that our country will be safe, that your own school days may be happy ones, and that at the right time a beautiful love may come to each of you."

There was a little spatter of applause and then a generous round, with the girls leaving quietly. Many, Katherine noticed, picking up a copy of the poem she had mentioned. The chairman, Kate, thanked her soberly.

"I think you did that very well," she said. "We've had several speakers before who talked about sex, but the girls either sort of giggled behind their hands, or else were indignant. You spoke as though you were one of us and I think they liked it."

"I do hope so," Katherine said.

Miss Darby was on hand to escort her to the car, bringing

Dr. Harris' thanks, praise, and regrets that he could not give her tea in his office. "He's in what he calls a terrific quilt meeting and doesn't dare miss it."

"That's all going well, then?"

"You wouldn't believe how well. That idea was inspired if ever I heard of one. Now, go home and rest yourself. Dr. Harris says he knows how much a first speech takes out of you. I forgot to say he has a secret listening post, as he calls it; so he heard it all. He's a caution!"

"Miss Darby, do you know what I've discovered?"

"No, what?"

"You're very fond of Dr. Harris."

"Fiddlesticks!" said Miss Darby. "I teach English. I've no time for romantic folderols. Now, you get on home."

Katherine laughed and started the car. A happy chuckle escaped her as she lay down to rest before dinner. What an ideal match! she thought. Well, stranger things have happened.

Tim came that evening, full of delicious wit and roundabout praise. It seemed the chairman, Kate, was a granddaughter of old Judge Wills and, knowing Tim had some slight interest in the speaker, had called up to report to him what he had heard.

"Now," said Tim exultingly, "aren't you glad you did it? But now let's drop the speech for a while. I've got some real news to make your eyes shine. The Sun Dial came today!"

"Oh, really. Oh, Tim, I'm so glad!"

"Wait till you see it and you'll be gladder yet. It came addressed to me, so I took Boles at the hotel into my confidence and at once you'd think he had planned the whole thing. He helped me unpack it and has arranged with a mason to come up tomorrow about noon and set it just where you want it. Then you can enjoy your gift. Aren't you excited?"

Katherine leaned her head on the back of the chair. "I'm really too tired to be excited, but I'm awfully happy."

Tim rose at once. "That's right. You've had a big day. What

you must do now is go right to bed, and don't let your new laurels as a speechmaker tickle your ears! I'm very proud of you."

The house was still and Katherine fell asleep with the warm, comfortable feeling of a difficult thing apparently done with satisfaction and the anticipation of something lovely to come on the morrow. She rose in the morning rested and lighthearted, but, as she opened the back door, a paper fell out which had been lodged next to the screen.

She picked it up in surprise and read it. The words were written in what might be said to be deliberately tipsy capitals:

> "Dear Mrs. Davenport,
>
> Our gang has heard about what you said to the girls this afternoon and we don't like it. When you get into the girls' private lives, you may get into ours too, which we won't stand for. Better watch what you say after this."

It was signed with some sort of hieroglyphic.

Katherine folded the paper and tucked it in the desk. She was disturbed. It sounded almost like a warning. Her happy chain of thoughts had been broken as she pondered what, if anything, to do about the paper.

When the children were gone, she called Dr. Harris and found she could see him at once. She went to his office and spread the paper before him.

"It scares me a little, somehow."

Dr. Harris looked it over carefully and smiled. "Here is the clue to the writer," he said. "Do you see the little curl on that last *s*? I've watched that coming up through the grades. It is the unconscious signature of Don Elkins. He's been living with a girl far above him in every way and who, I think, has been wanting to free herself. Your speech may have given her the final spark of conscience and left Don hurt and very angry; so he struck out at you. That's my feeling."

"But this *'gang'* business I don't like."

"Oh, that doesn't mean much. There are five of them who want to pose as hard-drinking, fast-driving desperadoes, but my spies report they usually settle for a bottle of beer. They're all terribly poor and there is only one car available, which my spies report is an old one held together by safety pins or the like. If anyone lives with a girl, she probably provides the money and he the strong masculinity which appeals to many girls . . . Just tear this paper up, Mrs. Davenport, and forget it. I've heard several nice reports about your talk; so be happy."

By the following day Katherine needed no advice for happiness as she stood beside the treasure which now graced her garden. It rested on the very spot she and Philip had once selected, with the hours deeply engraved, the motto showing clearly above and below the face of the clock as though to commend its strength to those who looked upon it:

L'heure passe
L'amitié reste

Around the edge of the large circle ran a delicately engraved wreath of leaves and roses, added, Katherine felt sure, by Philip to bring the garden into it. At what expense! But with what beauty!

And now, even as the garden had once been, the Sun Dial became a focal point of interest. The neighbors came, more acquaintances came, school children came, all to admire the beautiful gift and speak of the gentle gardener who had sent it. To Katherine the hours were filled with a peculiar joy as she watched them move around their daylight course.

After several weeks Dr. Harris himself came, bringing with him a tall, shabby boy with a shock of dark hair all but covering brown eyes.

"Mrs. Davenport," he began, "this is Don Elkins, the best artist we have in school. One of our girls would like to make a picture of the Sun Dial as the center of her quilt, if you have no objections. Don here, I'm sure, could somehow make the copy."

"I haven't said I would, mind."

"Of course you will. You're just too modest. Look at it closely now, and you can't resist it."

Don moved closer and studied the Dial intently.

"Pretty thing, ain't it?" he said.

"I knew you'd feel so," said Dr. Harris. "You and Mrs. Davenport can work out the details as to where and how you can best work. Thank you both so much." And he left.

Katherine and the boy looked at each other and laughed.

"That's him, all right," Don said. "He gets you roped an' tied before you can say a word. I'll have to take a try at this thing, but it's going to be a tough job."

"I'll do everything I can to make you comfortable," Katherine said. And somehow with the laugh and the short exchange of words a strange and pleasant friendship began between them.

"I have a little office inside where you can work when it gets too chilly out here," she sold him.

"I can't do much tracing over the engraving," he said. "I'll bet it will all have to be by measurement and freehand."

As the days passed into weeks, Don worked on steadily, after school hours and slowly, to Katherine's amazement, he brought out a picture of the Dial. There was a true artist's skill in the boy's work and at all times, when neither of them was busy, he seemed eager to talk to her.

"You know the day you gave that talk to the girls?"

"Oh, yes, very well."

"Did you find a paper in your screen door that next morning?"

"Yes, I did."

"Well, I couldn't go on here, with you being so kind, without telling you I wrote that, and I'm ashamed now."

"I think you were just a little angry."

"Man, I was, more than a little! I was furious. I thought you'd made me lose my girl. But you know what?"

"What, Don?"

"Well, it's funny, but us boys in our gang have heard a lot more about what you said and we've begun to wonder if there ain't more to it than we thought at first. I like to talk to you about things."

"Well, I like to talk to you too . . . very much."

"Well now, about love — the way you think about it," he said suddenly one day. "Now, I've been to weddings and when the priest comes to that part about just sticking to the one person for the rest of their life, I just thought it was sort of mumbo jumbo which had to be in the ceremony but nobody would pay any attention to it. No one does, do you think?"

"Why, certainly, great numbers do. In fact, if you look our whole country over, I believe you'd find most of them do."

Don looked at her in astonishment. "The people I know don't. That's for sure. It's a hard vow I'd say."

"Not when you really love."

"Well, I don't want to hurt you, mind, or speak out of turn or anything, but we all know your own husband didn't."

"That is true."

"Well, doesn't that prove anything?"

"No. He did break his vow, but I kept mine."

"Honestly?"

"Yes, truly."

"You've just had one man all these years?"

"That is right!"

"Even while he was gone and there were maybe other chances — I mean, other men?"

"I have loved only one man, Don, if that's what you want to know."

"You're some woman," he said. "Wait till I tell the gang that. They won't hardly believe it, but I'll tell them how you looked when you said it. I'm nearly done with this job now, but I want you to know I've been glad to work here and listen to what you say. I won't forget you, mind."

"Oh, please don't. And I'll try to see you when I can. I'm very interested in your talent. There might be a chance for art school later, let's hope!"

"Let's," Don said briefly.

At last the difficult task was completed and the large square of white on which the design was finally to be centered was removed from Katherine's table to the room at school given over to the quilts and new designs, as the plans progressed. Perhaps no one except the head of the art department realized the labor and skill that had gone into Don's work: the patient first tracing, then the freehand and measurements, the delicate corrections, then the final design, out of the many failures and successes, of the dial, on the last heavy inked medium which, when held face down upon the cloth, would yield the beautiful imprint.

It was, in its way, a triumph and Don, keeping well out of sight, still heard the exclamations and the praise. Katherine, who had come to see the hanging, wished she could be closer to him, but had only glimpses of his well-brushed hair and high color. When she left, Dr. Harris was speaking earnestly to him, so she did not wait to get through the crowd which had gradually gathered to see the work and its artist.

That night she felt more lonely than usual. She missed the boy whose afternoons often stretched to early evenings. She wondered if, in all their strange conversations, she had said anything of value. When the first darkness came, Don himself came. It was mild Indian summer and the door was half open. She hurried to hold it wide and welcome him.

"Didn't you get a lovely ovation this afternoon?" she began.

"What's that?"

"Oh, praise and hand-clapping. They were all so pleased,

and well they may be. Did you speak to the girl who is going to make the Dial quilt?"

"Yes. She's a nice girl. I was glad she liked it. You know, I came to tell you something."

"I'm glad. Please sit down."

"No, I'm just on the way to the other fellows. But today Dr. Harris talked to me again about that school and bringing my work up and all that. Last night our gang was just sitting around talking and I told them about your idea too and how we could all do better in school. We're smart enough." He paused. "This part is sort of funny to tell you, but I thought you might like to hear."

"Oh, surely I would."

"Well, we had just been talking about cutting out a lot of rough stuff and really studying and all at once Bill — he's one of our gang — and let me tell you, he's been around all right, if you know what I mean. Well, he just spoke up and he says, 'Sure we could make marks for college if we tried. Then sometime when we fell in love and got married, wouldn't it be wonderful on our wedding night to know we was *the first*?' And nobody said a word. We each just got up and went home. I guess to think it all over."

Chapter Six

DAYLIGHT SAVING was ended for this year and the shadows began to fall before the sunset was over. If there was no sunset at all, the darkness early swallowed up the last vestige of light.

Katherine Davenport sat on the lawn and mused sadly of the seasons. A light west wind was blowing, so different from the tumultuous craving cries of March which always frightened her. This was gentle but still held a faint threat of winter to come, even as the April breeze brought the insistent promise of summer. So many different winds blew over the earth; so many winds of love had their way with the heart.

For herself she felt saddened and discouraged. There was a terrible, unconquerable loneliness. In a sense, life was full. She had her children, her friends, and an increasing involvement in various kinds of community work. But it was not enough. Her heart was empty and longing for the love of a man for a woman, for the love of her own man, which she feared would never be hers again.

Of course there had been substitutes offered along the way. Dick Hunter, whom she had known and respected for years, who was now alone, had spoken to her once gravely.

"I wonder, when you really decide to be free, if you would consider marrying me. I would so love to make you happy."

She had lain awake a long time that night thinking, for, as at this time, she had been feeling deeply the loss of love and she knew Dick's fine qualities. But it was no use. The image of David came between her and the thought of her union with another man. She tried to explain to Dick, who accepted her words with the quiet chivalry which was a part of his nature.

The other time she had lain awake considering the varieties of love was for quite a different reason. Harry Kline, a neighbor, had called to say his wife had suddenly contracted the flu and would Katherine care to use the extra ticket to the concert series if he escorted her? His wife hoped she would. She accepted with pleasure, but, upon their return afterward to Katherine's house, Harry became passionate in speech and desire, convinced, apparently, of his own compelling charm. Katherine felt sickened and after she was rid of him, she locked the door and went upstairs slowly and weakly. She thought of the two opposite types of men who had somehow been drawn to her. At least, her pride noted, in spite of her being left "hanging alone on the bough," as it were, she must still be a desirable woman. But oh, what poor solace for an aching heart!

The darkness had gathered now and she rose from her remembered thoughts and gave herself a little shake. "Autumn evenings are not good for me," she said to herself. "What I need is a good, bracing tonic!" She went inside to the phone and a brisk, almost harsh voice answered her call.

"Miss Darby speaking!"

"Good!" said Katherine. "Would you consider coming over for a coffee nightcap? I can add coconut cake."

"Consider it? I had just decided to call you to ask if I could come."

"Is there anything the matter? You sound upset."

"The world is out of joint. 'Oh, cursed spite, et cetera.' "

"Well, come along and let us curse out spites together."

As she made the coffee and cut the cake, she wondered what was troubling Miss Darby and wondered still more when she saw that lady's grim face.

"What's the matter?"

"Wait," she said, "I'll not deny I'm hungry, for I couldn't eat my dinner. We'll save the problem until later."

There were few comments then except about the weather, until they were both seated in the living room and Miss Darby, as it were, "took the floor."

"What I'm about to tell you is an absolute, inviolable secret. I can trust you. If I go on keeping it alone, I'll wear myself out. It's pretty sad, but here it is."

Miss Darby swallowed with difficulty.

"I always make a last-minute check on our classrooms with darkness falling so early, to be sure there's no monkey business going on and that nobody gets locked in. Two nights ago, outside of my own English room, I was sure I heard someone in there crying. I went in. There was a slip of a girl bent over her desk, sobbing. It was Laurie Bradley. I put my arms around her and said to tell me her troubles if it would help. I supposed she had just had a spat with John Lester. They've been dating quite a while. But finally she almost flung herself on me and she said, 'Oh, Miss Darby, I'm so *scared,* and I'd rather die than tell Mother and Daddy what's happened to me. I'll jump in the river first.' "

"Not *Laurie*!" Katherine said in a whisper.

"I told her not to be silly about the river and dying and all that nonsense, but to brace up and remember what my mother used to say: 'Where there's a problem, there's always a way out!' "

"Has she seen a doctor?" Katherine asked.

"No, but she says there are signs to make you sure, and I know there are. She grew calmer after a while and I drove her home. My heart just melted as I watched her go up to the Bradleys' front door. She had wanted me to go in and tell her mother while she stayed up in her room. 'Just till Mother gets over her first shock,' she kept begging. But I couldn't do that. It would be harder for her mother to hear it first from a stranger. Do you know her Katherine?"

"Oh, yes, she belongs to the famous Bridge Club and is the very lively center of each meeting. She is what you would call volatile. She moans and groans when she makes a mistake and screams with joy when she makes a grand slam. She's a compulsive talker. She just can't keep quiet. But everyone loves her even when they know they would play better bridge if she kept quiet. Once in a while someone will say, 'Oh, *shut up,* Cele! I'm trying to concentrate.' She will smile and be still for ten minutes; then she'll say, 'Listen, girls, I just have to tell you this.' When she doesn't come to meetings, it's a relief, but at the same time things seem a bit flat. Do I give you the picture?"

"What about Henry?"

"Oh, he's as calm and steady as she is excitable. He will be stricken by this. He adores Laurie. Poor Henry! Poor Cele, and, oh, poor little Laurie! What can they all do when they're faced by this really tragic situation?"

"Well," Miss Darby said slowly, "they have several options, as you must realize. The first obvious — and the one you are probably thinking of — I would be against. I've no religious scruples, of course, but I have *woman's* scruples. The very heart of me goes against it. Life is so precious, no matter how it's come by. Then, even with the best doctor, there is some risk."

Miss Darby sighed heavily and then went on.

"There's another thing that keeps coming to me, since I knew. John Lester is a nice boy and he's nineteen, a year older than the other seniors. His father's company took him once to Mexico for a year and his family went along. John had to make up that year when he got back here. Now, I believe those youngsters are truly in love."

"You can't be thinking of marriage at their age?" Katherine was aghast.

"Well, we are doing a lot of talking just now about early days in our country and in Revolutionary times, and a good while later, a boy of nineteen was considered a *man*, ready to marry and set up a home."

Katherine shook her head. "Times have changed since then," she said. And then they sat on, discussing the other options, their faces sad with the vicarious suffering of woman for woman. In their recurring thoughts of Laurie herself, they had both perceived in her a peculiar brightness, almost a radiance of expression, along with a quick lightness of movement which in a musician might be called virtuosity. Along with great physical beauty, she had an inner loveliness of spirit. How, then, could she of all girls have allowed herself to be betrayed by a love too passionately expressed?

"I've heard of another option, though it seems a bit unreal," Katherine said.

"Tell it to me for heaven's sake."

"I have an old college friend with whom I've always kept up. She teaches in a girls' private school. She wrote me not long ago that she knew of a number of unmarried girls who kept their babies, if the parents are willing. She thinks it's really an offshoot of the Lib movement. The girl in such a situation in effect says, 'Why should I blush, hang my head, while the young man or boy, who is as much involved as I am, goes on his way as usual? No, I shall keep my child whether we decide to marry or not, and hold my head high.' She says she has seen this happen and the community, at first startled, comes to accept it."

"It certainly is startling, but then most things are nowadays," Miss Darby commented. "I really must go. We have been talking as though it was our part to make the ultimate decision instead of her parents and Laurie."

"And John," Katherine added.

Miss Darby hesitated at the door. "I might give you a little counterirritant to take your mind off the big trouble. It's pretty small compared to that, but Dr. Harris is quite concerned. Of course, he doesn't know about Laurie. This other thing has to do with the quilts. A sample of what is already done has been hung up, as you know, in the small gymnasium for a brief display. Jeannie McAllister is the girl who suggested the Sun Dial and she has worked beautifully on it. Now it seems her father is a sort of tyrant and she's to stop these folderols and study her books. Don, meanwhile — you remember him?"

"Very definitely!"

"Well, he's been haunting the room whenever possible to look at the Sun Dial and also, I think, at Jeannie. Dr. Harris told me he could cheerfully throttle McAllister, but outwardly he's as calm as a summer sea. My dear, try to sleep. I'll tell you any news I hear."

Katherine saw her off and then returned to her chair. She was not sleepy. It would be better to think things through again until her brain was tired. So she went over and over again all the options they had just discussed. None of them eased the factual pain. It was only a few days now until the club meeting, and what would Cele do then? Would she come, a parody of her old self, and somehow brave it out? No, she was too transparent. She could not cover this. She thought of the young lovers, fed, according to Cele's report to her once, on Romeo and Juliet and Cyrano! There had been a beauty somehow in their unfortunate intensity. She never thought of the quilt problem until she was upstairs. It did seem so small compared to the other.

When the members arrived for the next club meeting, there came a lull after the first burst of gossip, while they waited for the late comer. This was Cele. When she finally arrived, she took her place quietly without her usual fanfare.

"Okay, girls. Sorry I'm late. Let's begin."

There were anxious calls from all tables.

"What's wrong, Cele?"

"Why, you came in like a thief in the night. Not a word, not a call, not a scream."

"What's wrong, Cele?"

"I'm worried," Cele answered calmly. "It's about Laurie."

Katherine felt a chill creep up her spine.

"What's the matter with Laurie? Has she broken up with John Lester?"

Cele managed a small smile. "Oh, *that*!" she said. "It's her health that I'm worried about. She's had a little cough for some time. I paid little attention to it until she began to look pale and lost her appetite. Then I took her to the doctor and he says —" She paused to wipe her eyes. "He says there is no real danger yet, but the x rays of her chest make him feel a change of climate would clear it all up. He's an old family friend. He knows Sis, my sister, lives in Colorado. He advises me to take her there and leave her for some time."

"Oh, Cele, I'm *so* sorry," her partner said, "but you are catching it in time. And it's wonderful she can be with your sister. When do you leave?"

"We fly on Saturday morning. I'll have to stay a little while, but I hate to leave Henry so lonely."

The news was relayed from table to table. Katherine felt she was playing at random, thinking that there were two actresses now in their midst, for Cele had told her story as with utter conviction. When the evening was over, Cele came up to her. "May I run you home, Katherine? I heard you say you had walked over because your car stalled and would hitch a ride home. Come with me?"

"Gladly, and thanks."

The ride home was quiet except for Cele's confession that she had gone first alone to the doctor, who, as an old family friend, had helped them over the first part of the plan and had, indeed, suggested it.

"Do you think they believed me?" she asked.

"I'm sure they did," Katherine replied.

"When I looked into your eyes," Cele went on, "I felt you somehow knew the truth. Miss Darby knows and might have told you."

"She did. Oh, Cele, if I only could help you!"

"You can if you just let me come in with you and talk for a few minutes. I do need that, for I try never to let down for Henry's sake."

So at last they sat together in Katherine's living room and Cele broke down completely. "I've often tested myself," she said. "I've imagined what if Laurie was in a fatal car accident or had a desperate disease. But never, never, did I think of this that has happened. And now I simply don't know what to do beyond going to Colorado."

"What about John?"

"Oh, I must tell you that when Henry first knew, I thought he would kill John when he saw him. Then last night when the bell rang, we were both so nervous, we answered it together. There stood John, looking so pale and distressed and *scared* that Henry just put out his hand and said, 'Come in John. We have much to talk about.' So he came in and said he would do anything, *anything* we wanted him to do or Laurie wished —

"And as we talked, Laurie heard the voices from her room and came running down the stairs in her blue dressing gown, looking like an angel. John started up and they met halfway, both crying out to each other. 'Oh, Laurie, can you ever forgive me?' 'Oh, John, do you still love me?' And all at once they were in each other's arms and then we all talked together."

"But, Cele, don't you feel a little better about it all now?"

"How can it ever be resolved? John's marks are so high, he's been counting on Princeton. Laurie's are extremely good and we were hoping for Wellesley. Now the whole pattern of their lives seems broken."

"Don't be so sure of that at this point. Sometimes Providence takes an unexpected part in the affairs of men — and women. Try not to look too far ahead. Take Laurie to Colorado. That will do you both good. When you get back here, be natural and wait until her stay is ended. There just might be a solution."

"You really think so?"

"I really do."

When Cele left, she was calm and inclined toward a mild acceptance if not optimism.

Saturday was a bright sunny day for the travelers. Mary and Bill Hastings went to the plane with Henry to see his family off.

"Poor devil!" Bill reported to Katherine. "Cele hung to him like a leech while we waited. He finally pushed her off, almost roughly, I thought, but he probably couldn't take any more good-bys. Poor Henry will be pretty lonely now. Mary asked him to dinner tonight but he declined."

And the pleasant day wore on. Miss Darby called once to say she had thought of Cele and Laurie on their way to Colorado, also that Dr. Harris was still bothered about the McAllister man, who was making a nuisance of himself. That was all.

Katherine put the children to bed early that night and sat by herself, reviewing what had passed. At eleven she heard faint sounds which indicated another bad accident at the intersection where her own street crossed the main avenue a long block away.

"O-oh!" she shivered. "I hope no one was hurt." Then, later, the indistinct sound of the ambulance siren. Then quiet. At twelve the lights were still on at the Hastings house and she decided to call up and see if they knew anything of what had happened, but before she reached the phone, Bill Hastings was at the door.

"I thought you might be wondering — or would want to know — if you could hear any sounds from the accident. It was Henry Bradley."

"Oh, *no*! Is it bad, Bill?"

His reply was a question. "Was Bradley a drinking man, Katherine?"

"No," she said. "Never. I've often watched him nurse along one cocktail and refuse a second. What made you ask that?"

"Well, he was drunk as a lord when they got him out of the car wreckage. I'll tell you that. And the thing that even seemed to break up the interns who came with the ambulance was that he could just barely speak and he kept mumbling, 'Don't tell Cele. Don't let her come here or I'll kill you.' Pretty wonderful in such a time to be thinking of his wife. Didn't want her to be worried."

"But will he get over this? Did you get to see a doctor?"

"Mary did. She rode along to the hospital. He has no relatives here, you know. Luckily the Bradleys' own doctor was there on account of another patient, so he saw Henry when they brought him in. He told Mary it was pretty bad and they couldn't tell until morning what could be done. They feel sure one leg and one arm are broken, but they are so swollen they couldn't be set tonight. They will keep him on opiates now and watch him carefully. Even with his poor bruised, swollen lips he kept trying to talk to the doctor. 'Swear you won't let Cele come' the doctor told Mary. It certainly touches you, doesn't it?"

"Oh, it's utterly distressing. But there's something wrong with the story. Henry could not have been drunk."

"Well," Bill said slowly, "a man would have to have had a pretty big snootful to make him drive his car straight through a red light into another car. Tell you how I have it figured out. Henry was all alone yesterday and all evening. Laurie is a quiet little thing like her Dad, but Cele — you know how she keeps things lively every minute. And he missed that. He was lonesome, so he just drank a bottle of Scotch and started out. Not being used to drinking would make it all the worse. I've got to go to Mary. She was pretty shook up from the hospital experience. We'll keep you in touch."

When he had gone, Katherine put out the lights and dragged herself upstairs. This was sad news indeed. Poor Henry! His life hanging in the balance and his family far away. This was a heartbreaking situation. Now, if ever, he needed his wife with him. Laurie was safely under the care of her aunt. *If Cele came* — suddenly Katherine sat up in bed, repeating her last words. *"If Cele came* — I wonder," she said slowly, *"if we were all wrong."*

For five weeks, Henry Bradley lay quietly submitting to all that nature and the doctors did to fuse his battered body back to something like health again. The broken leg would still take more time, but the left arm was doing well. The nurses adored him. His bruised face was not swollen now, so he could speak with ease; but he seldom did. He smiled at the girls, though, and they smiled back at him marveling that he was so relaxed and often fell asleep even though he must be in pain.

The Bradleys' doctor and friend had done his work well. Cele was still in Colorado. She called Katherine frequently but gradually became reconciled. "Of course, I know, as Doc says, that if I got to see him, I'd just talk my head off, asking all about the accident and telling all my news. But it does seem queer not to go on now."

Katherine parried as well as she could. "He's only now getting really relaxed, Cele. He sleeps a lot. The doctor says if he got excited now it would undo half of their good work."

"Maybe so," said Cele, sighing.

It was six weeks when Henry sent for Katherine. He could write now, so it was a note she received.

Dear Katherine,

Could you call on me one afternoon soon and tell no one you are coming? I'm still pretty banged up, but actually getting better.

Henry B.

When she arrived at the hospital, she found he had been moved to a small private wing and was sitting propped up in a large chair with one leg extended.

"Henry!" she exclaimed.

"This is good of you," he answered.

She sat down opposite him and followed his lead as she told him quietly bits of neighborhood news. Very soon he began to speak himself.

"I'll try not to make this too startling for you, but I want to tell you at once. I may have to go to some sort of sanitarium when they finally discharge me here. But when I am well, I will be leaving Cele."

"I don't understand."

"Leaving by an indefinite separation or a divorce, or whatever she wants, but I will not live with her any longer. I am telling you because, of all my friends, I am most sure you will keep my secret. When it's all a fait accompli, everyone will know, but my reason is what I would not want known by the general public."

"Please tell me at once. As you may guess, I feel a little shaken without knowing the facts."

Bradley waved at a nurse for her to stay away for the moment. "It was like this," he began. "I was the only child of not so young parents. Our house was not the kind where youngsters gather and I grew up a shy, bashful young man. In college I hadn't much of a social life until one night at a party I saw Cele, and I was entranced. She was animated, vivacious, constantly talking, laughing, calling out to this one and that. I fell in love with her. Heaven help me, I still love her, but I can't live with her." He paused for breath, and then finished quickly. "By some strange alchemy of nature, she fell in love with me. We were soon married, but before a month was up I knew I had made a great mistake. The somewhat noisy animation of the party group did not fit into our home. She is a compulsive talker. I never had a quiet evening to read. I tried my best. I once booked on a deluxe fishing boat with a group of congenial men. When she heard how much it cost, she cried bitterly. 'That would almost pay for a cruise that we could take together,' she said. I gave up the trip. I must not go on citing examples. I didn't know until the Saturday she and

Laurie left how near the breaking point I was. Then the whole day of quiet taught me. I drank a lot of Scotch and, to celebrate my freedom, drove off. You know the rest."

"What about Laurie?"

"She has a nice boy. I have a strange feeling they are going to work something out. I will not leave, of course, until I know she is, in some way, happy. But I felt I must get the burden off my heart and I know you will not speak to anyone of what I have told you."

"Of course I will not. But have you thought of discussing this in plain terms with Cele — in demanding what you need for your own health and peace of mind?"

"My dear Katherine, of course I have been almost rude in my description of the situation. She literally doesn't understand it. 'You're just overtired,' she always tells me. I'm working too hard in the office and that's why I'm a little irritable. She's just icing a cake for the Smiths or Jones or Whosiz who are coming in for dessert and a little game of bridge. Do you get the whole picture? Twenty-four years of this I've had!"

"Yet you still love her?"

Henry hesitated. "I have loved her body and the qualities that everyone likes in her. If my nerves would still hold out, I would not think of leaving, but I don't think I can go on."

"It may all but kill Cele to lose you."

"Oh, I should have explained. I've talked with my manager. I've had some success with the company. They will send me to the Toronto office to come back in any emergency or for an occasional long weekend. It would sort of be a separation with *visiting privileges*," he said with a faint smile. "And of course I would always be in touch with Laurie and come when the child is born."

Katherine's face was still white from her shock at his first words when she rose at last to go.

"Would you mind if I wrote to Cele and, without giving anything away, advise her, just from my knowledge of many evenings with her?"

"Not at all. But I don't think she will know what you're driving at. You may only lose a friend and she's very fond of you. But you might write to *me* if you have any suggestions. I'm open to advice. And, thank you, my dear, for listening to me. I feel better already, having unburdened myself."

"When would you leave, Henry?"

"Doc says in two weeks he's sure I'll be discharged. Then I should go to a sanitarium for a little therapy and then be as good as new. I did get off relatively well, compared to the way they found me. Luckily, the man in the other car was not much hurt. I took the brunt. When I leave for the sanitarium, I'll go right from there to Toronto. I think I will write my decision to Cele. My nerves are still shaky. I don't believe I could get through a physical encounter."

Katherine did not reply except to wish him good health soon, and wisdom in all his plans.

Back at her home, she thought and thought. She wrote three letters to Cele and tore them up, one by one. After a sleepless night, she decided to do as Bradley himself had suggested. She would write to him.

Dear Henry, [she began at last]

Your confession of yesterday is sealed and sacred in my memory until you yourself make it public, but it has been going round and round in my mind and heart. I have not written to Cele, but at your suggestion I am now being bold enough to offer you some advice.

I do know what you have been through. Two evenings a month for years I have played bridge with Cele, and while everyone is very fond of her, there are always some cries of "Oh, don't talk, Cele; I'm trying to concentrate."

I feel that you, as the husband, should make your wishes felt so decidedly that you will achieve them. Could the little card room in your house not be made into a study for you where you can retire and have perfect quiet one evening, perhaps, a week? Later on, the cards can still be played there when you are not using it. But it should be made clear that it is *your* study.

As to the fishing trip you spoke of, perhaps you should have gone. You needed it and deserved it. If Cele cried for what she herself wanted to do, I believe you should have stood firm and gently promised her a cruise later on. Could your trouble have been that, since, by nature, you are gentle and chivalrous, but since marriage is a partnership, you needed to assert yourself and your wishes sometimes, and have not done so? If you now told Cele plainly what you expect in the future, there may be some tears at first, but it will be, in the end, so infinitely easier than the permanent cleavage of your marriage. That would break her heart and maybe, eventually, yours too. I do think, Henry, there is a better way. I'm copying some sentences from a wise old book. They have often helped me. God bless you both.

Katherine

Love is a great thing, yea a great and thorough good. Love feels no burden, thinks nothing of trouble: attempts what is beyond its strength, pleads no excuse of impossibility: Love is active, sincere, pleasant, courageous, long suffering and never seeking itself. Though weary, Love is not tired; though pressed, it is not straitened. If any man love, he knoweth what is the cry of this voice.

For two more weeks Katherine heard no news of the Bradleys except that Cele was home and Henry, discharged from the hospital, had not gone to a sanitarium. One day, in the mail, she received a brief card.

Dear K.D.,

You may be right. At least it's worth a try. Deepest thanks to you for your interest.

H.B.

And the days advanced toward Christmas, the second since David had been gone. Katherine wondered, as on the last one, how she could get through it. Boxes from Paris came early for the children and were carefully kept out of sight, except for an occasional peep to quell the youngsters' rising curiosity and wild imaginations.

But no matter how her own heart felt, she must go through the usual seasonal ritual. Tim took the children shopping before November was over, then later helped decorate the house with greens and put up the tree. Katherine baked the fruitcake and made the cookies and even laid the wood for the fire on Christmas Eve. At last everything was ready. Hearts might break, but certain things had to be done as they always had been. The trimming of the tree had been hardest, for David had always done much of that.

As they sat beside it on Christmas Eve to open their gifts, Tim said stoutly, "Now, I believe in having the grand opening Christmas Eve instead of morning, when the kids have lain awake all night in excitement and rouse the family at the first cockcrow. (That means rooster, Kit, if there is one left now in this sophisticated suburb.) Come on, let's get to the boxes. Children first, eh, Katherine?"

"Of course. Go right ahead, darlings."

With squeals of delight they each found their unusual toys and then looked in surprise at two small extra packages: "To Mother from Davey"; "To Mother from Kit."

"Why Dad never before sent things for us to give to you, Mother," said Davey.

Katherine flushed as Tim turned toward her and whispered, "A fit of conscience, maybe."

"Open them, Mother. Let's see!"

She undid the ribbons on the first, and a silk scarf fell from it, of incredible white delicacy.

"Oh, how lovely!" She exclaimed. It was a spontaneous reaction.

"Now mine," urged Kit, holding out her package.

This contained long, white kid gloves, which made Tim whistle. "This all means opera, for sure. I'll take you when I get back."

"Oh, Tim, are you going away?"

"I have to, dear. I didn't want to spoil Christmas so I will stay until after dinner tomorrow and then get a plane West. I have to see a man in Los Angeles. Writing or phoning won't do. I have to talk to him, face to face. It may take about a week and then on the way back, I'll have to stop to see Jack Paar. You remember him?"

"Of course, you were always bringing him home from college with you."

Tim laughed. "He sticks to his one introduction of me. ('This is old Tim Dalzell. Roomed with him four years in college and came out alive. Miracle of the century.') I'll be staying only a night, or a day with him and be back before you know it."

When the children had at last gone up to bed with their treasures, he gave them his good nights and when downstairs again, helped Katherine to tidy the melee of ribbons and papers and then they exchanged gifts they had not put in their separate heaps before. He gave her special information in connection with his absence. "Be good, don't worry. I'll telephone you. Remember I'll miss you too, my dear Kitten." And he was gone.

The holidays went fast. Katherine skipped the big New Year's dance, for it was one affair she and David had always made quite a point of enjoying together. She burned the greens on Twelfth Night, however, a tradition the children always loved and made much of. With them back in school, Katherine settled into the round of town activities. Cele was certainly home, but neighbors reported she seemed rather subdued. Only said Laurie was doing well and liked being in her aunt's home. But Cele had tears in her eyes when she told that the doctor had said Henry was on the verge of a nervous breakdown and no one must see him for a while or make any sound that might disturb him.

"Poor Cele," Katherine murmured to herself. "She's been pushed down an unfamiliar road and doesn't know how to walk it." Could her advice have had any effect?

Miss Darby, meanwhile, gave the news of the Terrible McAllister, who didn't want his daughter to waste her time on folderols, namely, the quilt. "But Dr. Harris has something up his sleeve," she announced with a fine mixing of metaphors. "There's more than one way to skin a cat. He's subtle, but he's also devious, meaning it in a respectful way. He'll get that man yet!" She added that Don, the artist, walked Jeannie home every afternoon.

It was when Tim had been back for ten days that Katherine noticed the childrens' behavior. She herself had barely seen him, for she had been plunged into committee meetings and Tim was working now, far into the night to make up for the days he had been away from the office and to use the material he had gone for. Then Katherine realized the children had something on their minds. They retreated to corners and whispered earnestly; they made queer signs; they spoke in little abortive sentences; worst of all, they looked unhappy. Knowing they couldn't keep a secret long, and assuming it was some little school trouble, Katherine waited. One evening at dinner it came out.

"Mother," said Davey, as though marshaling all his forces, "What's wrong with Uncle Tim?"

She looked shocked. "Why, I don't know. Is anything wrong?"

"Yes," Davey went on. "We're afraid." Here he stopped and let one hand circle around his head. "We're afraid he's gone bananas!"

Katherine laughed as she had not done for a long time. When she could speak, she said, "My darlings, you don't need to be worried about Uncle Tim's mind. It's about as sharp and keen as a steel trap. What made you think such a thing about him?"

Kit took it up. "It's the way he acts. He's come twice when you were out and he went straight to Peter, and he asked Davey —"

"'Will you please show me Judge Peter's new residence,' he said, just as sober as could be. So I showed him the nice new winter house the carpenter made for Peter. Then Uncle Tim walked round and round it and then he said — "

Kit took up the narrative. "And he said, 'Judge, could you please stop wiggling your nose in court? It disturbs the lawyers.' Then he made a big bow and swung us around a little and went off."

"And the *next* time," said Davey, "was worse. He came in from the car just for a moment, he said, and you weren't here then. So he went straight back to Peter and called him My Dear Old Chap and said he had come because of Peter's *tail*."

Kit went on. "He said it wasn't much of a tail but still it was one and Peter should be thankful he had even that much because there were some *cats* that didn't have any at all."

"And then he began to sing this song about these cats — "

Katherine broke in with a laugh. "Oh, I remember that song. Our father used to sing it to us as we were getting ready for bed. Now listen, children, Uncle Tim is just happy because he got the material for which he made the last trip, and also because he had a little visit with his old college friend, Mr. Paar. So that's all there is to it. Now just relax and enjoy his jokes and funny songs. You know how he loves to tease!"

"Well, I certainly am relieved," said Davey.

"Me too," echoed Kit.

"And he has just called," Katherine went on, "to say at last he has a free evening and will be over to dinner and help put you to bed. Isn't that fine?"

But when Tim came, even Katherine was a little mystified. After kissing them once around, he went to the piano.

"Now I'll entertain you with my present favorite song. Just remembered it the other day. It's a very serious song, so please give attention." In a good strong tenor, Tim began:

"All the other cats have tails
In England, Ireland, Scotland, Wales.
This is a rank injustice! [bang, bang on the bass]

To right it is my plan,
It is a burning shame, [bang, bang]
That the cats have got — [delicate treble]
No tails on the Isle of Man!"

"What! No applause? Well, here's another!"

"Tim, oh Tim,
He always dresses so prim
He's full of vigor and vim
Oh Tim
And the nectar is up to the brim
Of the glass for Tim
Oh, Tim!"

"I made that one myself. Pretty good, I think. Maybe I'll give up law and take to poetry."

Katherine suddenly stood, "Timothy Dalzell, you get up and look me in the eye!"

Tim did as he was bidden, a wide grin on his face.

"Tim, I know what's the matter with you. At long, long last, you've fallen in love!"

"My darling sister, I wouldn't deceive you for the world!"

"Oh, Tim, I can't believe it! Who is she? How did you meet her? How long have you known her? I'm simply bursting with questions. Tim, I'm so happy for you!"

"Well now, let's have a nice normal dinner. I'll promise not to cut up any more monkeyshines. I was just teasing the children, but from the looks on their faces, I must have scared them in some way. We'll all be good now, play a while after dinner until bedtime. Then after that, Katherine, you and I will have a real visit. All right?"

"Perfect!" they all chorused, and dinner went forward as usual except for a few pointed questions from the children.

"Uncle Tim," Davey asked, "if you fell in love with somebody, the way Mother said, would you have to get married?"

"Well, that's the way it happens sometimes, I believe," Tim replied.

"But," said Kit anxiously, "you'd still come here for dinner and stay all night and things, wouldn't you?"

Katherine and Tim's eyes met. Her face had lost some of its color.

"Of course," he said stoutly. "I'll have that in the bargain."

When the last bedtime story had been told and the cat song sung again, the children settled to sleep and Tim came downstairs and sat on the couch beside Katherine.

"Now for the grand confession," he said, his eyes dancing.

"Tim, I'm too excited to sit still. After all the years I've planned — tried to matchmake for you —"

"And then the scoundrel went and did it all himself. There's gratitude! Well, where shall I start?"

"At the beginning, and don't leave out a thing!"

"Very good. When I arrived at Jack Paar's house, it was a cold, wet evening and I felt like a drowned rat. All I wanted was a bite to eat and a bed to stretch out on if Jack would let me. But when he met me, I saw he was in high feather about something. It seemed that was the night of the Bachelors' Cotillion, the biggest social event of the year and he felt it was the very hand of Providence which had brought me there just in time. I tried to beg off, but it was no good and after Wesson, the old man who practically brought Jack up after his mother's death, had seen that I was showered and shaved and into a warm dressing gown, I began to revive.

"Jack explained while we ate in front of the fire that as soon as he got my wire, he had rented tails for me. I said 'Good Lord, not tails!' And white gloves — the whole works! He told me he thought I could find my way round at that! We're still the same size, so dressing was fun but no problem.

"When at last we entered the ballroom where the Cotillion took place, I was stunned by its beauty. It looked to me like the Old South before the war must have done. A huge dance floor with perhaps a hundred little gold chairs around the back and side for onlookers or those who wanted to rest. The orchestra was not on a balcony but on a dais, which gave the same effect. Then the flowers! Ropes of white around the fireplaces and great mirrors, shipped in from California, Jack said, by order of the bachelors or men in general, if bachelors were in short supply.

"We made our bow to the dignified old chaperone and her aides and then, Kathy, it happened. I've always heard about love at first sight, and I thought it was just a little poetic nonsense, but I swear to you, it happened to me. I looked across the floor and saw a girl and something like an electric shock went through me. I turned to an aide and asked if she would take me over to the girl in white with three men around her and introduce me, and she laughed and said I would soon realize there were always a number of men around that girl. When I reached her, I looked down at her and she looked up at me and as our eyes met, I really think things were settled there and then. We didn't even catch each other's name, for as they were being pronounced, the orchestra began. I held out my arms and she slipped into them.

"You remember that poem we read over and over during the war — 'The White Cliffs,' wasn't it? The girl in it says, 'I put my gloved hand into his glove; We danced together and fell in love.'

"So that's the way it was with Mary and me. Oh, that's her name, I forgot to say. The sweetest name in the world, I think. We danced, never speaking, but feeling that strange electric spark going back and forth between us. I remembered a number of little extra steps you and I had worked out as we practiced at home for your debutante balls when I escorted you because Mother thought you were too young. As I tried them, I found Mary followed every one. I could tell we were being watched. After we had circled the floor a few more times, we noticed that we were in a bare space just in front of the orchestra, which began to play 'I Could Have Danced All Night,' and then we heard the applause. It was all so strange. There were Mary and I thinking of nothing but ourselves, but putting on what, I realize now, was quite a show. As soon as the piece ended, we stopped, bowed to the orchestra and the chaperone, and slipped out a door marked Exit. It happened to be one of the men's cloakrooms, but it was dim and empty. It was there we had our first kiss."

Tim looked off into space as if the memory still overpowered him. Then he went on.

"Jack had been trailing us and caught us as we were ready to leave.

"'Well,' he said in his bantering way, 'for a man who is too tired even to look at a Cotillion, you shook a pretty fancy leg when you got here!' Then he looked at us closely. I swear his eyes were moist. He said, 'God bless you, my children! Where to now?' I told him we wanted a quiet spot where we could talk. Did he know one? He did and would call a cab and give directions. In the state I was in, he said I wouldn't remember them. Of course, he was right.

"The place where he sent us was perfect. Very French, very elegant, with couples looking like lovers coming and going. I waved the waiter aside but the old sommelier with his keys swinging took a look at us, then went below and brought up the finest champagne I ever tasted. And then, Kathy, we talked our very hearts out. We laughed sometimes, so happy that our sense of humor was a congenial one. But we were mostly dead serious with a tear or two when we described how we had each been miraculously prevented from making the great mistake when we were almost at the altar. We felt so sure we must wait for the ultimate, as Mary called it. So we talked on and on. I vaguely recall eating something at one time, but it isn't clear. When I looked at my watch at last, it was four o'clock and I was truly scared and ashamed. I told Mary we must call her father at once. And I would speak to him myself. 'You are my responsibility!' 'Since when?' she asked with a laugh. 'Since you let me kiss you as I did in the cloakroom.'

"When her father's voice came, it was husky and angry. I took the first word, told him Mary was safe and sound and, I thought, happy. I apologized for the hour and gave my name. 'What have you been doing till four o'clock?' he sort of barked. 'Talking,' I said. 'Well,' he went on, 'if it was with any other girl than Mary, I would assume you had found something more exciting to do than talking.' This rather nettled me, so I said, 'I resent your assumption, sir. Choose your weapons and I'll meet you at sunrise.' "

"Oh, Tim, you *didn't* say such a ridiculous thing!"

"Yes, I did. I was excited and a little mad, but luckily he liked it. He laughed and said I would notice he had cleared Mary at once, but he admired a young man with some principles. Then he said slowly, 'A lawyer, eh? Did you ever by any chance run into Judge Dalzell?' I told him it wasn't by chance. He had visited me in our old nursery when I was three weeks old and we had continued a very close acquaintance since he was my grandfather. Mary's father didn't speak for several seconds; then he said, 'Hurry along over then and let's have a look at you.'

"I liked Mary's parents on sight and luckily they sort of took to me. Of course, Granddad was my best introduction. He and Mr. Chadwick had once gone on a fishing trip together he had never forgotten. I didn't stay late, for I knew they had been waiting up, so I made my good nights as soon as was courteous. I said, though, that before I left I would like to ask for his daughter's hand in marriage. He sort of started up in his chair.

" 'Good God, man!' he said, 'you're a fast worker. Now, I move a bit more slowly. But I'll tell you what. You've been in a fairyland tonight; that's plain to see. If, tomorrow, in the cold, clear light of common day, you feel the same, come back and we'll talk things over.'

"Then Mary did the sweetest thing. She kissed her father's cheek and said, 'Do you know, night or day, I believe he will feel the same.'

"Next morning I was up at the Chadwicks as soon as I thought the older folks would have finished breakfast. So Mary and I became engaged, and that is the story!"

"Tim, it's a perfectly lovely one. I couldn't wish a more beautiful one for you — and you so richly deserve it. But when will I meet Mary? When will the wedding be? Oh, I've still more questions, though you've made it all awfully real."

"As to meeting her — I hope soon. Her mother has promised to bring her here for a week. Perhaps in the city. For I want Mary to help select the ring. And then you can go in there to meet them and have them out to the house. We'll plan it all. But as to the wedding —"

Katherine looked sober. "I was afraid a 'but' was coming somewhere. It all sounded so like fairyland, as her father said. Tell me what would delay your wedding?"

"It's like this," Tim said slowly. "Mr. Chadwick owns a little steel plant or some such toy. He has planned to hold the reins of management right in his own hands until he is seventy, which he will be on April 1, and then drop business completely and take his wife and Mary on a trip around the world. Mary says it has become a fixed idea with him. His study walls already are covered with maps, schedules, pictures of special places, and, in fact, he's almost living in the trip already and there was no reason to question the plan until I came on the scene."

"But, Tim, couldn't you be married first and just postpone the trip for a time?"

Tim's face had a smile she had never seen on it before.

"We discussed that along with the whole problem the night of our talk. Mary said she could go on the trip if we were just engaged, but when we were married, she could not and would not leave me. That decision is rather precious to me. When I was with Mr. Chadwick that last morning, he was very brave. The wedding must go on. The trip must be put aside. I told him I was thirty-five years old and had waited this long to fall in love; so surely I could wait a few months longer. After the trip," said I stoutly, "Mary will be free to take her time and plan her wedding, go to all the parties, and get her trousseau, as every girl likes to do. She will always have the trip to remember with pleasure and no regrets about missing it. I must say, he did his best, but we are going to wait. They will leave in April and be back in July at the latest."

"Oh, that's not too bad, Tim. I feared some dreadful obstacle was in the way. Do you have her picture with you?"

"Funny question!" he laughed, producing one from his inner pocket.

Katherine looked at it for what seemed a long time; then gave it back with tears in her eyes. "She's beautiful, but there is, I think, a sort of magnetic quality which drew you at first sight. I'm so terribly happy for you, Tim."

He stood up to go, took out his handkerchief to wipe away her tears, then blew his nose. "You know," he added, as he did so, "Mary has some sort of foolish notion I'm some sort of prize. I wish to God I were . . . for her sake."

"But you are, Tim dear. You don't know it, but you are!"

"Vote of confidence," he said with his old grin. Then opened the door and went out.

That night was another of many when Katherine lay awake, listening to the tall clock below strike the hours. She thought first, of course, of Tim. She had somehow never thought he would really fall in love and marry. And now she saw this new light in his eyes, this new tender smile on his face. Already he was changed by the peculiar alchemy she herself had known. And Mary! She must have great beauty from the picture, but there was more. There was a quality of expression, indefinable, but the one which had drawn Tim. They were taking a chance, these two, to allow the distance of a world to separate them just when they had found each other; and yet the greater chance might be in living with the regret of destroying an old man's cherished dream. They were probably right.

Her mind wandered to Cele and Henry. In retrospect, she felt her letter to him had been presumptuous. What must he think of her? To offer such detailed advice! And yet Henry's mind was determined upon a course that would definitely break Cele's heart and in the long run, as she had told him, perhaps his own. She wondered if in the wave of divorce which seemed to have swept over Lemming the last few years there were among them situations as peculiar and as relatively simple in solution as this one seemed to her. Yet the waves still dashed so many upon the rocks.

Above it all was Laurie and her great problem. Suppose, Katherine thought, it was her own little Kit grown to eighteen years and going to have a baby out of wedlock? What would she, her mother, do? How would she bear it? All at once, the possible solutions, the options, seemed to fall into pieces in her hands. Poor Cele with this on her heart and now Henry's trouble, still mysterious to her. She had truly been ''hit by both barrels,'' as the hunters would say.

Katherine decided she must do something for Cele. To invite her over might be the best help.

Her mind returned to Tim. Not since the day David had told her he loved another woman had she been shaken with so deep an emotion! There was no use putting it by with thoughts of others. She must feel it all now and, if possible, accept it. Tim, her brother, her childhood playmate, her close companion during her growing-up years; her adviser and counselor when she was a woman! And, most important of all perhaps, her supporter during the first unbearable days of her loss of David. Now this precious bond, the strength of which she had not fully realized before, which had bound brother and sister together over the years with its unsharable intimacies, would never again be the same. Her heart did not deceive her. There would always be now, a sweet shadow between them — that of Mary, the wife!

Chapter Seven

IT WAS the kind of morning which every mother of growing children experiences, and dreads. In the first place, it was early February with the weather capricious beyond belief. At eight o'clock, when Katherine was hurrying Davey and Kit with their breakfast, a torrential rain began to fall.

"We can't go through this!" Davey said cheerfully.

"My ear hurts," said Kit.

"Oh, my dear, does it hurt you badly?"

"Well —"

"I'll get the drops."

"Oh, it don't hurt now," amended Kit.

"Doesn't, Kit."

"Doesn't."

The rain had slackened and had become a thin, wet snow.

"I can't go to school, Mother. I simply can't go!" Davey said.

"Oh, it's not too bad to walk that short distance. I did explain about the car. The garage men promised it faithfully for yesterday afternoon and it's not here yet."

"That's not it, Mother. I've lost my workbook. All the homework I did last night is in it. And if I don't have it, the teacher will be mad — Gee, she gets so mad. I'm telling you!"

"All right, Davey. The thing to do is to start right in and look for that workbook. You've had a good breakfast; now hurry and *hunt*!" She felt her voice rising.

She rushed upstairs, got the ear drops, and joined the

search for the workbook until she was convinced it was not on the second floor. When she came down again, Kit glanced up, saw the dreaded bottle approaching, and waved her mother away.

"My ear's *com–pletely* well," she said with her mouth full of a muffin.

Katherine did not pause. "You've been playing games with me, Kit; now you are going to have the drops — just in case. Bend your head over. You know they don't hurt. Bend over, dear." Kit tried to oblige as the drops were going in, but choked on the muffin, had to be set up straight, patted on the back, and given sips of water while the drops oozed out.

"I've done my best," Katherine muttered to herself; then, "Now, Kit, you've had enough breakfast, I'm sure, and time is passing. Get up and help us hunt for that workbook."

Kit rose reluctantly and made her contribution. "Maybe Thomas has Davey's old book," she said.

"*Thomas*?" Katherine cried. "Why in the world would *he* have it?"

"Well, he likes to scratch things with his toenails," she said.

"Even so," her mother murmured. "Look at my chairs! You take the living room, Kit, and I'll go to the kitchen!"

Thomas was a large, beautiful black cat, acquired lately by grace of Tim, one of whose clients was leaving and wanted a home for her pet. Thomas had accepted his new surroundings with apparent satisfaction, lay in the softest seat and strolled through the house with his unusually long and furry tail held upright behind him like a banner. At loud mention of his name now, Davey scuttled down the stairs, calling, "My book's not up there. I can't go to school. Yippy! Yippy!"

But Kit had raised another cry which brought Katherine and Davey quickly to her in the small library off the living room. "There!" she panted triumphantly, "I told you he might have it!"

On the wide window seat lay Thomas, stretched at ease inside the opened workbook, his mouth meditatively chewing upon a page while with a paw he delicately scratched ribbons on the opposite one with his claws.

Davey, with one spring, slapped Thomas and rescued his book. "It's ruined!" he said, serious enough now. "Oh, I forgot I worked in here last night. What will I *do*?"

"Get your things on as fast as you can, both of you. I'll call your teacher, Davey, and make everything right about the workbook. Just hurry now."

They were soon in their sweaters, coats, and scarfs, *and* galoshes! Katherine thought with gratitude, there were two mated pairs. Many times there were four disparate ones!

"Your lunches are in your bags, darlings, for it will be a good day to eat at school. Now, walk carefully. Don't run. You have enough time. Good-by, good-by." She kissed each child and watched them trudging along the walk, then with a sigh closed the door and sat down for a needed cup of coffee.

The hot drink with a muffin and jam raised her spirits until she was ready to admit that even a grim February day might have certain elements of pleasure. She was picking up the plates to carry to the kitchen when the telephone rang sharply. The clock stood at nine-thirty, as Katherine glanced at it. She always averred she could guess the quality of the coming conversation by the nature of the bell's ringing. Long, lazy rings indicated merely conversational gossip; staccato ones meant trouble. The ring now was quick and continuous.

"Yes?" she answered.

The voice that came was that of Dr. Harris. "Mrs. Davenport? You are on a private line?"

"I am."

"I'm in strange trouble. Miss Darby is standing by, but has to be with her class. I don't want to confide in parents or any of the faculty yet. Could you come over and give me your opinion? Is your brother at home? I called him first."

"He's away, but only for a day. He'll be back tomorrow. I'll come down at once."

She got into her coat quickly. After hearing from the garage that her car would be back at noon, she called a taxi, since the distance was too far to walk, and was soon going through the halls of the High School. On the second floor before a door marked "Principal's Office, Private," she paused, catching her breath. Not a sound came from within. She waited longer and still all was quiet. She then moved the door ever so slightly and, through a small opening, saw a strange sight. Miss Darby was releasing herself gently from Dr. Harris' arms. She came on out, did not even see Katherine standing in the shadow, but went directly across to her own classroom. Katherine, startled and uneasy, pushed the door a little farther open, knocked softly, and was greeted at once by Dr. Harris.

"Oh, you're so very good to come. I'll give you a quick rundown on what has happened. Our young artist, Don, has some poetic talent too, it seems. He has fallen deeply in first love with Jeannie McAllister and has been writing poems to her which he has kept in a special notebook under other work in his desk."

Dr. Harris stopped for a moment and Katherine finished his quotation:

" 'Deep as first love, and wild with all regret —' "

"That's what I'm afraid of," he went on, "the last part of the sentence. Well, there is a boy in Don's room named Joe Parson, so you can see why he's nicknamed Preacher. He is bitterly jealous of Don — of his drawings, his good marks, and especially of the girl Jeannie. Preacher found the notebook, came early this morning — just as I was getting here — copied the most loverlike poems on the blackboard above Don's name and waited for the reaction.

"It came in great bursts of laughter just as Don entered the room. He saw the blackboard and Preacher's guilty face and struck the first blow. The boy who came up to tell me said they had soon gone to the back of the room to fight it out. Preacher was heavier but flabby; Don, taller and all bone and muscle. I got there in time to see Don land a terrific blow on Preacher's jaw as he went down, striking his head on the iron base of a desk. I called the ambulance, for there seemed no life in him. I've kept calling the hospital every few hours to inquire. The concussion is deep and the pulse weak. I have never felt so helpless.

"I should also have said I called Preacher's home, but his father and mother both work and I do not know their places of business. I'll keep trying to reach them."

Katherine sat quiet, thinking. "Of course, it is my brother you need. It might be possible he would get home tonight. If he does, where would you be?"

"Anywhere he could meet me."

"As to my opinion, I'm afraid it's not worth much, but here it is. I think it would be foolish at this point to get in touch with the police. They could do no good for Preacher and they would find Don going quietly on with his school work."

"I agree."

"The one idea I have — perhaps quite crazy — is this. Jeannie McAllister is involved in this strange triangle: her father worked in Scottish shipyards before he decided to come over here, and I dare say he has seen many a fight. He just might have something in the way of advice, if you were to go to see him. Have you ever thought of doing that?"

"Thought of it? I've just been waiting for the end of this marking period to take Jeannie's report to him. But your idea of my going right away is a good one. I'll act on it."

"If so, you can put in a word for Don's good character and, of course, give him Jeannie's report as of now."

"A ray of light out of the darkness!" Dr. Harris exclaimed. "It will certainly do no harm and the sure good will be that I will get jolted out of my stupid mental block. Thank you, Mrs. Davenport. I'll let you know what happens. I'm ashamed of my weakness, but I've had many things on my mind. I hope you will consider my request for you to come as a very great compliment and not a foolish intrusion."

"But I do. Thank you for asking me. My day looked a bit empty."

"You see," he explained, "I have so often found that in a ticklish or semitragic situation a woman's perceptive mind will go straight to an odd but valid solution. Usually Miss Darby does that. In this case, she is as stunned as I am by the possibilities facing us. But my deep thanks to you again. Can you get home now all right?"

"Oh, yes. And don't worry too much, Dr. Harris. After a bad concussion the patient may sleep for days or even for a week and then wake up and get well."

Katherine called her taxi from the phone on the first floor and rode back, thinking deeply. There were disturbing facts. Before a roomful of witnesses, Don had struck the first blow, white with anger. Unfortunately, he had also struck the last fatal one. If Preacher died, what sort of case could be brought against Don? She longed for Tim. Even with his natural preoccupation with Mary now, she found their old comradeship in great measure still intact.

But another problem teased her as she got home and began to put her kitchen in order. What she had seen of Miss Darby and Dr. Harris through the small opening of the door could not be imputed to the casual friendship of the years. It had certainly looked like the ending of an embrace of love. Good heavens! Could such a thing be? Of course, Miss Darby had indeed been transformed by her first trip to the hairdresser. Now, she went there once a week. Her dresses were often soft pastels with white cowl collars — a contrast to the dark ambiguous prints she used to wear. The tiniest bit of makeup, delicately applied, was, as she had once said, not real deception, but did make a difference. It did, indeed, Katherine thought. And one of David's quips came back to her. "When an old bachelor decides to try the water, he goes in up to his neck." One thing she had noticed from the bits and pieces of gossip that came to her from Miss Darby's students: They liked her as a *woman,* apparently not only as a teacher.

"Well! Well!" Katherine kept repeating to herself as she went on with her work.

Dr. Harris called at noon to say there was no change in Preacher's condition and the doctor did not like the weak pulse. He, Dr. Harris, had failed to get through to the boy's parents, but he was still trying. He had made an appointment to see McAllister that day and had attempted to comfort Don in some measure. The boy was distressed and frightened.

Dr. Harris sounded calm and in complete control of his emotions. He said he was very much ashamed of calling her up earlier. "I didn't know I could ever feel so weak and shaken," he added. "Do forgive me."

The house was quiet until after two. No more reports. Then the phone rang sharply and Katherine rushed to it. But it was not Dr. Harris. It was a happy voice, its owner bursting, it seemed, with good news. It was Madeleine Fulton and it was vibrant. "I just had to tell you, since you've always been so interested in the Thespians, though you haven't belonged. It's my only outlet since I've given up the idea of bigger things."

"You've been brave —"

"Had to be. But listen. We had a meeting last night to choose the next play and what do you suppose they've decided on? It's ridiculous, but it's wonderful! It's *Romeo and Juliet* and I'm to have the lead. I'm so happy I go through the house saying a few of the lines already. Of course it will have to be cut a lot, but the beautiful entity of it will be left. Isn't it amazing?"

"It's incredible! Oh, I'm so happy for you. You'll have something now worthy of all the work you always put into your parts. Who will play opposite you?"

"A new young man. A nephew of the Kincaids. Just got his Master's at Harvard and is going to Yale Dramatic School. He and I read a few paragraphs last night at our house and, Katherine, I don't want to boast, but it did sould like the *real* thing!"

"It will be. I'm excited already. I just needed this good news today."

"Why? Anything wrong but the weather?"

"Oh, I heard that a couple of High School boys had a fight," she said.

Madeleine laughed. "And what else is new? My boy isn't home yet, for he eats lunch at the cafeteria as a rule. Katherine —" Her voice dropped low. "I want to tell you that what you said to me once when I was about to make a fool of myself is true."

"What was that?"

"The greatest happiness comes from doing your duty, you said. I'm not talking now about the play, but of my own life. I'm happier now that I've been in many a year." And she hung up.

Katherine went about the house with a smile on her lips, except when thoughts of Preacher lying inert in the hospital came to disturb her. There were no more reports from Dr. Harris until three and then he said he had gotten in touch with the parents at last and they were amazingly unconcerned. "Him," the father had said, "he's got a thick skull. Just a dunt on it ain't going to kill *him*!" And the mother was even more cheerful. "Oh, he's been in fights before. I've seen him lay sleeping for a week an' then get up an' ask for a bottle of his Dad's beer with his dinner."

"The phraseology is mine," Dr. Harris laughed and Katherine joined him as though a bit of tension had relaxed.

"What do the doctors say?"

"Not much. The pulse is slightly stronger, but they will not commit themselves further. However, upon your suggestion I made a call upon McAllister. You were inspired to think of it.

He is inclined to an optimistic view of Preacher's condition, and at once was angrily roused to Don's support. 'Mebbe I'll be thanking him for taking up the matter for Jeannie's sake!' he said. He seemed rather proud of what Don had done. When we got around at last to the quilt and Jeannie's high marks, he quite melted. Said he'd maybe been a bit severe and she might as well finish it up, since she was doing well at her books. And as to this boy Don, he'd been polite enough each time he had been to the door. And at their age it was time for them to be courtin' a little. At least that was the way in the old Country. So, Mrs. Davenport, a double blessing and my thanks again!"

A little snow still fell and the wind was cold, so Katherine drove to school to bring the children home. They were nervous and eager to get there, for as they said, they had been anxious all day about *Thomas*.

"I did slap him too hard," Davey lamented.

"And I called him a mean old cat and I'm sure he heard me."

"How did he seem, Mother?"

"Well," Katherine admitted, "I was so busy with my own thoughts today, I didn't really notice."

"Oh, Mother, maybe he went out in the cold and you didn't call him in," Davey moaned.

"He has a good bed of leaves under the back porch and with his fur coat he could always keep warm. However, you call him as soon as we get back."

They did so, the two strident young voices ringing out from one end of the garden to the other.

"*Thomas! Thomas!* Come, Pussy! Come, Kitty Cat!"

But there was no response and finally the children gave up and came sadly back to the house.

"He's gone!" Davey said with finality. "And I did it!"

"Well, I called him the bad names," Kit insisted through her tears.

"I'll tell you what we'll do," said Katherine, thinking fast.

"We'll have our dinner later than usual to give him more time to come back. I'll open a can of sardines. He loves those but he hasn't had them often, because they've gotten so expensive. We'll have his little deep dish full of them, and I'll put some real cream in the milk for his shallow dish, and what a big supper he will have!"

"Sounds nice," said Davey. "You think he'll still come?"

"I've the greatest hopes. Now, when it's beginning to get dark, we'll put all the lights on. That may help. You children get some games out and keep your minds off Thomas except when you go to the door to call him every so often. Now brighten up!"

But Katherine did not feel very bright herself. The cat had been an old lady's great pet, used to nothing but kindness. Davey's slap had, indeed, been hard. It seemed sure he had run away. But how far? And would he ever return? A thought struck her. Could he possibly have made his way back to his old home? She quickly called the number Tim had given her and a man's voice answered. She introduced herself. "A large, beautiful black cat used to live in your home before you bought it. We have had it since, but it's now missing. Could it be there with you?"

The man laughed. "No black cat has been around, but if it had, we probably would have chased it. We're not cat lovers. Sorry."

So that was that. It was strange that she, with much more important things on her mind, should feel these genuine qualms about a cat. But Thomas had at once taken her for himself. He allowed the children to play with him, but it was their mother he followed about from room to room, making small mewing sounds as if in conversation. It was against her ankles he rubbed when he wanted to be petted and it was her knee upon which he jumped at every opportunity and curled himself, purring contentedly. She had never before known a cat intimately, and now she realized that Thomas had added something fond and mysterious and satisfactory to her day.

At a quarter to seven she told the children they must make their last call and then have dinner. As they prepared to step out into the chill of the night, Katherine spoke quickly, "Let me call him this time. He likes me. Maybe he will come."

"Thomas," she called in her sweet contralto voice, "come on, Thomas, I want you. (If anyone hears me, I will sound like a fool.) Come on, Thomas. I've your supper ready. Pretty kitty! Nice Thomas! Come on!"

And out of the shadows and the mist Thomas came, his fur wet and his paws pricking gingerly through the wet grasses. He went by Katherine without looking at her, entered the house, his tail high, his large green eyes barely glancing at the children who were waiting to receive him with due celebration. He walked to the kitchen still aloof, ate his dinner with no mews of satisfaction as he usually gave when food especially pleased him, then marched past the family with dignity, his shining green eyes again looking through them as though they were not there. He went to his best hiding place beneath the center of the dining-room table, where he stretched out comfortably and apparently went to sleep.

"I never dreamed he would stay mad after he came back," said Davey.

"I thought if he just came back everything would be all right," said Kit.

The children looked limp from emotion and hunger. "Come on, darlings," Katherine said. "Let's eat in the kitchen alcove as fast as we can. We are all worn out, but I'm sure by morning Thomas will be like his old self."

Bedtime came soon, the only untoward incident being that Thomas did not go upstairs when the children did, try each bed until he decided which one he chose to sleep upon, thereby making sharp rivalry between the children. Kit shed a tear or two over his absence, but the strains of the day had been heavy, so relaxation came soon. It came soon on the first floor also, as Katherine selected a book from the library shelves and started into the living room. She paused where she could see a dark shadow beneath the dining-room table. "Thomas," she said, "you have been very naughty tonight. You should be forgiving. Davey is sorry he hurt you and longed for you to come back. You spoiled his book, so you should forgive him. We all have to learn this, Thomas. Now, be a *good, nice* kitty."

She went on to her easy chair, turned on the light, and opened her book, her heart beating heavily. There was the sound of soft pat-a-pats on the carpet. Thomas was before her, looking up with a faint meow. She nodded and he landed on her lap, curled his long tail gracefully around him, and settled in softly purring comfort. "He can't break the spell," she murmured.

She opened the book. It was one of Shakespeare's plays. It was *Romeo and Juliet.* All at once, like great waves, the past swept over her. She was young. She was beautiful. Those attributes, plus a gift for acting and, most of all, her voice, had made her the choice out of all the senior girls for the role of Juliet in the college play. But, as she thought of it now, she knew without vanity, with only the clear perception of the years, that no one, the director, the dramatic teacher, the president, faculty, and students, as well as all the town who came to see, had expected such a performance! For, by a miracle, there had flooded through her such a sense of reality, such a passion, that her own identity was lost and she was completely the young girl Juliet, her heart breaking with love and sorrow.

Katherine leafed through the pages before her, and then, hearing the words as they formed like spoken syllables in her mind, she went slowly through the lines. And it all came back. That strange, wonderful May night, the applause from the audience, first for the cast, then for the principals, and, at last, for her alone. At that point the noise sounded like thunder as she stood trembling to receive her flowers and bow again and again. One face stood out to her from the crowd. It was that of David, with tears on his cheeks. She knew the great bunch of red roses was from him.

When it had all been over at last, the congratulations, the postplay party, and she and David were alone in the moonlit night, he had told her for the first time how much he loved her and asked her to marry him soon. He had been waiting to finish his Master's dissertation and to secure the sort of job he wanted before he felt he dared to speak to her of marriage. He had felt now, as he had come down for the play, a little bit pleased with himself because fortune seemed to be smiling upon him in his first ambitions. "But, oh, when I saw you tonight as Juliet," he had said, "every bit of courage ebbed out of me! I had to try at least, but I'm so frightened, waiting for your answer. Are you —" he had stammered, "do you intend to make the stage your career?"

"Not if I can be your wife," she had answered quickly.

Katherine drew a long sigh and came back to the present. She set Thomas down gently and placed the book back on the shelves. I'll read it often, she thought. It has a certain magic for me.

The next day brought good news all along the line. The sun actually shone, though a few clouds hinted that rain or snow should not be discounted. In the house Thomas the cat, after a comfortable night's sleep, was moved to be gracious, at least to the females near him. He allowed Kit to stroke his head, and followed Katherine wherever she went, making the soft mews which apparently were meant for conversation. He still maintained a show of hauteur when near Davey, who "didn't really care whether any old cat liked him or not."

From the outside world the report came through Miss Darby. "Doctors are funny!" she announced. "The one I talked to seemed to hate like murder to admit Preacher was even just a trifle better. I think he wanted the patient to confirm his learned diagnosis by dying! Anyway, there is a very slight improvement in the pulse. Dr. Harris is relieved even for that. I never saw him so upset as yesterday. He's still embarrassed about calling you to come over for what proved a ten-minute conference. That man!"

She paused and then went on with a shade of smugness that did not escape Katherine. "I thought I knew him in and out and still there are undiscovered depths to his character. McAllister told him that a good fist fight never killed anybody that he ever heard of and that Don seemed a polite chap. And also that since Jeannie's marks were as high as he said, maybe she'd better finish the quilt. I guess Dr. Harris told you all that, but I wanted to add it to the latest report on Preacher. . . Did you hear what the Thespians have chosen for their spring play?"

"Yes, I did."

"Well, they're pretty good, some of them, and they might as well aim high. It was Lucien, Madeleine's son, who told me. She's to have the lead and he's so proud; I think I'll start my class soon reading the play. Why *Romeo and Juliet* is not on every High School list is beyond *me.* Well, *I'm* putting it there. A better day than yesterday, Katherine." And she hung up as she often did when her message was completed.

It was nearly ten when Tim called. His voice still sounded sleepy. "Kathy dear?"

"Oh, Tim, are you really back? Have you seen Dr. Harris?"

"Seen him? I practically spent last night with him. I myself got through to the hospital about three this morning and got a straight report from my doctor friend that the boy was really, he thought, going to pull through. So Harris and I shook hands in relief and I, at least, got to bed. But that man Harris is quite a person. I never talked to him that much before. He acts as if every student was his by right of birth."

"But, Tim, if Preacher should die, Don couldn't possibly be accused of murder, could he?"

"Not that, exactly, but if it all came to a case in court, there might be a few sticky spots in it. Don, white with anger, struck the first blow in the presence of a roomful of kids and then, at the end, struck the one that felled this Preacher. His hitting the desk iron was accidental, but the blow was not. So there you are. I would, of course, have defended Don if it came to his need for me. But I hope I don't have to do it. Is everything well with you and the children?"

"Fine. Do come tonight if you can."

"Make it dinner at six-thirty and I'll be there. I need comforting. I talked to Mary in Honolulu and, golly, it seemed like a long way off!"

The snow did come that day toward noon — great, soft flakes this time, which would be mounds of white before long. The world seemed to have lost all sound; there was only the utter quiet of the snow as though from above, the word had come for the puny trafficking of men's affairs to cease.

Katherine got a bit of lunch and then, like a small boy stealing jam, went back to the library and took out once again, the small volume. Why should I not? she demanded of herself. Why should I be ashamed of reliving that wonderful night? It will do me more good than a doctor's tonic.

The house seemed removed from all intrusion, remote and still in the falling snow. She opened the book at the Balcony scene and spoke the words aloud. She remembered them! The echo of her voice was wooden. She tried again. She was feeling more now. The third time she forgot where she was, and came to herself with a jolt and a laugh.

"It's still there," she spoke, "whatever it is, and I'm glad of it." Her thoughts had buoyed her up. "I suppose I should have joined the Thespians when they invited me. But the children were so young when we moved to Lemming and membership would have demanded many evenings away from them and from David. After he was gone, there had come more insistent invitations. One of the High School girls had told her mother that Mrs. Davenport spoke like a real Pro after she got over her first embarrassment. But Katherine had no heart for it then and would enjoy the plays from the audience. Until now, with one evening's deliberation, the Thespians had unconsciously put her in command of those resources which had so long lain dormant.

Dinner was lively and Tim kept glancing at Katherine. "What's happened to you?" he said curiously. "You look as though you had swallowed a firecracker."

"I'm just happy over some news I heard. The Thespians are doing *Romeo and Juliet* for their spring play."

"Egad, they have courage! Who's to play the lead?"

"Madeleine Fulton. As you know, she's practically professional. Do you remember when I did it, Tim?"

"I could hardly forget. The women and a lot of men had tears at the end and even hard-shelled old *me* blew my nose pretty often!"

Katherine spoke to the children's questioning eyes. "We're talking about a play I once was in."

"Were you good?" Kit asked.

"Wonderful! Incredible!" answered Uncle Tim. "Kathy dear, do you ever have regrets about giving up a career? I happen to know how the night ended after that play!"

"Never, if the career I chose hadn't been broken. Oh, let's talk now about Mary."

This was a fruitful topic, because all could join in praise. The meeting had been in the city on a day stolen, at least from time, when Mary and her mother had flown there to join Katherine and her children with, of course, Tim. The sense of loss which Katherine had determinedly tried to throttle seemed almost to disappear as she and Mary clasped each other, both saying the same thing: "Now I have a sister!" The children, while excitedly adoring, had behaved well. Davey, as usual, summed up his impressions. "Uncle Tim, I really don't think you could have found a nicer girl than Miss Mary."

"Me too," echoed Kit.

"That's just the way I feel too," Tim responded gravely. "And thanks for your opinion, children."

Now on this evening they all reviewed Tim's joy as their own, and, each in a different way, thought of happy prospects for the future.

When the children had gone to bed, Katherine and Tim sat quietly discussing the traveler's great journey and when the wedding could likely take place. As Tim rose to leave, pleading sleepiness, the phone rang and when Katherine found it was Dr. Harris, she motioned Tim to come over to listen.

"The latest report on our friend Preacher is that the slight movement in arms and legs continues and the doctor seems a little less pessimistic. The whole thing has worked out in the most amazing fashion, as though Providence actually had a hand in it. Please thank your brother for me when you see him." Katherine nodded to Tim, who made a stiff salute to the telephone.

"One more thing," Dr. Harris went on, "I am calling a very important meeting of the Special Quilting Committee on Friday afternoon at three. Can you come?"

"Of course."

"Royal Command," she said to Tim softly.

"I have a few plans I want to discuss. Thanks again and good night."

"So the quilting business goes on?"

"It's more popular than ever. There must be at least thirty-five girls, maybe forty, working on a quilt. You see, the wheel has come full circle. Their great-grandmothers made quilts and sewed their girlish hopes and dreams into them. Now this new generation is doing the same. I think there is a moral therapy in it. At least we'll hope so, for that was the original idea."

"A good one. I hope it works. Wasn't it great the way the kids took to Mary at once?"

"They adore her and so do I!"

"Well, that makes four of us. Good night, dear. Don't work too hard at all these meetings. How do you get into so many?"

"Try saying no to Dr. Harris and you'll find out," Katherine laughed.

By Friday the snow had made its benign visit and from a day of warm sun had largely disappeared. Preacher was better and time now would complete its healing work. Within the Davenport home all was as usual, with Thomas graciously allowing Davey to stroke his tummy and tickle his chest. Katherine went with a feeling of interest to the meeting at three. She was relieved of responsibility; for she had engaged Mrs. Weagle to come for the afternoon and evening.

There was a full complement of members in Dr. Harris' office, and after his first greeting he plunged into his plan.

"As you all know, we started the plan of the quilts because we had come to know that in our very High School — as probably across the country — there were numbers of young people, fifteen to eighteen years old, who were, as it is called, 'living together' and having sexual relations because of it. I can report to you that because of Mrs. Davenport's fine talk to the girls, and because of the natural charm of the quilting activity, there has been a lessening of this 'living together,' as my spies report to me.

"But we need to do more to vitalize our quilting program. So this is my thought: I would like to enlist the cooperation of at least six of the owners of the largest houses in town, in which would be held that number of 'quilting parties.' At these parties I would have the girls bring their quilts to work on steadily for an hour or a little more, while the boys put on some popular records for a background and keep up the fire in the fireplaces perhaps and also take a good look at the quilts. Then, after this work period is finished, let there be dancing!"

"How wonderful, Dr. Harris! What kind?"

"The kind that belongs to the quilts. You see, it would probably be the great-grandmothers of these girls who would be making them. So we would keep to those times. We're looking back this Bicentennial year anyway, so I mean the so-called Play-Games, which are really simplified Square Dances."

"Oh, tell us more about them," Katherine said. "I never saw a square dance."

"I was hoping I would be asked to illustrate," Dr. Harris said, smiling. "Well, the most classic one, I suppose, is 'Peel the Willow,' a form of the old Virginia Reel. The girls line up on one side, the boys facing them upon the other. There should be music for this — perhaps a waltz. The girl at the head of her line starts slowly in a diagonal direction to meet the last boy in his line. When they meet, they bow and then he swings her round and round and they step backward into their places. Then the next go, and so on. When all have done this, the last girl in her line and last boy in his meet, bow, and swing, then, holding hands, chassé, dance, or whatever, up to the head of the line and all the others then follow their example, edging down, if space is small, for the new lines.

"Now I would call your attention to the fact that in all these games the important thing is the *swinging* of the girl by the boy. He can hold her close, you know, and I've been told it's a very pleasant sensation."

There was a great burst of laughter from the ladies and then he went on:

"The next one I'll speak of has a rather unclassic title. It is called 'We Kept the Pig in the Parlor.' A circle forms with one boy in the middle; then it moves round and round as the players sing, 'We kept the Pig in the parlor and it was Irish too.' When the circle turns, the delicate lines begin, 'We'll all go down Rouses and get some lager beer.'

"These lines are repeated over and over until the boy in the center chooses a girl from the circle and her former partner steps to the center and becomes the new Pig.

"The game you may have read of or heard of most is 'Skip come-a-lu, my darling.' This is another circle, a singing and swinging one, but somehow very captivating.

'Flies in the sugar bowl, shoo, shoo, shoo,
Little red wagon painted blue,
My wife's gone and I'll go too,
Skip, come-a-lu, my darling'

In this too there is a boy in the center who choses a girl, and so on. But the one I like best of all, for I've played it as a youth, is 'The Dusty Miller.' There is the circle of boys and girls, hands tightly clasped, moving around to the song as one boy as the Miller stands in the center. I think I can sing you that little song:

'There was a dusty miller and he lived in a mill,
A-grinding corn, he made his will
One hand in the hopper, and the other in the sack
Ladies go forward and the gents turn back.'

With this the girls continue and the boys turn, proceeding in a ring outside the girls. Then the song goes:

'Sailing, sailing,
Sailing o'er the ocean,
Young man, look out or you'll miss your wife,
If you don't be quick in the motion!'

You can guess how it ended, with each boy grabbing the girl then beside him, while the one who lost out becomes the new Dusty Miller."

There was warm applause from the audience. "We never knew you had such a lovely voice, Dr. Harris," Mary Hastings said, and the others added their compliments. He only grinned a bit sheepishly. "I'm not a performer, but I did want you to like 'The Dusty Miller.'

"Now I have a question to put that frightens me. You have heard my skeleton plan except that after the dance we would serve old-fashioned refreshments such as gingerbread and cider, then maybe have some spontaneous singing, ending with 'Aunt Dinah's Quilting Party' which I would want them to sing on the streets going home." He paused and then looked at them bravely.

"We are dealing here with very sophisticated young people. Will this plan of mine work? Will the boys and girls think it is all childish and laugh at it? Please be honest."

There were a few seconds of terrible silence, then Sara Barnes spoke: "I suppose you might call my daughter and son sophisticated, but I've found that under that veneer they are pretty young at heart. I think they would like these parties with the singing and the swinging and the movement. It would all be a new experience and young people like new things."

Others spoke quickly. There was some laughter, but it was all *approving* laughter. When it came to the matter of invitations, Dr. Harris was adamant. If they were sent to any, they must be sent to all.

"It's a small High School, as they go, and I can't face any boy or girl who missed the fun by not getting an invitation. We'll have to manage somehow. As to their distribution, to save postage we can give them out at school. If we have the promise of six large houses, I think we could consider fifty for each house, allowing for the five percent who, for some reason, would not come.

"I must leave you now for another meeting. Why don't you stay here and discuss more of the details? But you've lifted a big burden from my heart. Next time I won't talk so much. I'll listen to you."

When he had gone, they all settled to the problems at hand, growing more interested in the project as they did so. The six big houses would take searching, but could certainly be found, since Lemming was a wealthy suburb especially "on the hill," as it was called. Should there be a bus to convey those who had no cars to their place of entertainment? Should the groups be divided with some basis of congeniality? How many quilters in each? Also, should there be at least two faculty members in each to teach the game songs and start things moving? How would the refreshments be apportioned? There were many details still untouched.

"As you can see," Miss Darby said, "there's more to all this than meets the eye, but I believe it's a good plan and we can carry it out. I think at this point we ought to adjourn."

When Katherine got home, she found her "sitter" there, Mrs. Weagle, (with a long *a*) pronounced *Waggle* by the children, who liked her. She was speaking respectfully to Thomas, who eyed her dubiously and switched his tail. The children were playing games in the library.

When Tim dropped in one evening a week later, he asked at once for Preacher. "No news, I assume, is good news," he ventured.

"Most of it is. He can sit up, is eating normally, but his mind is still not clear."

"Whew! I don't like that. If his parents would bring a mental suit, it wouldn't be too good. Are they upset about this?"

"Not at all, Dr. Harris reports. They saw Preacher a few evenings ago and he didn't know them and talked some kind of gibberish. His father just slapped his arm and said, 'Snap out of it, Sonny, you know us well enough.' And his mother told the nurses not to pay any attention to him because he always talked silly when he didn't want to do something. The doctors think, however, that he's not pretending. So that's the way it is."

"Well, I hope he recovers first for his own sake and second for all of us."

When Katherine started to tell him about the Play-Games, she found, to her surprise, that he knew about them already.

"That was what that long night's talk was about," Tim said, "and, by golly, I think that man has a great idea. Why I feel underprivileged that I never got to play them in my youth, especially 'Pig in the Parlor.' That one charms me."

"Don't make fun, Tim."

"I'm not. I'm dead serious as to the plan. I *know* some of these boys. They have run the whole gamut from drug trips to sexual experiences, and they've gotten a little sick of the whole modern setup, as I read them. When they start stomping around shouting these crazy songs at the top of their lungs, and swinging the girls, they're going to like it! Dr. Harris put a lot of emphasis in this *swinging*. Do you know, for an old bachelor he has a lot of old-fashioned sentiment in him. Now, how are you planning these parties?"

"In the first place, we have our six big houses all 'on the hill,' as you might guess. But every one of the owners seemed pleased to have them used for a party. You see, in that section, there are so many older, retired men, with their families grown and gone, and their big recreation rooms empty. Several of them seemed actually elated as they heard the plans. Then we have about finished apportioning the refreshments among fifty different women. But, oh, Tim, the biggest preparation for it all came a few nights ago. It was due to Dr. Harris' wisdom, of course. He suggested that our committee, and as many of the faculty as he could prevail upon, would meet in the small gymnasium Wednesday night and practice the Dance-Games. So we did, and Tim, I haven't had as much fun or laughed as much since I was a girl. If you could have seen us going round and round in the circles and changing hands and being swung, as far as the ladies were concerned, by some of the older professors who looked as though they were committing an indiscretion! Then everybody warmed up, the singing was louder, and the swinging was absolutely uninhibited. It was all simply hilarious." Katherine stopped to laugh. "And I tell you, all of us who were there are now more than able to teach the students at the parties!"

"Sounds marvelous," said Tim. "I'll call up for a private lesson. Give me a few more details and then I've got to go. I'm calling Mary up."

Katherine went to bed that night in a happy mood and woke to a bright winter's day. When alone, she went to her desk and noted free hours on her calendar except for some phone calls. One to Madeleine Fulton she put in effect at once, since she had heard nothing from her since her first ecstatic report of the play. Her voice, when she answered now, sounded flat.

"I was just about to call you, Katherine. Could I come over and talk to you? I'm worried."

"Oh, do come. At once, if you care to. I'm free as air today."

"I will be over, then, soon. And thanks so much."

When she arrived, she plunged at once into her problem as soon as they were seated. "It's about the play, as you probably guessed. Of course, I read the book years ago, but, oddly enough, I've never seen it on the stage. As I studied it, I realized what an enormous amount of skillful cutting it must have. This Mr. Lawton, the retired actor — he's just had supporting roles, but he's good — volunteered to do it. Now, it develops, he finds it too hard and his eyes won't stand it, etcetera. But where would we turn for another 'cutter' with a month lost already?"

Katherine felt the color rising in her cheeks as she hesitated. "I didn't mention it before, but away back when I was a college senior, we gave this play —"

"And you were Juliet?"

"Incredibly, yes. But the point is, our drama director cut the play, had the manuscript typed and printed and gave each member of the cast two copies. In a box on our third floor here I have all sorts of mementos and I'm sure these copies are with them. Would one of them help you?"

"You really played Juliet?"

"Yes — in my fashion."

"With your voice you must have been wonderful. Were you frightened?"

"Isn't everyone at first? Then, with an audience, you forget that. But do you want my copy?"

"Of course. It will save the play. But I have a confession.

I'm scared. You see, in all the other roles here, I've felt just a little above them, so gave them my best, but with no fear. When I had my thoughts of the real stage, they were only of musical comedy perhaps, or a supporting role in a good play. The thought of Shakespearean heroines never entered my head. Now I wish it never had! I'm so afraid I'll muff it and let Lucien down. He's as excited as if I were Duse herself."

"My dear, don't be foolish. You will be sure of yourself once you get started on the rehearsals. I'll go through that box and then drop the copy off to you this afternoon. And please cheer up."

By the end of February a number of interesting things had happened. Katherine's cut version of the play had been received with delight, and rehearsals were now in full swing, with a rumor, hastily quashed, that Madeleine's gift ran rather more to comedy than tragedy. Dr. Harris had taken Miss Darby to the Harvard Club in the city to dinner and to a show afterward. A sleepless neighbor had noted their return at 2 A.M., and the long pause at Miss Darby's doorway. Davey had carried off academic honors in his grade. Kit had received more Valentines than any other girl in her class on the Saint's Day, which she felt offset Davey's distinction. But best of all, the six Dance-Parties, as they came to be called, had each been set down as a smashing success! Such shouting and singing and swinging and general jollification had not been known "on the hill" for many a long day. The trays of gingerbread and doughnuts had been consumed to the last crumb and, as Dr. Harris had dreamed, the strains of "Aunt Dinah's Quilting Party" floated through the streets of Lemming at midnight, as cars and buses made their circuitous routes to the various homes.

So February passed and March, as though to atone for its reputation, came and went with lamblike docility. Never once did Katherine have to cower in bed from a tempestuous storm.

But in April, the winds of love — if such they could be

called — had beat fiercely upon the husband of one family and the wife of another. The two had gone away together, leaving only notes behind. Since Sally, the woman, was a member of the Bridge Club, the light beating upon it was strong.

"If they just didn't both leave young, half-grown families, I could stand it better. But this somehow hits us. They are near our own ages. What moves people to take an action like this? I suppose this case is not unique. Oh, Katherine, what do you think? We oughtn't to ask *you* such a question, and yet —" one member said sadly.

Katherine spoke slowly. "I'm not sensitive about my own situation. But because of it I suppose I've done more thinking about the problem than most of you. I don't like to offer an opinion, but we have all been struck hard by this last glaring experience in our community's life, so I'll try to tell you some of my own ideas."

"Go on, Katherine!" came from all sides.

"Well, this may sound odd to you, but I believe that our modern advertising has to bear some of the blame. Even if the big heyday of the magazine has past, we have some good ones left which come into our homes. And the stunning ads in them usually deal with young and very beautiful women. Husbands see these as well as their wives. When you couple this with the constant emphasis on sex which pounds away at us all the time in books, articles, and programs, the effect could be to make some married people discontented.

"But the big reason, I think, for the prevailing breakup of homes is that the old-fashioned word *duty* has apparently gone out of our language. Have you ever seen it or heard it spoken lately? A man did so-and-so because he felt it was his *duty;* Jane Doe once thought of a divorce but decided it was her duty to remain with her family. I know this sounds old-fashioned, but isn't it just a part of what we are trying to do before this year is over — get some of the virtues of those early days into our own times? I do believe that, if the partners in any marriage fulfilled the *duty*, the obligation that lay upon them, there would be fewer needless divorces. Now, I really must stop."

"Please go on if you have any more ideas. Some of us need some concrete thinking. At least I do."

Katherine laughed. "I feel ashamed; I'm afraid I sounded so *preachy*, but I have another thought that haunts me. That is the number of divorces among the very young marrieds. After only a very few years some of these marriages become dissolved, and I believe it is because there seems to be now a new and, I think, a mistaken concept of *happiness.* It, or what they conceive it to be, must be had at any price, even at the cost of a new partner. Surely, we all know it is not like that. You can't pursue happiness or clutch at it. It comes unbidden to the inmost heart, usually, I think, when you aren't thinking of yourself at all, but perhaps of others.

"I often wish that at every marriage ceremony the minister would make the couple answer to one extra vow: Do you solemnly promise to try to bring *contentment* into your home? This might help. Oh, girls, do forgive me this long speech. I'm afraid it's been very disjointed. But you *did* bring it on yourselves!"

"And I'm glad we did," Mary Hastings said quickly. "I would suggest we take these ideas home and think about them. And perhaps play a little bridge now to get our minds off the world's troubles!"

The various threads of experiences which had become entangled with Katherine's own had become gradually smoothed out. Preacher, released at last from the endless tests, was pronounced fit to leave the hospital. Dr. Harris made sure he would be welcomed by his class and the homeroom teacher had reported that his face actually shone when Don shook hands and apologized. The word went around that John Lester was going to marry Laurie and still go on to Princeton. A number of boys had asked Dr. Harris if there could not be a repetition of the Dance Parties. It was said he had smiled benignly and said something might be worked out later on.

The one report which was discouraging was, strangely enough, that of the play. Madeleine came over fairly often to discuss it. "I'm not satisfied," she kept saying. "I'm better than I was, but there's not enough feeling yet. I'd like to just sit and *listen* to the story. Why don't you read it for me, Katherine? I'll cue you in."

"I guess I know it pretty well. I've been going over the script just for my own pleasure. I won't emote; I'll just go through it so you can hear the sound of the words." And they began.

Halfway through, Madeleine stopped her. "I think I know what's the matter . . . the quality of the voice. Mine is too light. Even as you read it, there is feeling in it. But what can I do now?"

"Not a thing. You are used to speaking on a stage. So just forget yourself and your voice and think only of Juliet, the way *she* might have spoken. She was only fifteen, we are told. Now you are *good* and you know it. So why not enjoy this role and stop worrying?"

"I'll try. At least one burden is lifted. I know I have an understudy."

"Mercy!" Katherine cried, the blood all at once going out of her cheeks. "Don't dare to say such a thing even in fun! You scare the wits out of me. Let's make some sandwiches and have a cup of tea to settle our nerves."

"Good! We'll forget the play for I've a lot of gossip to tell you."

Over the impromptu lunch, Madeleine gave the news that Lucien had brought. It seemed that John Lester had left school with the promise he could finish his work and take final exams in midsummer. He was going out to Colorado to join Laurie.

"And the boys have it all figured out that Laurie's trouble was not a weak lung at all, but a pregnancy and that John is going out to marry her before the baby comes. Isn't that amazing: But, you know, I feel it's true. What do you think?"

"I quite agree. If this is the way it is, then it will surely be the happy solution to a sad situation."

Madeleine's face relaxed and she gave a slight giggle. "It's serious, really, but it has its amusing side. It seems John Lester has been very popular with a large group of boys who always stick together. Lucien is in it. But now the thought of John as a possible husband and father has them 'all shook up' — Lucien's words. And a few of them who have been living with girls are going to break it up, because they feel they don't know as much about the facts of life as they thought they did."

The boys' theory had further support when it became known that Cele and Henry had also left for Colorado to visit and eventually bring Laurie home with them. They had told Katherine just this much and no more, but she too had drawn her own conclusions and inwardly rejoiced with her friends.

As a matter of fact, as May moved on, she had been fighting the old battle in her own heart. She loved spring but a recurrence brought back poignantly that other in which David had said he was leaving her. The tender leaves, the shy crocus, as well as the strong bright glory of the daffodils and tulips all reminded her of those first terrible days of her loss.

But was this now only the pain of a memory? Was it only the remembrance of a wound which she had once felt and not now a present stabbing of her heart? She pondered, and then raised her head for breaths of the spring air. She had come again to her usual answer:

> "Love is not love
> which alters when it alteration finds."

So it had been with her. So it was now. And the ache continued, unqualified, unabated.

Chapter Eight

AND THE WEEKS moved swiftly toward June, the time of roses, weddings, and graduations. In her more formal garden Katherine paused often to read the Sun Dial and look at the rich profusion of red, pink, and white blooms which the gentle gardener's hands had arranged must be there.

> "Roses, roses blowing,
> In my garden growing,
> Scent the air, everywhere,
> Mine to wear — mine to share" . . .

He had often quoted this old song as he planted the bushes. "Come next June," he always added, "there will be a perfect glory here." And now this had come true.

The remembrance of him now was not painful. It was, rather, a tender reliving of the days they had spent together in the garden, laughingly tossing botanical names back and forth, or quoting bits of poetry they both loved. The Sun Dial with its wide frame of bright flowers brought all this near, only as though a peaceful dream had passed, leaving only beauty behind.

There was another dream, however, which did not slip peacefully into the past. This one demanded all her restraint. It had to do with the letters to the children from their father. He wrote more descriptively, now that they were a little older. He told of the boys and girls sailing their boats in the park lake, of the time he had gone to a wonderful palace called

Versailles — Mummy would pronounce it for them — where there were many, many fountains on the lawns, throwing up great sprays of water; of the church with the most beautiful stained-glass windows, called Sainte Chappelle; of the pussy cats everywhere, lying asleep on steps or windowsills . . . All this and much more David tried to picture to Davey and Kit. Did he not realize how she had longed to see Paris herself and show its beauties to the children with him beside her?

If emotional discipline was needed, she had it, she thought, when the letters came.

One evening early in the month two cars drew up before the Bradley house. Out of one came Cele and Henry and out of the other Laurie with John Lester carrying a large basket. The watching neighbors said Henry had laughed once and said, "Don't drop it!" Then they all went into the house. Katherine waited for the phone call she felt sure would come. It did — at late bedtime. It was Cele, her voice kept low but vibrant.

"Oh, Katherine, I imagine you've heard by now, for I saw several women outside when we all got home. We're all *so* happy. You know, don't you?"

"I want to hear it all from you!"

"I'll just give you the high points with details later. Well, John Lester, bless his dear heart, came out, determined to marry Laurie if she was willing. He'd been talking a lot to Henry. They were married in a little church near my sister's home. Laurie had decided to give the baby away, but after it came — a darling little girl — John took one look and said, 'Nobody is going to get this.' So here we all are together."

"Cele, I can't tell you how glad I am for you. It is the most perfect thing . . ."

"I know. Almost too perfect, as though we didn't deserve it. Sometimes in the night I think of the girls caught as Laurie was, but with no boy friend waiting to marry them and the family to make the way easier. I try to tell myself our case is not unique, but I give thanks very humbly just the same."

"And enjoy all the blessings you have."

"Oh, one more thing. I've never seen Henry so utterly happy over anything before. Whenever we miss him, he's upstairs looking at the baby — little Cecilia!"

"When can I see her?"

"We haven't had time to get settled, but I think a little later I'll give a tea for the club girls. That will start it off right. I must stop, Katherine. Thank *you* for everything!"

While this news was thrilling enough, Katherine waited anxiously for further reports of the play from Madeleine, who had been strangely silent of late. When phone calls came, they were brief. She felt she was doing much better in her part, but that Mr. Lawton continued asking her to repeat lines which injured her pride and made her nervous. The scenery was finished and was nothing short of marvelous. She always ended on the same theme. "I wish it was all over and I could relax. As it is, I can't sleep for thinking about it."

On the afternoon before the dress rehearsal Katherine was surprised to find Mr. Lawton at her door. She liked him at once — gravely courteous but making no delay as he stated his business.

"Have you heard of Mrs. Fulton's illness?" he began.

"Oh, no!" Katherine cried. "It can't *be* — with the play tomorrow night! What has happened?"

"I'll try to be brief. No one can question Mrs. Fulton's talent. I feel she's close to professional, but her roles here have been comedy or drama, never tragedy, and it was evident that the Juliet role threw her as the slang goes. She's been doing much better, but it was clear she was very nervous and on a strain. I've just talked to her doctor before I came here. He said in her condition she was ready to catch any bug that came along. But what she has now is a bad case of flu. She tried to get out of bed this morning and fainted. So that's our sad story."

"But what will you *do*?"

"Here are the facts. The house is sold out. We can't postpone this play because our Romeo, who is *excellent,* leaves almost at once for a summer course. The cast is ready and good. This brings me to the only alternative I can imagine. Mrs. Fulton once said jokingly that you knew the lines as well as she did. Is this true?"

Katherine felt herself trembling, but she kept her voice calm. "I think it is," she said.

"We have used your own cut version, so the action must be familiar and I know you have played the role once before. Could you — *would* you go through this rehearsal tonight and see if you can go on with it? This is a tremendous thing to ask of you, but I feel quite desperate."

Katherine's hands gripped each other, but her voice, when it came, was calm. "Of course I'll try, Mr. Lawton. If I fail, you would be no worse off than you are now, would you?"

"Not at all. But I can never thank you enough for trying. I have no words. Rehearsal is called for 7:30. I'll send a car for you. By the way, is your hair long or short?"

"Long. My husband liked it so."

"Good. The robes, caps, et cetera, are in the dressing room at the theater. Bless you, my dear, bless you! Oh, I forgot one thing. We have a narrator, a man who can't act but reads beautifully. He will use Shakespeare's own introduction. We can't improve on that. Then I have written what is needed to introduce the scenes and made the necessary omissions so the story will go smoothly. Now, once again my eternal thanks and don't worry. If you can't do it, as you say, we'll be no worse for trying." And he was gone.

Katherine sat down until the trembling left her, feeling, first of all, waves of pity for Madeleine that almost made her sick. Oh, poor Madeleine! She deserved this triumph. This would be a crushing loss to her.

But slowly thoughts of herself began to come. Rising within her was an almost stubborn sense of pleasure, a joyous excitement which she could not now restrain. She would once again use the gift she had given up for David. Now as a recompense it would be, for this time at least, given back to her. She began to feel steady, so she got up and called Mrs. Weagle, begging her to come soon and take over the meals and the children, staying all night and on through the following one if she could. I'll need rest, Katherine thought, and no cares. I want to run over a few long speeches to make sure. She would not tell Tim until tomorrow after they all had decided on the outcome. More and more she felt an intense eagerness for the time of the rehearsal to arrive. She tried to be ashamed of her assurance but gave up the struggle. For she longed to speak the immortal words as she knew she could speak them.

She told the children she was going to a play practice and if it was given tomorrow evening, perhaps they could go. They took the news calmly and were playing with Thomas as she left. At the back of the theater Mr. Lawton greeted her and at once turned on the stage lights. Katherine gasped in amazement.

"We have a wonderful stage crew — several men who make a hobby of wood-working, a professional artist, and several interior decorators. They use many screens, painted curtains, and real carpentry. I wanted you to see your balcony first!"

"It's unbelievable," Katherine whispered. "The whole garden is there."

"The balcony scene is the one people always remember and I think this will be worthy of remembrance."

"It's incredibly beautiful! Even the wall is there which Romeo over-leaps!"

Mr. Lawton laughed. "One of the triumphs! Painted bricks on pasteboard. But come now and meet the cast."

Katherine had been conscious of a small group in the front seats, heads turned toward each other as if in discussion. Before she and Mr. Lawton had gone far up the aisle a young man had started down to meet them. When he arrived he looked disturbed as he was introduced.

"Mrs. Davenport, your Romeo! And a fine one he is!"

"I'm truly embarrassed," the young man said, "but I've been deputized to give a message from the cast and I guess I must do it. The thing is, we've all been talking the situation over and — do forgive me, Mrs. Davenport — everyone feels that after our hard work and the sentiment we have now for the play, we can't bear to put it on with the main character untried and unsure. We do thank you for your kindness, Mrs. Davenport, but we'd rather not go any farther."

"I can understand perfectly how you must feel," Katherine said at once. But Mr. Lawton interrupted.

"I can, also, but I want to remind you that I have worked very hard on this play as well as the cast. And now I only ask one favor. I would like you to go through the dress rehearsal now. After that you can take a vote and Mrs. Davenport and I will be quite willing to abide by it. Could you do that?"

"Yes, I think we should, when you put it that way. I'll tell the rest. We can be ready soon. Good luck, Juliet!"

"Good luck to us both, Romeo!"

"You have a lovely voice," he added, as he went to join the others.

Katherine found her dressing room where a young black girl with an eager smile had been placed to assist the women with their costumes and make-up. The nurse was already there in her voluminous robes and nightcap and Lady Capulet in the cloth of gold befitting her state. They greeted Katherine pleasantly, but she could feel their dubiety. They watched with keen interest as her hair was let down and brushed, falling sweetly around her shoulders. Their eyes widened as they saw how slender she was when she slipped into the white robe, adjusted the tiny cap, and received the touch of make-up.

"Not too much rouge," she begged. "I always flush up when I'm excited."

She climbed softly up a few steps, paused on the one behind the curtain, from which she would make her entrance, and waited as the general movements subsided, a bell rang, and the voice of the narrator began clearly to repeat the brief story of "the star-crossed" lovers; going on to give the synopsis of the opening scenes. At last came the familiar line from Romeo which was her cue.

At once she felt the burden of the play falling upon her. She was Juliet, her heart torn by love and longing. She leaned upon the railing, her cheek upon her hand and a sigh escaped her. "Ah, me!" With that heartbreaking sigh the whispering behind her ceased. There was an utter stillness as the words of love went on, which she spoke, as she thought, to herself, alone.

> "O Romeo, Romeo! wherefore art thou Romeo? . . .
> What's in a name? that which we call a rose
> By any other name would smell as sweet . . .
> Romeo, doff thy name;
> And for that name . . .
> Take all myself."

It was a yearning cry, but as she was answered by her lover, her voice held both surprise and fear. How had he come, since the orchard walls were high and the place meant death if any of her kinsmen saw him?

> "With love's light wings did I o'er-leap these walls;
> For stony limits cannot hold love out."

Juliet's voice still trembled with fear.

> "If they do see thee, they will murder thee."

But love was too strong, their tender vows continued past the repeated calls from the nurse, until at last the time was arranged for Juliet to send a message to him next day to find what plans had been made.

The farewells were repeated many times until Juliet felt for safety he must be gone.

> "Good-night! Good-night! parting is such sweet sorrow
> That I shall say good-night till it be morrow."

The narrator gave the scene in the Friar's cell when Romeo arranged to marry Juliet; then came the only really amusing part of the play, when the nurse returned to give Juliet the message from Romeo. She, using every possible excuse to delay her news, drives Juliet to petulance and near despair before she heard at last that she was to meet Romeo in the Friar's cell that day for the marriage.

The narrator told briefly of the later street tragedy in which Romeo unwittingly kills Tybalt, Juliet's cousin, and is at once banished from Verona upon pain of death if found there. And he just made a bridegroom!

The dialogue of the following scene, coming at the end of the wedding night, had always seemed to Katherine the most tender and most poignant of the play. Romeo had climbed to Juliet's bedchamber by a ladder under cover of darkness and now, as he had heard the early morning lark and seen the breaking light, stood, dressed, ready to leave. Juliet in her lacy gown approached him and grasped his arm.

> "Wilt thou be gone? It is not yet near day.
> It was the nightingale, and not the lark . . .
> Nightly she sings on yon pomegranate tree.
> Believe me, love, it was the nightingale."

Romeo's voice came, anguished but firm:

> "It was the lark . . .
> No nightingale: Look, love . . .
> Night's candles are burnt out, and jocund day
> Stands tiptoe on the misty mountain tops.
> I must be gone and live, or stay and die."

Juliet's pitiful pretense went on:

"Yon light is not daylight; I know it . . .
Therefore stay yet; thou need'st not to be gone!"

Finally Romeo's love grew stronger than his fear:

"Come, death, and welcome! Juliet wils it so.
How is't, my soul? let's talk; it is not day."

And then Juliet could pretend no longer. The whole burden of the facts and the danger fell upon her. Her voice broke in one last yielding, despairing cry.

"It is the lark . . .
O! now be gone; more light and light it grows."

Romeo clasped her to him.

"Farewell, farewell! one kiss, and I'll descend."

Juliet's heartbroken voice followed him.

"Art thou gone so? my lord, my love, my friend . . .
O! think'st thou we shall ever meet again?"

Romeo looked up to her at the window. He made his voice strong:

"I doubt it not."

But there was doubt in both their hearts, and the play moved on to its tragic ending. Romeo reached his haven in safety but Juliet's father was forcing her to marry the County Paris within a few days. Knowing herself to be already a wife, she went to the Friar for help. He gave it in the form of a sleeping draught which would make her look and seem dead, although really asleep. He would wake her at the appointed time as she lay in the great Capulet tomb, and by a letter to Romeo have him there to rejoice with them at the success of his skillful planning. But this did not happen.

The letter from the Friar did not reach Romeo, only the news from others of Juliet's death. He purchased a phial of poison and hastened back to Verona, determined to lie with his love in their last sleep. He found her dead, as he thought, and drained the poison, falling at her feet. There came then the small bit of action which would move any audience, strained by emotion, to tears. One of Juliet's hands slipped from her breast and slowly, gently the arm drops to the floor. She was waking, found Romeo dead, and with his own dagger ended her own life.

When Katherine had reached the end of the play she lay a few minutes where she had fallen, feeling the full stress of the emotion she had been depicting. Then as she got up, knowing herself in the real world again she heard cries and a rush from the wings as the whole cast gathered around her. Young Romeo kissed her, as somewhat incoherently the others expressed their wonder and acclaim at her acting. Mr. Lawton brought a break in the excited tension. He came up to the stage, blowing his nose, and said, "Well it's time now to take the vote. Do you want to go on with the play?"

There was immediate laughter. The man who had played the County Paris said, "Please don't make us look more foolish than we feel. We've all had a tremendous shock, but a fine one. I guess we can skip the vote, and just give our heartfelt thanks to Mrs. Davenport. But," he added, turning to her, "how in the world did you do it without rehearsals?"

"But I had them," she said. "Just for my own pleasure I spent night after night going over the lines, and also several times Mrs. Fulton wanted to hear how the words sounded, so she gave me the cues and I went through it all. So in a way I was prepared."

"Well," said Mr. Lawton, "in any case it was marvelous, and now we'd better be getting home and rest. I'll take you myself."

On the way he was very curious. "Mrs. Davenport, how does it come you never went on the stage?"

"I wanted something else more. I wanted to marry the man I loved and make a home."

There was little conversation after that.

Katherine relaxed with a feeling of deep contentment. She had done it, and from the testimony of her own senses she had done it well. Tomorrow night it would be easier still. The eagerness she had felt before still claimed her. She tried to put it aside and think again of Madeleine's disappointment. But here she ran into difficulty, for the whole cast, as one, had told her they had never felt the beauty or the reality of the play as they had done tonight through her interpretation. Perhaps, she mused, since she had known such sorrow, it was fair and right that she should have this happiness. I'll rest on that thought, she decided, and then roused quickly. She had forgotten to call Tim.

She reached for the phone and when he answered told him all the story.

"Goodness gracious, Kathy, this is absolutely tremendous! But do you think you *can do it*?"

"I've just done it. I'm trying to tell you I can't wait until tomorrow night. I've got three seats in the reserved section, for the whole theater is sold out. You'll come and bring the children?"

"Try to keep me away! I'm simply stunned with surprise and pride. You're not nervous?"

"I'm sort of ashamed that I'm not. I'm just happy to be doing it."

"Well, get to sleep and rest up. I feel tense as a string myself. You know, Kathy, this whole thing shows how much inner courage you have to draw upon. Now, good night, dear. 'Parting is such sweet sorrow' and all that. You see I remember a few lines myself."

The next morning, relaxed and refreshed, Katherine received her breakfast from Mrs. Weagle's hands and enjoyed the company of the children, who stood beside her bed while she ate.

"Are we going to the play, Mother?" Davey asked.

"Indeed, yes. Uncle Tim is taking you."

"Is it a funny play?" Kit inquired.

"No, I'm afraid it isn't, but even though it is very serious, I think you will be interested in it."

"What's it about?"

"It's about a very pretty young girl named Juliet and a man called Romeo who fell in love with her."

"Goody!" said Kit. "Did they get married?"

"Yes, they did, but Romeo had done a very bad thing and had to go away and leave her."

"Like Daddy left us?" she persisted.

"Oh, not at all the same. Romeo had accidentally killed a man with his sword."

"Will there be sword fights in the play?" asked Davey with new enthusiasm.

"Yes, there will."

"You know what the kids say about Daddy, Mother?"

"Shut up, Kit. You don't have to tell all you know. Watch me now." Davey took a fine dueling posture, extended his arm, pointing through thin air, and shouted, "Have at thee, bastard! I'll spit thee in the gizzard!"

"Do you want that extra muffin, Mother?" Kit asked, unimpressed.

"No, dear, you can have it, but I'm sure there are more in the kitchen."

"Come on, then, Kit. Let's go down. I could eat another one myself. Good-by, Mother. See you later. Have a good rest! I know I'll like the play."

"Me too," came the echo.

Katherine rested against the pillows not now quite so relaxed. She felt like laughter and tears together. Davey had been *so* funny, and as to language Tim had prepared her for what she must expect to hear from a growing boy. As to the other aborted news, that hurt. She knew that her situation with ugly but true rumors would still crop up in family conversation here and there; the sharp ears of children would somehow overhear and report without mercy to Davey and Kit. She had long ago fought out this imaginative battle. The thing now to relieve her heart was that her own children were trying to protect her. That was sweet. She would rest on that.

As she was brushing her hair, the door opened slightly and Kit stuck her head in. "Mummy," she said using the old nursery name, "do you think Daddy will ever come back?"

"Of course," said Katherine stoutly. "As soon as he finishes all this big business he has to attend to in Paris."

"That's good," Kit replied. "I just thought I'd ask."

Katherine heard her calling to Davey as she descended, by way of the banisters.

The day was one of June's most perfect — blue sky above, pink roses in the gardens, little thrills abroad as canopied church entrances here and there told of weddings, and in all public places large placards proclaiming that the Thespians would present scenes from *Romeo and Juliet*. And this was the day of it. At last, this was the night. Katherine was ready when the car came for her, with Tim to see her off with his final good wishes and admonitions.

"Don't feel too excited, Kathy. You look flushed to me."

"Don't ever tell on me, Tim, but I'm eager to begin. I love doing it."

"Best of good luck! I can't wait myself. And, of course, I'll take care of the kids."

When she reached the theater now her welcome was quite different from the one of last night. The cast clustered around her as though to make sure she hadn't vanished overnight. All at once they seemed like a warm, family group. There were some last comments, a few suggestions, and then they all repaired to the dressing rooms to await with what patience they could muster until the audience was finally in their seats and the voice of the narrator began the play.

Katherine listened tensely from behind her curtain. There was the usual medley of voices, low or clear, of seats raised or lowered, the words of the ushers correcting mistakes in tickets, whispering and subdued laughter — all a mélée of sounds until she heard Tim's voice followed by Miss Darby's and then faint chirpings from the children — a good combination.

The theater apparently filled quickly; for before she would have thought it possible, all the normal confusion ended and a great quiet took place. The heavy outside doors were shut, the lights went off in the house, she could tell, and only the bright strip in the front of the curtain remained for the narrator and for Mr. Lawton, who was now addressing the audience. He explained that only a day ago Madeleine Fulton had been taken suddenly ill with flu and Katherine Davenport, who was familiar with the play, had with great kindness agreed to accept the role. Because of the nature of the scenes there would be no intermission and the cast asked that there should be no applause until the end.

Katherine could hear a faint ripple of dismay and disappointment, like a small wind, among the listeners; then there was quiet and the narrator began to tell of the star-crossed lovers and explain the bitter to-the-death feud between the two great rival families, the Montagues and the Capulets. He stepped back then into the shadows, and the curtain went up on the softly lighted but distinct "balcony" scene. There were small cries of surprise and delight over the setting and then hushed silence as Romeo came forward from the wall behind him and Juliet emerged from the curtains to lean upon the railing of the balcony.

While Katherine was still conscious of the eager assurance which had before possessed her, she knew now that she must bring to the very hearts of perhaps hundreds of people the agonies of endangered love as Juliet had felt them. This, in a sense, was a greater thing than she had ever done because of the larger number of people to be affected. But as this scene advanced she knew that she had done just that; for she had been aware of that strange, subtle transference between the emotion of the actor and that of the listeners. From now on they would come to her as she poured out her heart to them.

In the little scene later on in Juliet's bedchamber the morning after her marriage to Romeo, which had always been Katherine's favorite, she could feel now a certain rapt quality in the attention of the audience as it began. Romeo is ready and must leave to save his life. He tells Juliet he has heard the lark, the "Herald of the morn," and it is growing more and more light. Juliet pathetically insists it is the nightingale that sings and it is not yet near day. But when at last she accepted the terrible truth she confesses it in the one yielding, heartbroken cry, *"It is the lark."* As this reached the limits of the theater there was here and there a muted sob.

So the play went on with its mounting complexity, its developing tragedy and the audience did not stir. When the curtain fell at the end and the lights went on in the house, the applause began.

Katherine felt exhausted and sat down to recover a little. She could see Mr. Lawton directing the cast to go out for their bows once and again. She could see the nurse going through the break in the multiple curtains and hear the clapping grow louder. Then Romeo went out alone and the applause was wild as again and again they called for him. Then Mr. Lawton came to her.

"Now it's time," he said. "They are all waiting for you. Come! I'll help you to the edge of the curtain."

So at last she stood before the sea of lights and faces while the applause became a storm, and then the real ovation came.

The whole audience rose! As she realized what was happening, tears came into her eyes and rolled down her cheeks. If the effect had been long studied it could not have been more perfect. For she stood there smiling through her tears, reaching her arms out unconsciously toward them in gratitude for their beautiful tribute for what she had done. She bowed again and again, and then slipped quickly behind the curtain. There were no more calls. The climax had been reached.

Back on the stage the whole cast gathered around for a few minutes of high jubilation and the cracking of champagne bottles. Everybody talked at once. The men hugged each other and kissed the ladies. Joy was rampant until suddenly young Romeo called out, "Listen! We've got to get to the party before it's any later. Let's get ready, folks."

"A *party*?" Katherine said. "Oh, I'm afraid I couldn't go through a party now. All I want is to get home, if you will excuse me."

"She's right. We must not ask anymore of you tonight. I'll take you home as soon as I have changed."

But a man appeared suddenly at the entrance to the wing which had an outside exit. It was Tim. Katherine gave a cry of delight and introduced him to the cast. Tim was at once at ease, as he shook hands all around.

"It was wonderful! Marvelous! I've no words to tell you. And I was so glad my sister here was able to sort of stumble through it," he said, with a wink in her direction.

There was a roar of laughter.

"Oh, that's just what I needed," Katherine said. "I'll get ready at once, Tim."

The farewells as she left were genuinely tender — Romeo's the most. He put his arms about her and gently kissed her forehead. "You performed a miracle for me. I'll never forget my lovely Juliet."

"Nor I, my Romeo."

When she and Tim reached the car he explained about the children.

"They slept through the last half, Kit against Miss Darby's shoulder and Davey on mine. At the end she and Dr. Harris suggested taking the children on home. They knew we would be delayed, and I knew Mrs. Weagle would put them to bed. So all is well."

When at last they were back in the familiar living room, Katherine begged Tim to stay for a while. "Just until I unwind a little. I couldn't possibly go to sleep right away."

So Tim stayed and after he had arranged Katherine comfortably with her feet on the hassock and cushions behind her head, he told her quietly all that he had felt from her performance. "I had something with which to compare it. You looked as young now as at that other time . . ."

"The make-up, and my hair being down."

"Perhaps, and you're still slender. But I was thinking of the voice. There is more in it now than there was then. This is your own suffering coming through. You are not play-acting. There was a reality there that touches the audience."

They sat quiet for a little while; then, as Tim went to make cool drinks, Katherine kept whispering to herself, "Why should I not ask him? What harm can it possibly do?"

She spoke first of the children's conversation with her that morning as she sipped her lemonade thirstily — a beverage Tim said would be safe after champagne — and then, turning to him suddenly, said, "If I ask you a question will you promise to answer honestly?"

"Certainly, if I can."

"Do you think that David will ever come back?"

He was startled and showed it, "Why in the world do you ask me that at this moment?"

"Well, Kit asked that of me this morning. And why do you look so distressed? Have you actually heard anything from him lately?"

"Yes, I have but I certainly had not planned to tell you tonight, of all times."

"What, Tim?" she asked quietly.

"He called me up late last night from New York."

"Oh, what did he say?"

"Just that he had finished in Paris and since things there were now running smoothly, they wanted him to come back to the States and establish another office in San Francisco. He was leaving for there last night, but had been trying to get me so I would know of this plan and have his new address if there was ever direct need of it."

"Did he say *it* or *me*?"

"He said *it*. He would hardly say *me* when talking to me."

"That's true. Didn't he ask for me?"

"Not directly. He asked particularly if 'all the family' were well."

"Did he say how long he would be in the West?"

"He said a good many months. He couldn't tell now how long. Does all this make you feel better or worse, Kathy?"

"Not much change, I guess. If anything, maybe a little better, because the thought of Paris has been intolerable for me. You have not yet answered my question, you know."

"That's true. And it's a hard one, full of imponderables. But in all honesty, from my human viewpoint I don't see how he ever could come back after the way he left."

Katherine sighed. "I believe that's the way I feel myself though I tried to answer Kit positively. I do keep on hoping, though, irrational as it is."

"Keep on, then. 'Hope springs eternal,' the poet says. Let it keep springing in you. It can certainly do no harm."

They spoke then of Mary, of Tim's own longing and his checking each day and week off on his calendar. "It doesn't hurt you, does it, Kitten, when I talk like this?"

"Never," she answered. "I enjoy it all vicariously. This is as if — how shall I say it? — as if I warm my heart at your fire."

He held her close as he was leaving, whispering the praise most precious to her of all she had received that evening. Then, strangely relaxed, she went to bed. The play with its tensity receded. The news about David took its place. But it was an old sadness . . . one that her brain had somehow been accepting for a long time. She fell asleep.

The next day, though Sunday, was peppered with phone calls. Davey proudly answered all unless compelled to have Mrs. Weagle's aid. Katherine lay still, knowing what the old country expression "bone tired" meant; for she ached all over. But it was a good ache when she could give in to it and rest all day. When she left her door open she could hear Davey speaking in his most grown-up voice, with Kit beside him to gather what crumbs of importance might be thrown her way.

"Sorry, sir. She can't be disturbed right now. Orders, sir. Who am I? *I'm her son*!"

Kit's voice came plaintively, "Davey, let me have the next one. You get them all."

"All right. If it's a woman."

Later, "Here you go, Kit. Now watch what you say."

"Oh, yes, good morning, I mean, hello! Yes, this is Mrs. Davenport's residence, but she was in a play last night . . . oh, you were there? Oh, thank you! I thought she was pretty good too. Yes, I could take a message maybe. No, she's not sick; she's just tired, I *think*. But she does look sort of white this morning. I suppose you could . . ."

"Kit, give me that phone. I *told* you to watch what you said."

"Well, she just wanted to come over to see Mother, and she sounded so nice . . ."

Katherine closed her door and returned to bed. Her friends would understand and the strangers didn't matter. She did take the call from Tim about noon. "Hello, there," he said, "is there anything left of you now?"

"I'm a little limp but all right. The children are answering the phone. I'm speaking only to you. So feel flattered!"

"I am. Also my own phone has been ringing, I think, since

daybreak. People have the idea I am vaguely related to you, so I sail in on the tail of your kite. There are only the most extravagant comments on the play and on your acting in particular. Did you sleep last night?"

"Strangely enough, I did. And it is a comfort to wake up and know Mrs. Weagle is here. The best news is that she says she likes us and will stay on. I was concerned how Thomas would react. He's been a bit standoffish when she came just for a few hours. Now he evidently feels she's part of the family and he is won over completely. I think it's because she puts cream in his milk! Are you coming over?"

"Perhaps to supper, if I'm invited. You know I've just been thinking how flat and dull everything will seem after the excitement of the play. Nothing can top that and Lemming will sink into quiet monotony — nothing but the usual mild school graduation."

"I don't think so," Katherine laughed. "My experience has been that, as one high spot disappears, another takes its place. We'll see."

And Katherine was right. Two weeks after the play, when she had gone to call on the Fultons, she heard the news. She found Madeleine still weak and pale. She had been, indeed, more gravely ill than anyone but the doctor suspected. Her determination to keep going had brought on pneumonia with the flu. She was now glad to hear about the play but apparently had no regrets.

"I think Providence just got me out of that, Katherine. I knew I wasn't doing well and I was so tense and unhappy. When I simply had to give in, I believe I felt relieved."

The two women were still discussing the strange events when Lucien, now on half-day session, burst in at noon.

"Mother," he called. "Oh, hello, Mrs. Davenport. Listen to this. Here's some news! This morning we were all asked to assemble in the auditorium for an announcement. We wondered what was up. There was Mr. Keith, you know, the Assistant Principal, with a paper in his hand. When everyone was quiet he read that there was a purpose of marriage — that's what he said — between Dr. Joseph Harris and Miss Darby to take place in St. Mark's Episcopal Church following the graduation exercises. A reception would be held in the High School gymnasium. Now what about that? Isn't that fantastic? Everybody is running wild. We have to have committees now and heaven knows what else. I'm going back as soon as I get some lunch; it's really sort of *our* wedding in a way. Well, aren't you both amazed?"

"I'm thrilled," Katherine said, "but not exactly amazed. I've been wondering if there might be a little romance going on there."

"Of course I don't really know them, but I think it sounds terrific! Count on me, Lucien, for anything. Don't you think you students ought to be the hosts at the reception? Neither the bride or groom has family here, I've heard. So you all will be their children."

"Why, that's wonderful, Mother. No one ever thought of that yet. Of course there hasn't been time, but this afternoon I'll suggest the idea to them. They'll take to it, I'll bet you. Now how would you work it out?"

"Well," Madeleine went on, the color coming back to her cheeks, "I would suggest a long bride's table at the end of the gymnasium, set up in the loveliest way possible. I'll lend my big silver candlesticks and the rose bowl for the center. There the bride and groom, best man and bridesmaid would sit and maybe your class officers. Then serve them as nicely as you know how with whatever you all agree will be the refreshments and let the students get something easy to eat from a long buffet. Oh, and have a table near the bride and groom for presents. There may be many and no chance to display them. How does that sound to you, Katherine?"

"Perfect! Now I must go and help spread the good news! Thank you, Lucien, for bringing it, and I'll be talking to you later, Madeleine."

All that day Katherine went about with a smile on her lips.

She had been right. As she had told Tim a new event would rise above the plain of quiet living. And what an event! Why had Miss Darby never whispered her secret? That evening she found out as that lady came herself when she had ascertained the house would be quiet. She came with a tender light on her face, a large diamond on her finger, and put her arms around Katherine.

"I can't believe it, even *now*," she began. "*Me*, the spinster, the old bag, as I know the youngsters used to call me before you transformed me. *Me*, engaged and going to marry the man I've loved for so long . . ."

"Did he never suspect?"

"Never. He wanted to speak long ago but he was afraid I would just toss if off. He thought I was too independent, and wouldn't want to give up my freedom. Imagine!"

"How did he come to change his opinion?"

"Oh, that's a nice part. One day a couple of months ago I was *so* tired and everything had gone wrong. It does, you know, sometimes, and I had to speak to Dr. Harris about a problem I had with one boy. His office door was open, so I went in and sat down beside his desk and all at once everything came over me and I put my head down and cried my heart out. He came in so quietly I didn't hear him till he put his arms round me and lifted me up." Miss Darby drew a long breath. "After that it was sweeter than I can tell you. I shouldn't pour out all my happiness to you. It's not kind of me."

"Oh, yes, it is! I'm so thrilled over this I can't wait to do something for you. What could I do?"

"I was just coming to that. I want you to be my bridesmaid. Dr. Harris is having his assistant, Mr. Keith, stand up with him. And, Katherine, I would like to have you come along when I buy my wedding dress. I *could* wear white. It would be truthful for me, if you know what I mean. But I am in my early forties, and I don't think it would be suitable. Yet I *do* want to look like a real bride for him."

"I know the very thing now," Katherine said. "You must have a pale gray chiffon dress, beautifully made. I'll talk to the florist about a little circlet of tiny gardenias or roses for your hair. That with your long veil will give you a real bridal appearance and still be suitable to your age. You'll look young that day in any case. When do we go shopping?"

The day was set and Providence and good taste combined to bring success. When the pale gray gown was ultimately found and Miss Darby stood in the fitting room, arrayed in it, Katherine turned her head so that the tears in her eyes would not show.

When several hundred people feel themselves pleasurably involved in a project, difficulties vanish and orderly arrangements fall into place. Not only did the excitement of the coming occasion spread like wildfire but there was a deep underlying personal interest, as parents recalled with gratitude something Dr. Harris had said or done to help their children. So, with a kind of holy zeal, the work went on. Dr. Harris at first said the idea of the students giving the reception must not be thought of, but soon found it was one of those kindnesses one does not refuse.

Representatives from the various clubs met in amity to consult about gifts, so that the larger ones would not be duplicated. Everything had to be done without delay, since the time was short.

"Oh, why did you not tell us sooner?" Katherine lamented to Miss Darby.

"Because this is just the way Dr. Harris wanted it, and I may tell you I will continue following his wishes."

But the hurry lent its own pleasant excitement. Even great stores can feel a romantic heartbeat, so the silver was engraved, arriving just in the nick of time, and some linens monogrammed.

The great interest of the men in all this was a surprise at first to Katherine. Then as she spoke with some of them in person or heard of their reaction from their wives she understood.

"I'm certainly glad of a chance to do something for Harris," one man told her. "I'll never forget what he did for my Tom three years ago when he was getting a little out of line and I felt I wasn't handling it right. Harris talked to him a few times and damned if he wasn't a changed boy. I tried to get him to tell me what Harris said, but he was vague. Well, he seems to know just what goes on in a fellow's head and then he shoots for that. He's a pretty smart guy."

Christine Hart, the woman who played the part of the nurse in the play, came to see Katherine, who was on the Bridge Club committee for gifts. "My husband, Dick, would like to contribute to the silver present. Of course I'll go in with the Thespians' plans, but Dick would like to give something on his own, because he never gets over what Dr. Harris did for our Jimmy when he got into a little trouble. He says all the boys tell the same story — that whenever one of them gets into a scrape and has to go to the office they're ashamed but not scared. He says Dr. Harris listens to the whole story, whatever it is, and makes sure they leave nothing out; then very quietly he lays it on the line what he expects them to do, and, upon my soul, they *do it*. I think the man has real magnetism."

"I think he's got *love*," Katherine said, "for every student there, and they feel it."

So the encomiums multiplied with Miss Darby too getting her share, especially from the mothers who remembered the days of their children in the old fourth grade.

The usual arrangements for the graduation ceremony were made, the auditorium seats put into place, the whole great room ready for the final arrival of the florist. The bride's table stood in a far corner behind screens. The piano and orchestra chairs crowded into as small a space as possible. Dr. Harris had addressed the school assembly just once after the famous announcement.

"My dear young friends," he said, "you know I have always had a reception for the graduating class, after the exercises. This year, thanks to your amazing kindness, we shall have it and a wedding reception as well. I hope you will find this innovation a happy one for you and your parents."

After everything had been minutely thought of and every contingency prepared for by — it really seemed — concerted action on the part of practically the whole town, the day before the wedding broke late in a bank of dark clouds and a steady little rain began to fall, growing consistently heavier as the morning advanced. Katherine's phone rang with pessimism until she had an idea.

"We all feel wretched about the weather. Why not come over and have soup and sandwiches with me and try a little exorcising!" Cele, Madeleine, and Mary Hastings accepted and soon news and comments flew.

"Oh, I could just weep for the poor bride and groom. Of course as far as the graduates go, they'll have fun anyway, rain or shine."

"You think the others couldn't have any fun when it's raining?" Cele asked slyly.

When the laugh subsided, Mary Hastings spoke practically. "Of course I'm sure you all have heard what Pete Murray has done. He wanted it kept quiet, but you know how impossible that is here."

"I haven't heard," Cele said.

"Well, it seems he owns a big part in the Foster Catering Service — it's the finest around — and he has engaged two of their best men to come over for the reception and help those poor girls. They won't get nervous or flustered now with the professionals there. They are giving each person a tiny little chicken pie and an ice cream cone. No fuss or bother then with cutlery or paper plates and cups. I think it's pretty smart."

"Lucien's girl is on the food committee and she snitched a little pie for him. He told me it was out of this world; I guess fifty mothers each made eight pies, but he says the girls were still worried for fear they might run out. You see quite a few parents of the graduates may go to the buffet. And also since they are having the tent on the lawn to help with the overflow in the gym, they are afraid, with all their watching, some of those monkeys may take a pie inside and one outside too. Fred's daughter is on the food committee and he gets news firsthand, so he has ordered the men to bring one hundred more little pies with them. I think it's wonderful of Fred."

"So do I," Katherine echoed, "but he is another who feels he can't do enough for Dr. Harris. Their older daughter, I believe, was somewhat of a problem and Dr. Harris worked his magic somehow. I don't know the whole story, but she's a lovely girl now, doing well in college. I'm glad we are all eligible for the church. Lucien and Rose Hastings are both graduating and how about John Lester, Cele?"

So the talk went on and so did the rain. The weather report was ambivalent as usual. There was a chance the downpour would stop before midnight but with a certain bank of clouds and an eastern wind blowing in, the prediction had to be uncertain.

Madeleine giggled. "When I was a girl our rector was old and sort of dotty. He tried to read the prayer 'O Lord, send us such seasonable weather, et cetera' and his eyes were poor, so he read 'send us such *sensible* weather' and the whole congregation laughed. They thought it was the best prayer they had ever heard."

"Well, we'd better say a few ourselves if this keeps up," Cele remarked. "What more can you tell us about the guests for the church, Katherine? That's been kept quiet, but I suppose you know."

"I think they're chosen very well and no one will feel hurt. There will be, first, the graduates and their families; for after all, some of the glory from their day has been stolen from them. Then all the faculty from kindergarten to the top, with whatever husbands or wives go with them; then the School

Board and wives; and finally the families of close neighbors who are their personal friends. The church is not large, so this will make a comfortable congregation."

The women left later, cheered from their exchange of gossip, even though it was still raining. There was one secret, however, which Katherine had not divulged. It had to do with Tim who ten days ago had come and thrown himself, a little distraught, into the biggest chair.

"Well, I've done a good many odd things in my lifetime, but I've never given away the bride." His clear tenor rang out spontaneously.

"Who will give the bride away?
I could, he said, *but shouldn't."*

"Tim, don't sing that crazy song, especially if you're thinking even remotely of Miss Darby!"

"Oh, the thing just came into my head. Anyone can see she's a virgin undefiled. But here are the facts. She called me up to ask if I'd come over for a few minutes that evening. It was very urgent. I thought she'd run into a law quirk, so I went. I found her in real distress. She said the one thing lacking was a man to escort her up the aisle and 'give her away.' There was no male relative and the president of the school board was not a great favorite with either of them; so Dr. Harris had suggested me. He said after a very long talk with me — please note carefully — he held me in high esteem! So he would be most happy, as would she, if I would agree to do this."

"But that's beautiful, Tim!"

"Of course I refused at first. I was thunderstruck. But finally, after all my excuses, she kept on urging until I, the softie that I am, promised to do it. I'll probably feel like a fool. Don't tell anyone until the thing comes off. What about a present just for her? Should I, now? I've already sent something to the two of them. It was right nice," he added.

"Nothing more. This is just the way she would like it best. It was dear of you to send something. But this new plan makes it all perfect for me. I will be going over early on the wedding afternoon to help the bride dress; then we must be driven to the church, and you will be there to do it, and also to take me to the reception later."

"And bring you home from same. Well, if it works out for everyone's happiness, I'll be glad to be the martyr. Don't mention it, though, until it all comes off. And I'll tell you one thing: If I get through this wedding, I'm not going to another until I go to my own. Mary gets back next week!"

"Oh, Tim, that's wonderful!"

"Past all whooping," he rejoined.

In spite of all the half-hearted tentative weather reports the morning of the great day dawned clear and cloudless, with the sun sending down showers of bright warmth upon the newly washed earth. All over town there were tremors of pleasant excitement which seemed to be caught up in the very air. Katherine felt them as she packed the picnic basket for the children, who were going with some of their friends to the park, supervised by Mrs. Weagle.

Ever since the play Katherine had felt a great uplift of spirit. There were still messages and calls of congratulation; with a sort of amazed delight, Katherine, trying to maintain due modesty, still felt a deep and thankful pride, as though her own personality as a woman had been justified.

But running concurrently with this through the stream of her thinking was the news that David was back from Paris. It was irrational perhaps, but she felt he was nearer now than before. At least the ocean did not roll between them. Such a tiny thread of hope it was, and yet she grasped it.

At two o'clock with her matron of honor's gown in a long box, she set out for Miss Darby's prim little house. To her dismay she found the bride-to-be nervous and on the edge of tears. "Oh, my dear, has anything gone wrong?" she asked.

"Not the arrangements. Everything's going like clockwork. It's me. I'm so awfully scared."

"What about?"

"Tonight," Miss Darby almost whispered it. "I feel I must talk to you about that, or I'll never get through the day. You see, I'm forty-two years old and I've been a spinster so long and I've never even talked about sexual matters. I've shied away from all that and I'm actually ignorant. I don't know what I should do. I'm so afraid I'll not start out being a good wife to Dr. Harris . . ."

Katherine fought down a faint desire to laugh. "My dear," she said, "let me tell you just what to do, and then relax and enjoy your lovely wedding day!"

"If only you *would!*"

"Here it is: Tonight put on that exquisite, sumptuous nightdress I helped you select — the one I said would make a stone catch fire. Then tell your bridegroom how terribly much you love him . . . how you trust him. Don't keep anything back. Pour it all out on him, and *then* leave everything else to him."

"You mean that?"

"I certainly do."

"You think he will know . . . will understand?"

"I'm quite sure he will know and understand. So now, let's get on with our dressing."

Miss Darby breathed a long sigh.

"I'm so relieved," she said, "Now I'm ready to enjoy everything."

When their flowers arrived, there was a flutter of delight. White roses and gardenia for the bride, and for Katherine roses with larkspur, which were perfect with her pink gown. This had been bought for an important occasion before David left and had since hung mutely swathed in the closet. It was a lovely dress and right for the present moment.

When Tim called for them, his sudden attitude was not a

pose. "I'm a little bowled over by so much beauty, but I can at least pay my own homage to it. I do like that little crown you are wearing, Mrs. Harris-to-Be!"

"You don't think it looks as though I were trying to be girlish?"

"Not a bit. It's so tiny but sort of significant. Now I think we should be starting. You're taking this small bag with you, Miss Darby?"

"Oh, I mustn't forget it. You see, Dr. Harris was so anxious for us to leave *from* the High School; so we'll change there. The big bags are locked in his car, with six boys guarding them. I would have been afraid of a garland of tin cans myself, but he said that if they promised him, they would guard it with their lives. Oh, Mr. Dalzell, we cut out 'Who giveth this woman?' You won't have to say a thing. The Rector said we were old enough to give each other away."

From a small room at the back of the church they could see the pews filling up. The organ played softly as the Senior Girls' Chorus sang "O Perfect Love." Then the wedding march began. The groom and best man entered with the Rector from the sacristy and took their places, and Katherine began her slow walk up the aisle past the ribbon-bedecked pews. It was as the bride on Tim's arm moved forward that little half-audible expressions of surprise and pleasure escaped from those along the aisle. For Miss Darby had come radiantly into her own at last.

When the wedding party was back at the High School they found, instead of the chaos there could have been, an orderly arrangement. The orchestra was quietly playing in their corner. The honor guests were escorted to a place in front of the bride's table, where the graduates who wished could come to greet them. This long line quickly formed and passed, and when other students and friends from the church service had given their good wishes, the wedding party was seated at the table and had a chance to relax and look about them. There were flowers everywhere and garlands of laurel, but most beautiful of all there hung on two of the walls like tapestries the quilts the girls had made. All but one . . . Even as they looked and admired, there was a stir about the door, and the famous Sun Dial quilt seemed to be walking in. It was soon apparent that its upright position was caused by Jeannie and Don holding its upper corners. When they reached the bride's table, Don made a little speech telling how he and Jeannie both had a part in the quilt and wished now to make it a wedding gift.

Dr. Harris rose and accepted it with moist eyes. "Fold it carefully, Don, and place it on the table with the other gifts. We are deeply touched by this."

There were many things of value on the gift table, so two policemen stood inconspicuously behind it, ready to receive the property into their care later.

There seemed to be no end to the steady stream of well-wishers until it was time for the toasts to be drunk and the enormous wedding cake cut by the bride with the groom's hand upon hers. It was borne away, after the table had been served, by the caterers to be cut into tiny pieces and passed among the crowd of students. Then Dr. Harris waved to one of the boys appointed for this moment. Through his small megaphone he shouted, "Dr. Harris says, 'Let there be dancing!' Form your circle for 'Dusty Miller'!" The orchestra struck up the tune and in an incredibly short time three large circles were moving through the wide spaces of the gym and the words rang out:

"There was a dusty Miller
And he lived in a mill . . ."

The boy who had been chairman of the dancing came up to the table.

"Oh, come on," he said, "all of you. That will make it perfect!"

So they went, wedding clothes and all, and broke into several circles where the boys stamped and whistled, and the girls laughed and sang. It was noticed, though, that Dr. Harris, breaking all rules of the game, always managed by devious tricks to swing his wife rather than another. It was all lighthearted and gay. Word came that there was dancing too in the tent. At last Dr. Harris stopped and gave a sign to the orchestra. It, the singing, and the movement all slowed. Dr. Harris stood beside the table and raised his hand.

"May we have quiet, please?"

There was a general laugh at these very familiar words. They were obeyed, however, as usual.

"I want to tell you that my wife and I are unspeakably grateful to you for giving us this beautiful reception. We shall remember it always in our hearts. And now our best wishes to the graduates who go out to new experiences and also the hope that the rest of you students will be here to meet us next fall. Once again, our great thanks, and now let us close with the school song."

But before a note could be struck Katherine caught Dr. Harris' arm and whispered to him. His face looked startled and for a moment distressed, then cleared as he raised his hand again.

"I've just been reminded that I've forgotten something very important. The bride has not yet thrown her bouquet."

There was more laughter as the new Mrs. Harris came at once to the table, lifted her lovely bunch of white roses and tossed it out over the waiting girls who had already massed in front of the boys. There were screams of excitement and then of delight as Rose Hastings, a prime favorite, caught it.

"Now the song!"

It was a sweet and tender song, its melody written years ago by a fine musician who had paused in Lemming for a few years on his way to later eminence. As to the sentiment and words, those who sang now did not know that much the same were being sung in thousands of schools the country over. It was *their* song, they truly believed, and they sang it with their hearts.

When it was done, the wedding party left for the back exit. Katherine and Mrs. Harris went into the latter's own classroom and Dr. Harris and his best man into the principal's office across the hall.

"Wasn't it simply wonderful!" the bride exclaimed. "Didn't Joseph look handsome? And weren't the chicken pies out of this world? I was so hungry I ate all the caterer's man put on my plate. I hadn't eaten all day. Oh, I'm so happy! I hope you'll like my 'going away' outfit."

Katherine did. "Now, calm yourself, dear, and let me help you put on a new face. Then into your darling suit and away you'll go."

"I got the hat to match, because Joseph so likes a hat. I think it is rather becoming, though." Her tone held a new assurance.

She was ready in the rose silk suit and tiny hat which Katherine adjusted, with the least tilt, over her lovely hair. When they reached the corridor outside where Dr. Harris was waiting, his expression, as he took a long look at his bride, left nothing to be desired.

In front of the building a crowd of the students had gathered to see the couple off and the car with its honor guard was waiting. The boys guarding it had kept to their promise only at the last allowing themselves to paste a dignified white bow on the back of the trunk.

Dr. Harris handed his wife carefully to her seat and then took his own in the driver's place and started the car. At once a loud voice shouted, "Keep your hands on the wheel, Doctor." This was followed by a roar of laughter.

"Eyes on the road, Doctor," came another shout, with the same result. The crowd was growing hilarious.

As the car began to move, one final instruction came clearly, "Mrs. Harris, see you make him behave."

At this point Dr. Harris all but stopped the car and put his head out of the window. "And you behave *yourselves,* you rascals!" he yelled. But there was no reprimand in his tone. Rather, as most of the sharp young eyes of the students could see, his face was overspread with a wide, delighted grin.

Katherine had thought that perhaps some repetition of the school song would waft the travelers on their way but it was not so. As the car moved on down the school road, another tune was raised and caught on like wildfire.

"For they are jolly good fellows," they all sang at the top of their voices until the car was about to make the turn into the highway and be lost to sight.

> "For they are jolly good fellows
> And so say all of us!"

The Great Day was ended as though with a special blessing, under blue skies and with laughter and song.

Chapter Nine

"WHEN THE DUST of all this excitement has settled," Tim remarked one evening, "I'll have time to think about my own affairs."

Katherine watched his face. The old whimsical, half-cynical expression always changed to tenderness now as he spoke of Mary.

"What's the latest news of the landing date?" she asked.

"It will be, they hope, in the morning of July twelfth. I will meet them in New York and then join them for the flight to Mary's home. I have my affairs in order, so I can stay until we have a little visit and settle on the wedding plans. You know the awful thought that has just struck me? When she sees me again after just two brief meetings, what if she doesn't like me?"

Katherine laughed. "My dear boy, you are the most modest man in the world. And the most foolish. I think you can safely put that preposterous thought out of your mind. But if it's not too nosy, I would like to ask if you've been making real money over these years. Don't answer if you don't want to."

Tim was greatly amused. "In other words, am I prepared to keep Mary in the state to which she is accustomed? Well, I don't own a coal mine or anything like that, but I have had a good deal of success as a lawyer. I've had very many big juicy toads, grateful for being pulled out of the puddle, with resultant fat fees. Made me able to help a few small toads, incidentally. Yes, I've done pretty well. There is, too, the substantial amount the blessed parents left each of us. And then, by some peculiar strain in my blood I have a flair for investing! I'm no gambler, but I've bought good stocks which have done well. And once in a while I've treated myself to a 'dog,' as they call it, a fifty-to-one chance, and upon my word each one has exploded into something big. Yes, I think I can give Mary all she wants. I believe after my long bachelorhood I'll love having her bills come in to me. I'll be sure then that I have a wife."

"It's my impression," Katherine answered, "that she loves you so much she would live on a crust if necessary, but I'm glad you told me what you did."

The lull, which Tim had once predicted too early, fell now with a comfortable lethargy upon the town. Pleasant showers kept the grass green and the gardens in bloom, but the general populace seemed to move slowly. There was one bright social event in July and that was the tea which Cele had planned in order to introduce the new baby to her closest friends. Her house was full of flowers on the day, and the novelty of the occasion sent a small ripple of excitement through the guests as they were greeted.

There was a short time of chitchat in which the Harris-Darby wedding was reviewed, and new compliments, still filled with wonder, for Katherine and the play, were given over and over. Then Cele disappeared for a few moments and came back with Laurie, flushed and happy with her baby in its beribboned basket. And all problems and misgivings concerning the birth melted away before the beautiful child. For little Cecilia was, indeed, beautiful: the perfect features, the soft moist hair already suggesting curls to come, the incipient dimples, the little waving hands. The women were in rapture. When the exclamations had died down, Laurie received their good wishes and disappeared with the baby.

Over tea Cele answered the flying questions. Yes, Laurie and John had been married as soon as he went out to Colorado. They were very happy. They would have an apartment in Princeton while John went on with his studies. The only thing to dim the general joy was the thought of what she and Henry would ever do when they left and took the baby with them!

"Oh, I hope," Cele went on in her old impulsive way, "that John and Laurie will want to take many little weekend trips — and, of course, there will be vacations when they can leave little Cele with us!"

As Katherine and Mary Hastings walked home together, they discussed the strange story that had ended in such happiness for all. "But in spite of it," Mary said, "I still feel somehow there is a piece missing."

"So do I," Katherine answered. "I was thinking of it as I looked at that *perfect* baby. No one could wish it had arrived by any other route, and yet as you lay out the whole puzzle there is a tiny jigsaw bit not there. It's the moral piece, isn't it?"

"Oh, yes," said Mary. "We miss it because we're old-fashioned. The quilt my Rose copied was one her great-grandmother made. I remember her when she was very old. One story she told me was that if a baby came too soon after a marriage, the parents had to stand up in church and confess to antenuptial fornication. Those were the very words. Weren't they awful? And the minister rebuked the couple publicly. What a change time has brought! A little for the better, I think. But the only thing is that young people seeing this happy ending of John and Laurie's story may feel there's no need to wait for marriage in their own lovemaking."

"I'm not so sure," Katherine said. "Lucien Fulton, Madeleine's boy, told her a lot of the boys are pretty scared. They can hardly picture their friend John as a husband, let alone a *father*. So they're playing it cool, he says. Maybe if our one little jigsaw bit is absent here, it may turn up in other places."

"Meanwhile, we can enjoy the happiness of the Bradley-Lester families."

And they fell to discussing the tea until they said good-by at their own front doors.

July was a beautiful month, warm but not hot, with beneficent showers at just the right time. It seemed made for lovers' meetings, Katherine often thought, as she imagined Tim's reunion with Mary and the news he brought back at last about the wedding. It was to be in September — the 28th, he said. There would follow two weeks in a quiet spot they knew — "no traveling" Mary had said, and then for the present at least Tim's own house in Lemming.

He had talked to Katherine about this. "Of course, our main office is in New York and I go there three times a week, as you know, but I can't work my best there. I don't like the city. But if Mary wants to live there, I'll manage. Out here though, I not only have my small office but I do have a very nice house. I bought it years ago, you remember, because I wanted a home. With your help I've made it into a place, I think, of real comfort and charm. So we'll see! By the way, you and the kids are to fly out for the wedding. I hardly need to tell you that."

After Tim had left, he returned as he often did for a sort of postscript. This time he came only to the door.

"Forgot to say she still loves me. Miracle of miracles!"

In later years Katherine remembered the months through which she passed as a kind of kaleidoscope — unreal scenes which flickered brightly and quickly passed into nothingness. There was the regular August visit to David's mother in Vermont, where the older woman and the younger one shed their tears together over David's defection. But there was a certain soothing in the great mountains and also in the children's joy, as they picked berries, waded in the stream, and watched the farmer with his sheep. As usual they were all loath to leave.

"And you'll tell me if — if ever . . ." the old woman begged.

"Oh, I promise," Katherine answered, trying to make her voice cheerful.

It seemed only a breath of time until Katherine found herself ushered into the front pew on the right of the church as the groom's family, then trying to quiet her nervous heart, for Kit was to be flower girl and Davey the ring bearer. They had all flown out two days before to be sure of being there for the rehearsal. Now, as the wedding march chords were struck, the audience rose and the Rector with Tim and his best man, Jack Paar, came from the vestry.

Katherine watched her brother in something like amazement. Was this tall, handsome, grave man Tim? Could it really be that at long last he was to be married? Then she saw his head turn slightly and his fixed expression melt. She turned also and could now see, in her long ruffled dress, Kit advancing slowly, scattering her rose petals with meticulous care as she prepared the path for the bride. And then — Katherine caught her breath — Davey, the image of his father, walked sedately, bearing the white satin cushion *and* a ring, but not the real one! (The Rector had said he had seen too many accidents with that.) The one with its sacred inscription was safely in the vest pocket of the best man.

And then Katherine, the watcher, saw Tim's expression change again. Behind the bridesmaids he had caught sight of the white vision which was Mary, moving forward on her father's arm. When she reached him, he did not extend one hand to grasp hers, but both of his, as though he must always give more than she expected. The ceremony began with the time-honored words. Katherine heard them dimly in her heart until a different line startled her. It was spoken in Tim's voice, clear but with a catch of love within it:

"With this ring I thee wed
And with my body I thee worship."

How beautiful! Katherine thought. But why . . . where? . . . Then she remembered. It came from the old form of the English wedding service, agreed upon here, evidently, by the Rector and Tim, for there was not to be a double-ring ceremony.

"I don't like to see a ring on a man's finger," Tim had explained before to Katherine. "Just one of my little oddities. As to protection, as I've heard it called, if anyone I ever meet doesn't know by my actions that I'm a married man, a ring wouldn't help. Mary feels as I do. So there is to be one ring and I'm the one who gives it."

The reception, to Katherine, was a blur of strange, friendly faces lighted here and there by Tim's old college friends and their wives who lived near enough to come, and his law partners and their families, who had flown out. The big Chadwick house was opened to its fullest extent, and a tent of extraordinary dimensions on the side lawn was prepared for dancing. Katherine with the Chadwicks was, of course, in the receiving line, never feeling more lonely for her husband. For Tim's sake she had been outwardly gay and, she *hoped*, charmingly so. It was hard to represent a whole family for Tim by herself.

The children circulated freely among the guests, but because they received many plaudits on their wedding performance and because the whole excitement over Uncle Tim and Aunt Mary was much to their liking, they behaved unusually well and were finally spirited off to bed by Mary's own old nurse.

Mary had wanted a gay reception and she had it. The music and dancing and bright voices kept on until late, until the toasts, the cake cutting, and the tossing of the bouquet had all been accomplished. Then, by the quiet manipulation of Jack Paar, the floor was cleared and as the orchestra began, Tim and Mary alone danced the waltz as they had done when they first fell in love! During the applause they slipped off to dress for their leave-taking.

Mary had some little oddities too in the realm of opinions. One was that she did not intend to sneak away from her guests like a thief. "I'm going to walk down my own front stairs like a lady, with Tim waiting for me at the foot, and go away through the front door with everyone calling good-bys."

The guests crowded into the wide hall and the entrance to it to wait, with Tim in his own position. When Mary appeared at the top of the stairs, everyone clapped; in a dress as blue as her eyes, laughing and waving, she came slowly down. Near the last step she added an unexpected fillip to the sight; for tripping upon it she literally fell into her husband's arms.

The bridal couple did not make a mad rush for the door. Rather, they went slowly, waving and smiling between the good-bys and good wishes. They were escorted outside by the ushers and into the car where Jack Paar waited in the driver's seat to take them on the first leg of their journey. The guests with little bags of confetti pelted the car as it started and the irrepressible ushers, all Eli men like the two in the car and Whiffenpoofers, at that, shouted out the memorable song to waft the happy bride and groom on their way.

"Such a sad song for a wedding!" one girl was heard to remark as the singers drew out their "little lost sheep who have gone astray" to the last possible note. But to the Yale men involved it was not all nostalgic but hilarious with youth.

When many skilled hands had brought something like order to the house, and the distant relatives had gone quietly to bed, Mr. and Mrs. Chadwick and Katherine sat down in the living room to talk it all over. The two women shed a few quiet tears, but Mr. Chadwick was expansively satisfied.

"Beautiful wedding! Wonderful reception! And, best of all, the young man I've always hoped Mary would find — one who would be a son to me too. As to Mary — I ask you, Katherine, could there be a lovelier bride?"

"Jim, you shouldn't boast of your family."

"Why shouldn't I? I'll begin on you next. You look like a bride yourself!"

"Don't pay any attention to him, Katherine; he's just happy. As am I, over Tim. As you can imagine, there have been plenty of young men along the way and one or two so determined I thought Mary might weaken. But she always told us, 'It's not right yet — not the way I want it. I'm still going to wait.' "

"Well, she did a good job waiting; that's all I can say."

Mrs. Chadwick suddenly took Katherine's hands in her own. "My dear, I want to tell you how wonderful you were tonight when you must have felt a sort of double heartache — for your husband, first of all, and then for having now to share Tim. I can imagine all the constant little bits and pieces of your lives you have told each other. Now it may be just a little different. But you will find you have a true sister in Mary. She's always longed for one."

"That's right," put in Mr. Chadwick. "Over the years she was always saying, 'Please, Daddy, give me a sister.' Only thing I've ever denied her. Until tonight. I think I've given her a beauty now."

"You have been so kind to me. Tim and I have been so short of family and now we both feel we have one. Your relatives and the guests too seemed to take me in, and this warmed my heart."

"You have to leave tomorrow?"

"Yes, school will be calling the children Monday, so we must be on hand. But we'll certainly carry delightful memories with us."

They went over again the high spots of the evening until at last Katherine said if they would excuse her she would go up to her room, as she really was rather tired.

"Of course you are. We've been selfish to keep you up longer because we wanted to have you with us. Come, my dear, we'll walk you to the stairs." They both kissed her fondly and Mrs. Chadwick said, "I know my husband is dying to say this, but I claim the last words. First, we'll count you as a daughter now; second, you look perfectly lovely tonight; and third, you can think of this if you ever feel depressed — you simply captivated the reception guests as well as your new family. And now, my dear, our thanks and good nights."

Once back home in Lemming, Katherine settled into routine living, trying always to allow the thrill of pleasure over the wedding festivities to win over the little ache she felt now in always being second place in Tim's life. But the sweetness of Mary seemed to drive away the latter unworthy thought.

Dr. and Mrs. Harris had returned by the end of August after a most fantastic European trip, they reported. They were installed now in the bride's house as the larger of the two and Dr. Harris would sell his, with plans afoot to add two large rooms to the other. In school there was a difference. The Principal was in his accustomed office, but a new young woman would now be teaching English. After so many years of work Mrs. Harris was now to rest and enjoy herself, so the dictum ran.

As usual Katerhine was consulted. "I'm not a very good cook," the bride explained. "He likes pie and I've made so few. Could you teach me?"

"Dead easy," Katherine cheered her. "I've a never-fail recipe for crusts. Come over and we'll practice here. Then if you should make a mistake we'll let Thomas eat it and Dr. Harris will never know."

The cooking lessons progressed steadily and well. The bride was an apt pupil. Before long she had made a lemon chiffon pie of elegant proportions to carry home to her Joseph.

"I'm so glad I never knew this before he asked me to marry him. I would always have been afraid then that he had fallen in love with my cooking instead of me."

"I would say you had always been perfectly safe," Katherine assured her, "pie or no pie."

The bride drew close to her friend.

"I want to tell you about — about what you said to me on my wedding day. It was all so true. Joseph understood all about my feelings and he was so . . . so kind and dear. I loved him more that night than I had ever done before. I just thought I should tell you."

The first obligation Katherine felt upon her was to check Tim's house, give it a new touch here and there. She had not been in it for some time and when she went one day she was struck by the severe masculine quality of it. Tim had said not to buy more furniture until Mary was there to select it, but surely there were some things she could do to brighten the place up. She decided, first of all, that the window hangings should be cleaned and perhaps sheer white straight ones at the windows themselves. She called her handyman, Henry, who also served Tim's needs, and the next day work began in earnest. The hangings were dispatched to the cleaners — only heaven knew what the color and design had been originally! A beautiful carved round table was brought out from a dark corner, ready, as Katherine thought, to greet the newly-weds, with a great bowl of flowers upon it, when they arrived; the Persian Oriental Tim had picked up in his travels needed cleaning badly but would, after that, brighten the whole room. It was sent out at once with the date of its return firmly agreed upon.

When she reached the master bedroom, where presumably the bride and groom would sleep, Katherine stood, surveying it in deep thought. It was very large and with its three pieces of furniture left one wall quite bare. The effect was almost austere. With Henry at her heels, all interest, she moved into the two guest rooms, where Tim had evidently been thinking of her own room and that of their mother.

"Make them pretty but not fussy," Tim had adjured the decorator, Katherine remembered. "Keep one rather plain, for my men guests."

But in the "pretty" room Katherine found removable treasures. She had Henry take the dressing table into the master bedroom and set it along the bare wall, where fortunately a good light would fall upon it. What a change! she thought gleefully. It alters the whole atmosphere of the room. The smaller room had been a bit crowded; so for the present, at least, the change would not be too noticeable there. I'll be careful not to do too much, Katherine advised herself . . . She decided to get some new curtains and nothing more.

When the rug and hangings for the living room came home from the cleaners, she could have cried for joy. She did not know how long they had been in steady use, but now the rug was a very light beige with delicate flower designs of pink and blue, and the hangings — the great surprise — had evidently been made by a professional hand to match the rug. They hung now with the same soft coloring against a light background. When she had finally hung the straight sheer white curtains, Katherine looked about her and said happily, "Tim need not be ashamed to show Mary his house!"

While she was awaiting the return of the bride and groom, she heard a piece of news which strangely pleased her, and brought its own small excitement. It had to do with the boy Preacher, who had been involved in the big fight and later been a puzzle at the hospital. Dr. Harris, it seemed, had kept, as it were, a finger upon him, and after the wedding trip and the opening of school, he decided to stroll over one afternoon to Preacher's home and see if he could find him. His wife told the story.

"And when he got near to the house he heard music. It sounded a little like a mouth organ but different. Whoever was playing it made a real instrument of it. My husband says it was an aria from an opera and beautiful. Joseph went up to the house and knocked and the music stopped. Preacher came to the door, red as a beet."

"I heard you playing some music," Joseph said.

"Me? No, sir."

Joseph just kept on very quietly and finally got him to pull his mouth organ from his pocket.

"Joseph can be subtle when he wishes," she went on, "so then he said, innocent as you please, 'A little aria from *Faust* I think you were playing?' And Preacher as quick as a wink said, 'No, sir, it was from *Traviata*.' And Joseph just said, 'Of course, my mistake. Now do begin and play it over.' "

The result had been that Dr. Harris was amazed at what he then heard. Once in the midst of his music Preacher had lost his shyness and music sweetly cadenced came from the ordinary instrument. The boy had a gift which until now had been hidden. Dr. Harris took action at once. The head of the music department must hear this. Preacher must have some lessons in note reading and then he could play in the orchestra. A solo now and then, at least. The boy gave up his secrets. He had so longed to be in the orchestra and play a fiddle, but they couldn't afford to buy one or to manage music lessons. So he put the little bit of money he earned into records and getting a really good mouth organ. He just practiced when no one could hear him.

Dr. Harris, his wife said, had asked a last question.

"You like music?"

"I love it. The good stuff."

So a new and wonderful life opened for Preacher. Music lessons were made a part of his school time and a violin was placed in his hands. His movements were instinctive, as though of remembered things long forgotten. The violin was given him as a stimulus to his other lessons, but one day Preacher drew from it one long, pure, sustained note. After that he worked on the violin too.

When the time for the fall concert came and the orchestra showed its fresh skill, Preacher was not yet ready to join the string section, but on the programs in bold letters were the words,

Harmonica Solo............................Joseph Parson

It was reported in town that this was the "hit" of the evening.

The return of Tim and Mary in October was to Katherine a happier occasion than she had expected. Mary's delight in Tim's house and Katherine's own had sent a little thrill over her, enough to counterbalance any thought of having even Mary supercede her in Tim's affection. In no time at all it seemed as though they had always been all-one together. There was much entertaining for the new couple until Tim called a halt.

"Darling," he said one evening as they were dressing to go out, "this round of festivities is delightful and all that, but I really have to do some work with a clear head. That means I can't do without normal sleep. Could anything be done, without disappointing you?"

"Oh, Tim, my precious boy, I'm worn out too. We never seem to have a quiet night at home. You have such a big circle of friends all wanting to do you honor some way. But I have an idea. I used to do this at home when social affairs got too thick. I would go to bed with a mild case of grippe. Even a good sniff can quickly put me to bed for a few days, allowing one to get up in very negligee robes for dinner and a quiet early evening at home. Do you get the idea?"

"It's the finest I ever heard except the one I had when I fell in love with you. Oh, this is going to be beautiful. We'll get Kathy over to make the telephone calls, and I can make a few more this evening. Half of the incoming ones are from my clients who have really become friends, but I know they may feel some obligation and may even be relieved now themselves. Come on, darling, let's go on to this affair now, which I know will be a nice one and we can be as charming as we please, knowing relief is in sight."

Katherine herself was relieved to hear the news, for she had been fearing both bride and groom were showing some signs of weariness; so she went over to Mary's to offer her services.

"I'm the best little social prevaricator in Lemming," she announced. "Show me your date book, dear, and let me get at it. I'll make every hostess feel she's practically distinguished because you can't accept her invitation. Not so far from the truth at that," she added. "Now, let's begin. Did I hear you cough?"

"Oh, just a little one. I may have a very slight cold, but I'll keep it down just enough to ease my conscience. Here we go!"

Katherine's dulcet voice had never been more convincing than when she explained she was calling for her sister-in-law, Mrs. Dalzell, to say she was so terribly sorry but since she was in bed with a troublesome cold she would not be able to accept her lovely invitation to dinner on the twenty-eighth of November. She hopes you will understand.

A voice came back at once.

"Is this you, Mrs. Davenport?"

"Yes, I'm doing some telephoning for her."

"But, oh, I'm so happy to have this opportunity to speak with you. We are still talking about the play. May I tell you now how wonderful everyone thinks it was?"

"You are so kind. Thank you very, very much."

Katherine turned to Mary. "I'm afraid the play which you may have heard of is going to be dragged in now on all the phone calls."

"Tim has told me. You must have been marvelous. Take all the compliments as they come and store them up in your heart. You can take them out and look at them again later," Mary said with a little laugh. "I only wish I had been here to see you earn them all."

The telephoning went on and, while Katherine was often interrupted with more happy comments about the play, the matter in hand was steadily and gracefully carried out. At last the date book was clean for two weeks ahead.

Katherine prepared a salad, and French Fries ready to heat while the steak was broiling under Tim's supervision, and left.

When he got home that night, the house was dark; his call when he entered was not answered. He put on lights and hurried through to the kitchen, saw the dinner prepared but still no voice. He ran up to the bedroom, thinking, "Now I have a ghastly anxiety I never had before."

He lighted the room and saw then a small figure curled up in a soft ball and evidently still sound asleep. He went over quickly, his pulse beating wildly from his fright and from desire as he gazed on the beauty before him. He stooped to kiss her and she woke sleepily with her arms around him.

"Oh, darling, I didn't know I was so tired. I've been asleep all afternoon, but now I feel so much better. It's so wonderful we can be all alone . . . no dinner to go out to this evening, isn't it?"

"Words cannot say how much I love you."

It turned out to be a beautiful evening indeed, with dinner arranged by both of them on the table in Tim's office which Mary had at once admired. They sat before it, side by side, on the brown leather love seat, and while the meal was excellent they were not too conscious of it nor even, indeed, of the champagne Tim insisted upon opening to celebrate their "new freedom," he said.

At last Mary noticed a tiny wrinkle in his forehead and at once took action. "Timothy," she began, "there is still something bothering you. Now tell me please, at once."

"Nonsense, darling. You have the most lively imagination . . ."

"My dearest one, I can read you like a book. Please go on with the story."

"Is a man never to have a private thought?"

"Not from his wife if it pertains to her too. Come on, Tim."

"Well, since you will have it. I was suddenly struck by the awful thought, won't we have to invite all these people back here, to *our* house, for more and more dinners? If this is so . . ."

Mary put a gentle finger on his lips. "Listen! This is Mrs. Timothy Dalzell speaking . . ."

"Those words sound so beautiful to me."

"And to me too. I practice saying them every once in a while."

This demanded a little interlude, but when it was over Mary began again.

"As I was saying when most pleasantly [*giggle*] interrupted, I've been thinking this over. When our quiet 'grace' period has ended, we'll be well on into November. Why not then begin to prepare for a big Open House the Saturday after Thanksgiving. Everyone loves a party then. And we can send out a card to everyone to whom we're indebted. Make it a four-to-seven affair and do it all in one glorious big *bash*! What do you think?"

"I think you're inspired. I know Kathy will love hearing the plan. And I couldn't be more pleased over it, or relieved. But I'm a little frightened too."

"Why ever, Timmy?"

"Because I'm just getting used to your beauty and you begin to produce brains also. That's too much for any mortal man. What shall I do?"

Mary's eyes were dancing.

"Oh, I think you had just better accept all this you've been talking about. Somehow, I think you'll manage." And she found herself again in Tim's arms.

Katherine heard the plan for an Open House with a great sense of relief. She had feared she should return the social debts herself and now this would be the most delightful way in which it could be done. Tim's friends, many of them, had never been in his home, since he had entertained at the Lemming Club or occasionally with a theater party in the city. Now all who got cards would be agog to see the house, the bride against its background, and to see Tim himself, the erstwhile charming but confirmed bachelor, now as *Benedict, the married man.* Yes, Mary's suggestion had been a stroke of genius, as Tim had said. The party in prospect would be completely gracious and yet, knowing the host and hostess, and the generally light spirits of the guests, Katherine felt sure there would be plenty of fun. Good! she thought.

She had been invited once to the Harris's for dinner — an excellent one — but after Dr. Harris had excused himself for a meeting, Katherine remarked that he seemed worried.

"He's about wild," his wife explained; "he's learned that three young couples, all of them graduates of the High School here, are getting divorces when they've been married only six, eight, and ten years respectively. Joseph walked the floor last night, saying there was something badly wrong — that there must be a reason for all this, and it had to be corrected. He told me he had been to dinner once with the eight-year couple and he was worried then. He said they seemed to him too brittle and sort of hard. They kept passing clever little wisecracks back and forth, but often with a little stab in them. He saw and heard no sign of real tenderness. So this evening he's going to stop off a moment to see this couple and give them a paper he's taking for them. It's some words from Tennyson he thinks everyone should know."

"Do you remember them?"

"Oh, yes. I've always known them but perhaps haven't thought much about them. Here they are:

'As through the corn at eve we went
And plucked the ripened ears,
Oh, we fell out, my wife and I
We fell out, I know not why,
And kissed again with tears.
And blessings on the falling out
Which all the more endears,
When we fall out with those we love —
And kiss again with tears.'

"That's beautiful in its own way, but do you suppose young people will pay any attention to it?"

"Dear knows. If anyone but Joseph were offering it to them, I would say *no,* but he has a way with him!"

"I well know it!" Katherine laughed. "I hope it works this time."

"I'll tell you what happened last month. The Principals of this whole area hold a meeting the first of every school year to exchange views, and at this one Joseph said there was enough fine, highfalutin psychology tossed around to fill several books. Then Joseph spoke and told them very simply what the problems are and how we had been facing them here."

"I hope they listened."

"Oh, they did, he said, most of them a little smugly but at the end one man stood up and said, 'We have heard many theories expressed here today but now we have just listened to what I would call a *Pragmatic Principal,* who has used common sense and said it works. There was also running through his talk a strong affection for his students. Maybe we need to look more deeply into our own feelings. We are dealing with warm-blooded young boys and girls, not with Cases 7 and 10 in our Psychology Manuals. I thank Dr. Harris.'

"Joseph said that word pragmatic just turned the tide. When they could all roll it sweetly upon their tongues, they accepted him and his opinions and a number of them came to him when the meeting ended, asking his advice on their own problems. He came home really very much cheered."

The effect of the old-fashioned Tennyson lines upon the young couple planning a divorce did not reach Katherine directly. At the first Bridge Club meeting, as general gossip was being freely reported and commented upon, there was a sad reflection upon the number of what seemed very young couples breaking up.

"Well," Mary Hastings put in, "you can count the young Woodleys out now. They have made it all up and are very happy. My Rose runs into the older crowd occasionally at big parties. She said Bill Woodley had confessed to someone that when they realized how little it would take to make things right again, they just went at it."

Katherine bid her hand and played it very well, considering that her thoughts were often upon the pragmatic Principal.

October seemed to drown its admirers in beauty. Never such glorious foliage, never such deep gentian blue skies. And November brought the delicious haze of Indian Summer.

The cards were out for the party and the three of them, Katherine always included, met usually at Tim's house to arrange the details. She was constantly surprised and delighted to see how Mary dealt with practical matters as well as the more "dressy" elements. It was planned that they, Tim and Mary, would have Thanksgiving dinner with Katherine and the children. No time-honored detail would be omitted. Tim would drive the children out to the country to buy pumpkins; he would also be available to carve them just before Hallowe'en. Davey, who had been a bit edgy lately, feeling his world had become a little out of joint, now relaxed.

"And you'll be sure to take us out to the country the way you always do — for you know what?"

"Sure as pumpkins, and we'll carve them the way we like, right, Davey?"

"Right, Uncle Tim. I have been a little worried. You see [trying to be honest and tactful both] you haven't been over here as much as usual. Kit's been the worst. She has cried sometimes, but we don't tell Mother."

"That's good. Now listen, Davey. You see, it's so wonderful to get married, but we have been going out to so many parties and things, and Aunt Mary has been pretty tired. We'll get it all settled soon."

"But you like being married?"

"Oh, it's simply . . ."

"Fantastic," prompted Davey.

"The very word."

"That's good. You know what? When I'm old enough I'll just bet you I'll have to marry old Kit here. She's always hanging on to me."

Uncle Tim laughed. "I can promise you that you won't ever have to marry Kit."

"Sure?"

"Sure as that Peter wiggles his nose."

"You really oughtn't to keep bringing that up. He can't help it, you know."

"Right. I apologize. Did you know Aunt Mary likes Peter?"

"She does?"

"Thinks he's the prettiest rabbit she ever saw. Now, relax, Davey. All is well."

Everything went according to plan. The Thanksgiving turkey was a truly magnificent bird, with everything else in keeping. Tim, in finest form, entertained the children and saw to it the story of the first Thanksgiving was duly repeated. There were jokes and riddles and cracking of nuts before the big wood fire, since the weather had elected to remain cold. There was at the last pumpkin pie and cider. This brought back stories of Hallowe'en, for the farm trip had been made and the pumpkins lined up in Katherine's kitchen, waiting for the artists' hands, as usual, to the delight of the children.

There had never been seen such delightful grinning faces!

"Are you nervous about the party, Mary?" Katherine asked once, as the afternoon advanced.

"Not a bit. I love a big come-and-go affair. I have a feeling ours is going to be a success."

It was, unquestionably. The guests came early and stayed late. Those who should have left couldn't bear to leave the fun. There was warm hospitality, delicious foods, just enough drinks and no more (Tim's orders), constant chatter and laughter. Music ran through the rooms also: some choice selections from the town's finest pianist and a barber-shop quartet which moved around, always drawing a crowd with it.

When the hour set on the cards for the end of the party had long since passed, there were half a dozen of Tim's closest friends still there. Mary came up to him and whispered, "What shall we do with them? The food is practically gone. Just the remains on the buffet. The caterers have left. What shall we do?"

Tim studied his last guests with a smile almost tender. This small group had been very close to him over the years.

"I'll fix them, darling. Don't you worry."

He went to a spot where the six guests were happily disputing.

"O yez! O yez!" he intoned. "Listen you! My wife tells me . . ."

"My wife, he says. He can't speak a sentence without bringing those words in."

"Well, since you've seen her, do you blame me?"

"No," shouted the group. "Excuse me, Timmy, my lad. I was just teasing. We think you've done us all proud in bringing us your beautiful Mary. Now, go ahead, what were you about to say?"

"My wife has just told me that the food is practically gone except for some odds and ends on the buffet. The caterers have left. If any of you feel the need of a sandwich before you ultimately — we hope — go home, you can go out and make them for yourselves." There were some gleeful shouts and a surge to the dining room. In a short time Tim and one of the men were making coffee in the kitchen; Mary, a pinafore over her lovely gown, was cutting the cakes left by the caterers and the rest of the half dozen were wrangling happily over the bits and pieces of meat and fowl on the platter. So ended the Open House just before daybreak.

As Katherine had always said, the calendar did not leave enough room between Thanksgiving and Christmas. This year the gap of time seemed less than ever, for plans must be made early, with Mary now in the family. Tim had to make a trip to California again early in the year, so Mary's wish was to be with her parents while he was gone. This left just Christmas itself to be settled.

Tim talked it over with Katherine.

"I can't leave you alone all of Christmas and I won't. We have to find a way for you and Mary both to be happy. She is so gentle about the plans, leaving it all to me. But I know what it means to her to be with her parents on Christmas."

At last Tim came up with a compromise. Suppose they would all have their big Christmas dinner here at Katherine's on Christmas Eve, after which they would open their presents as usual and he and Mary would stay on for the evening to enjoy the tree. He would help trim it and so would Mary that afternoon. Then he and Mary would take the earliest flight west on Christmas Day itself and be at Mary's home for Christmas with her parents. How about it? It was at best a compromise but, all agreed, a good one.

As Katherine went about her own preparations, she tried not to think of the long Christmas Day with herself and the children alone. She watched eagerly for the package that always came from David . . . It did not come until a few days before time for opening. With Davey's help she put up the holly and the greens and Tim, as usual, brought and set up the tree. Before dinner on Christmas Eve Tim and Mary came and, with the children, decorated it with all the bright immemorial baubles. On a carefully held ladder, Davey mounted and put the star on the top.

Mary kept constantly exclaiming how lovely it was to have Christmas with *children*. "We never seemed to have any little ones in our whole connection."

"There is always time," said Tim wickedly from behind a bough.

"That's right, Aunt Mary," said Davey, the all-wise. "It does take a good while sometimes to get a baby. Mother said they had to wait for several years for me."

"And what are you giving to Peter for a present?" Mary asked sweetly. And then the talk flowed into safe channels.

The dinner was elegance itself, with Katherine helping with the plum pudding and mince pies, while Mrs. Weagle did the rest with an accomplished hand. Then, replete with food, they all sat around the fire to open the gifts. What delightful tangles of satin ribbons and gold and silver paper! What exclamations of surprise and delight! Everyone was completely happy. Tim was always very generous, but now Mary was also. One fancy little package was the same for Mary and Katherine. Each contained a ticket for an opera in February.

"It's always sort of a grim month," Tim explained, "and I thought you girls might want to go into the city for a little *toot* all by yourselves. They can be exchanged," he added.

The children had received so much already that they were a bit slow about opening their father's package. Katherine's heart beat fast as she waited. The package was unusually small. Davey drew his small box out first and gave a wild whoop as he opened it.

"A watch! A real one! A good one! The first I ever had. Look, Mother, it's an Elgin. Oh, I am thrilled! Open yours, Kit. See what's in your box."

It too held a watch. Not like Davey's, but a smaller one with a border of tiny mosaic flowers around the face.

"It's a *baby* watch!" Davey cried.

"No, indeed," Uncle Tim said. "Yours is a sturdy boy's watch, Davey, but Kit's is a delicate, pretty watch for a little girl. It's a good one too. Is there another package?"

Davey withdrew it. On the card was written: *From Davey and Kit to Mother.* He handed it over.

Katherine opened it, wonderingly, for it was carefully wrapped. When she drew it out, she found a small but perfect snapshot of the two children, now in a charming silver frame embossed with violets. She cried out in her pleasure.

"Oh, what a lovely thing to send me!"

"It surely is," Mary said. "Perhaps we'll put it tops of all the gifts. When was the picture taken?"

"The last time he was here. He took the children for a ride and snapped this to take with him on his travels, I assume. Now he feels I'm the one who should have it. I'm very happy he sent it."

The stars burned brightly that Christmas Eve, and the flame of hope which Katherine had kept alive in her heart seemed to have a tiny bit more warmth. The picture frame must have been specially designed and David had remembered her love of violets.

The New Year came and passed. The strange habit of remembering it fell upon people as usual. At midmonth Tim and Mary returned and Katherine realized how terribly she had missed them. Small but secure cords of affection were binding the two women more and more together. When February, gray and chill, arrived, they had one glorious day in the city, lunching in elegance and going to the opera in style, as Tim's good seats demanded. There was a good deal of quiet visiting back and forth between the two houses that month, and one or two heavy snows to change the scene.

Then on a certain morning a new wind began to blow, so far a gentle one. Bright bits of budding life showed here and there; white, rolling clouds chased each other over a blue sky; and, as men and women drew long breaths of the newborn air, they smiled and whispered in their hearts, "Winter is over at last. This is the beginning of spring!"

It was the season of kites and school trips here and there. Indeed, as March progressed the children's life seemed unusually full. Katherine set to work to find new interests or new duties for her own.

On an evening when the wind was rising a little, and the children, weary, went to bed early, Katherine felt immeasurably lonely. She couldn't call Tim or Mary. She had tried *so* hard never to infringe upon their privacy. It was Mrs. Weagle's night and day off, and even Thomas roamed about mewing for his latest ally. At any rate, Katherine thought, I'll put on my hostess gown in case they might drop in later.

It was a pretty garment and, she knew, very becoming. She had bought it thinking of evening visits from the bride and groom. It fitted her mood now, though, for it bolstered her spirits. She went down to the living room and lighted the fire already laid, because the air was chilly. There were fresh flowers on the table which Tim had sent the day before as he was buying some for his own house. The whole scene, Katherine felt, was a very pleasant one, and she would rejoice in what she had. She selected a book and sat down beside the lamp. In only a few minutes the telephone rang. She jumped up quickly. It would be Tim, after all.

It was a man's voice, but it was not Tim's. Katherine caught the side of the stand as if for support.

"Oh — *David*!"

"Yes. I should explain. I flew in from the West today and this evening I borrowed one of the company cars and drove out here to talk to Tim about some matters and also to get a breath of fresh air. But Tim is nowhere to be found and no one knows where he is."

"He's married now, you know."

"Yes, I got word from the company. I've been thinking — I mean, I've just been wondering if you could possibly allow me to stop in to see you for a few minutes, and tell you some things I would like you to know. It's a great deal to ask. Could I come?"

"But — but, *of course*." Katherine could think of no other words.

"Would it be convenient now? Are you alone?"

"Quite alone. The children are in bed. Of course, you can come."

"Thank you," he said simply.

Katherine was stunned. It was David! Just as she had dreamed it might one day happen. But now there was a sickening fear. He had come to see Tim, but waited also to see her. Could it be to plead again for the divorce? She shook off the idea. At least she would see him and talk with him. That much was certain. She stirred the logs to a blaze and then answered the bell. David stood in the hall and followed her into the bright warmth of the living room.

"Oh, what a beautiful place!" he said. "And I'm glad there is a fire." He stood with his back to it. "May I have a few minutes just to look around and take note of everything again — especially you. Oh, Katherine, you have grown lovelier."

"And you look a little older, but I think much more handsome, David."

"I don't *feel* handsome inside me. Could I begin soon to tell you what I came to do?"

"Please do. Sit here facing the fire and don't look at me as you talk, if that would make it easier."

"It would. Thank you. I'll begin at the beginning and try to be fair. You know much of the story. Miss Mills had a devastating beauty. All the men in the office tried to keep away from her. I did but at times had to work with her. Before long I was at the point where — you must think the worst of me — I felt myself madly, irrevocably in love like all the great lovers of old. When you refused me a divorce — for which I now thank you with all my heart — she was perfectly willing to go with me unmarried to Paris. She is an artist and Paris was to her a lodestar. So we went."

David paused and found it hard to go on. "I arranged for her to have lessons from a good art teacher and for several months she was deliriously happy. For the most part so was I. But steadily I realized that outside of sex and art and my business, about which she cared nothing, we had little to build upon for just pleasant everyday living. After six months I found she was having an affair with her art teacher. Of course, there would be many more. I was not only disillusioned to find she had used me as a means to get to Paris and that I meant nothing to her beyond that, but most of all because I had been so blind, so weak, so lacking in a sense of values that I had turned away from a great reality to clutch at a tawdry phantom. This sickened me. I left her as soon as we had made our positions clear to each other. So, Katherine, that is my story. I feel better, having confessed it all. Thank you for giving me the chance." Katherine still seemed unable to speak.

He rose just as the wind, gathering force, swept, crying, around the house. "You have been very kind, as you would be. I ask nothing. I deserve nothing. But once again I appreciate your letting me talk to you. Now, I should be on my way."

Before he reached the door, a furious burst of wind, moaning and raving, tore across the roofs of houses, rattling windows and doors as though bent upon utter destruction. He turned to look at Katherine standing trembling beside her chair, her face white. He hurried to her and put his arms around her. He cradled her head against his breast and smoothed her hair as though she had been a child.

"There! There!" he kept saying quietly. "It's just the wind. It will die down in a few minutes. Don't be afraid."

"I'm not afraid now," she whispered.

And then as his head bent over hers, their lips unaccountably met.

When the wind was still, David released her and they stood looking at each other, shyly, as first lovers might look — her eyes shining through misty tears, his humbly beseeching.

At last he said, "I think I should say good night and leave you to think over what we have just now shared. You can always reach me . . ."

And then Katherine spoke firmly, as though trying to master a faint hint of laughter, or was it emotion?, in her voice.

"I think you should run your car into the garage, David, for you can't tell when the wind might rise again. And bring your bag in with you. It must be growing late!"